THE AMBASSADOR

DAVID BELDING

David Nulls is chosen by a superior race to be the respective for Earth in the federation of planets who use mental powers to communicate. David with the help a female space jockey Kitaracate soon learns to use his mental powers to help the planet Earth move into the space age with their own Space explorer space ship. Then goes on to help others in the federation who thought Earth people were a primitive race. David learns to further advance his mental ability and becomes a major figure in the federation to solve problems in other Galaxies using his unorthodox ways.

WORKBOOK PRESS LLC
187 E Warm Springs Rd,
Suite B285, Las Vegas, NV 89119, USA

Website: https://workbookpress.com/
Hotline: 1-888-818-4856
Email: admin@workbookpress.com

Ordering Information:
Quantity sales. Special discounts are available on quantity purchases by corporations, associations, and others. For details, contact the publisher at the address above.

ISBN-13:   978-1-955459-11-2 (Paperback Version)
                978-1-955459-12-9 (Digital Version)

REV. DATE: 08.03.2021

INDEX

Chapter 1

The beginning

It was a rainy dreary day in Washington. To the twenty-five to thirty people standing in the cemetery it was more depressing than usual.

The cancer had taken their friend away, even more so for David. It had not only taken his wife of 28 years, but his soul and will for living.

David really wasn't listening to the fine speech the preacher was giving. He was thinking of how he was going to, just get on his bike and ride off into the sunset. Oh hell he is on the west coast at the beach. Change that plan ride off into the sunrise. He kind of smiled thinking about it. I guess if anyone who saw him smiling. They would think he had gone crazy, with grief or that reality had sat in. Either way it didn't matter. He didn't care what they thought. All He wanted was to be left alone.

After the finial A-man, everyone came by shaking his hand, or giving him a hug. Telling him how sorry they were. And asking what was he was going to do now.

David just stood looking at his wife final resting place. Thinking, now she out of pain, and would just shrug his shoulders. He was also thinking sense they only had a few big material possessions, the motor home he would give to their son. The beach house he would give to their daughter and let them fight over the cars.

That night when everyone had left, except the kid and his mother, He told them of his plans. He gave the son the title to the motor home and the pickup; to their daughter he gave her deed to the house and the convertible. He decided it was better than them fighting.

David hugged his mother; she kissed him and told him to keep in touch. He then got on his bike and without looking back rode off, with no particular place in mind to go.

Two days later he was on a road. That followed a river in Colorado. Still feeling depress, that his wife was not on the back of the bike with him. David was thinking that would be a good river to fish in. When all of the sudden my hands started disappearing and he was being lifted off the bike. He looked down his body had vanished. He could see his bike, when it realized, that no one was on it. The front wheel swerved back and forth, the bike slid off the road and into the river.

The next thing he knew he was standing in a room that looked like the cockpit to an airplane. It had big windows and three men sleeping in chairs. Looking to his left, his heart skip a beat and he about peed my pants. There stood three things, only way to describe them was they were aliens.

David went on the defense imminently; you know like you see in the movies, Kung Fu David). He didn't know any Kung Fu, but hope they didn't know it.

In an instance they turn into humans in blue uniforms. This had to be one of those flash backs they told him would come he thought.

Mr. Nulls It's not a flash back. We are not going to harm you.

They speak English, but their mouths, were not moving. Harm me, you just kidnapped or should I say abducted me and wrecked my bike. By the way how do you know who I'm?

All that can be explain. We know all about you, because we have been watching you for the past year. We have a proposition for you.

What a proposition from aliens. Oh this I've got to hear, relaxing a little.

Sorry about that first appearance. I guess it would be a surprise.

Yes you can say I was surprise. It happen so fast, if I would have blink I'd have missed it.

As for our proposition, we represent the Kula. What you would call an inter-space federation. There are currently seven hundred and thirty seven planets represented in the Kula federation. We have selected four of you humans, from this planet to take back to the Kula council, for them to decide on one to be an ambassador on the planet you call earth, But only if they wish to join the Kula.

What if I say no?

Then we will put you back on your bike five minutes before we pick you up and you will remember none of this. But from what we know about you. You will not say no.

Well that would even be a better trick, than the change from aliens to humans in uniforms.

Not really space travel and time travel are related. What will it be an Ambassador or a biker.

Well your right I have always been one for adventure and have nothing to loose. After all you say that you have studied me and know that I won't say no, so what is next.

It will take four of your days to reach Tistana. That is the planet where the Kula council is held. So would you like to sleep for four days like the other applicant?

Hell no, I want to see where I'm going and study your ship. you said I might not remember anything. Hey, do you think I can fly this ship, he asked looking around.

We might be able to arrange that but it is what you call computer control. Come on let's get you a uniform, in case we collide with a planet. That way they will know that you are from this ship. That is if there is anything left. Traveling at twelve times what you call warp or the speed of light. If we hit a planet theres not much left to dig out.

What? David asked looking a little nervies.

No just kidding, as you call it. It's a space joke, you are perfectly safe. We will not hit any planets, the computer will direct us around any danger and there are four back up computers. The suit will help you blend with the crew members.

A joke is supposed to be funny, that was not funny. What crew members?

All space travelers think it's funny. As for your other question there are forty two members on this crew. Come on I'll get you in a uniform. Then she headed towards the door, I'm called Kitaracta.

After trying to say Kitaracta so that it would sound like she said it. David asked: I don't think I can pronounce that. Do you mind if I call you Kit for now?

Yes Kit is fine my name is a hard one to pronounce without rolling your tongue she answered.

Now at the door, things really got strange. When Kit got to the door she walks through it. I mean through it, not opening it and going through the door , I mean through the door.

A few second later she opens the door from the other side. Sorry I forgot you don't know the secret of materializing yet. Don't worry we will teach you.

Kit led David to a room with rows of uniforms hanging from a rail, But without hangers. It was like they were just stuck to the rail. Kit pulled one down and handed it to him. Here put this one on, Let's see if it fits.

David stood there looking for a dressing room.

Kit just looked at him is there a problem?

A dressing room he asked.

Kit just laughed, oh thats right your spices has that hang up, about covering your bodies from the other sex. I'll just go out in the walkway.

Hey do you have a shower, David asked?

No need, you were sanitized, when you were brought aboard. We don't use showers, sanitizing is faster and gets you cleaner. I'll be out in the walkway, after you're dressed. I will show you the rest of the ship.

The uniform was more like a jump suite. Fit good but had no pockets. David steps out in the walkway with his clothes in one hand and pocket knife and wallet in the other.

Kit laughed again, you could leave your clothes hanging in there and your personal things you can put them in your pocket. They will be safe and you can have them back any time you want.

David was sure she was laughing at him for not knowing things. He went back in the room and hung up my clothes on the rack, more like stuck them to a rail. The wallet and pocket knife were still in his hand.

Kit smiled looking at them, then leans over and touches his hip you can put those in there.

David touches the same spot she mentions with his wallet and the uniform open up making a pocket. He put the wallet in then did the same on the other side and a small pocket open. When he put his hand in the pocket it opens wider. And yes the pocket knife was there. He looked at Kit, he could tell she wanted to laugh but did not out of politeness. She probably will tell her friends how dumb these earthlings are David thought.

Come I'll show you around the ship, she said still smiling.

She showed him all the parts of the ship from the main bridge to the engine room. Every door they came to she would tell him think your way through it and walk in. After a few times of running into a door, not through and Kit telling him to keep trying, sooner or later he would get it. One time as he reached for a handle, and thought his hand went through the door. He jerked his hand back and looked at it.

See you are starting to get it, Kit said

Still looking at his hand and, he wasn't sure he wanted to get it.

On their tour they passed a door several times, Kit never offered to go in. after the whole tour and meeting the crew. Kit asked him what did think of her ship.

It really great but what's in that door you stopped at but never went in.

Kit laughed the little laugh she dose. You're quite observant that is our relaxing room. I was not sure you could handle that yet, but if you think you can. Come along, but be warned you might be surprise.

After what I have seen so far not too much more can surprise me David said.

They walked back to the door she called the relaxing room. Kit open the door as David walked in, he took a step backwards.

She was right, it surprised him. He wasn't ready for what he saw. It was a bar and a seen right out of a movie. There were aliens of all kind. Some strange creatures, all of the crew members he had meet were human.

Kit step up beside him well what do you think?

Think, he could not tell her what was thinking. All he could say was who are these people?

They are the same people you meet all day. They just don't have their visualizer turn on. It makes other see what they want them to see. This is what they look like normally.

And what do you look like normally he asked her?

Like what you would call a frog. No just kidding as she reached in her belt. (David guess to some control) instantly she turned green but keeps the human form.

Would you like some refreshment she asked? She then went to the wall, and said something then reaches into the wall and brought out two drinks.

As they walked to a table, several crew men welcome them. They asked how he liked their ship or what did he think about it.

David could see they were proud of their space ship. Then another strange thing, they all spoke English. At the table he asked Kit about it.

She shows him her wrist that he thought was a watch. Then she pointed to a small ball on the side of it. This is a translator it translates, any language into the language you can understand. Then she pointed to his wedding ring.

There was a small ball he hadn't notice before.

That translate everything you say into their language.

They finished their drinks and David yawned.

Are you tired Kit asked, come with me I'll take you to the resting room?

OK, but will I wake up in after a couple of hours or like the others, in three days David asked?

You will wake up after your normal sleep. As they entered the sleeping room there was several so called beds. They looked like glass slab leaning at 80 degree angles. There were about 10 or 11 aliens sleeping. Just lay back you will like it. Kit could see the look on his face as she led him to one of the slabs, just lay back.

David did and surprising enough it was soft as a bed and felt like lying flat. Also strangely enough it felt like he had a blanket on him. He laid there thinking of all the strange thing that had happen today. Had it only been one day or two. You couldn't tell day from night up here. He did know that he was really tired like he had been up for two days.

The next thing he knew he was wide awake and felt like he had slept for hours. David walked out of the sleeping room, in the hall way where he meets a crew member.

Hungry the crew member asked.

Why yes David answered do you have any coffee?

We have krista; I think it is like your coffee. It's a wake up drink the crewman answered.

In the cafeteria David saw Kit, Sleep well she asked.

Short but the best sleep I have had in a long time

Short she answered in surprise over 12 hours, in your time. How long do you usually sleep.

Twelve hours never that long. How long before we reach Tistana, and I get to meet this Kula council.

It is still a day and a half away in your time

How long it is in your time, David asked.

One and a quarter cycles she answered. Your day is a little longer than ours.

David spent the rest of the day exploring the ship and talking to the crew members. He wanted to learn as much as possible. He also keeps trying the walk through the door trick. A couple of times he got my hand through, but nothing else. One time Kit saw him stick his hand through then walk into a metal door and bounce back. She laughed that silly laugh she has, and told him to keep trying and that he would get it. David was not sure he would get it before knocking himself out.

After what he figured was a day, because he was tired he went to the resting room. Found Kit sleeping .He laid on the slab next to her and was imminently a sleep, Once again waking up rested and refreshed.

David met up with Kit in the cafeteria; she informed him they would be landing in a half cycle. Would he like to go with her and wake the other three applicants?

David answered sure, thinking he didn't like the word applicants. Suppose they were better than him and one of them got to be the ambassador job, and he would be back on his bike and not remember any of this. That would be disappointing, after all he had learned.

David follows Kit to where the other three had been sleeping, these last four days. Kit pushed some bottoms and the others started waking up. All saying it was the best sleep they had ever had.

David was studying my competition, one was British, one Russian, and one Chinese. They all spoke English, due to the translator on his ring.

Kit introduces everyone and told them they would be meeting the council, in about three hours. Then asked if they wanted some refreshment, like coffee or tea?

David thought it strange she mention tea. Then remember that not only the Chinese but the British liked tea. The aliens probably studied the others before picking them too. He did notice that Kit did not offer them uniforms. Later she did ask David if he wanted his clothes back. David thought about it, then how the others were dressed. How his leather jacket and shirt with born to be wild on it with a hand and middle finger extended. Just might not be appropriate to meet this counsel. So he told her he would like to wear the uniform if it was OK. Beside it was more comfortable than his clothes.

Chapter 2

Meeting The Counsel

David didn't feel the landing, but did feel heaver when they turned off the artificial gravity on the ship.

At the space port the four of them got their first look at the strange city. It looks like Hongkong with its tall buildings the China man said. David had been there and had to agree with him.

After leaving the ship they were lead to a walk way. That Kit pointed at; there will be someone at the other end to meet them. Then she said good-bye.

You're not going with us David asked, a little disappointed?

No my job was just to get you here. Maybe I will see you again. Now step on the walk way.

David was glad to walk and get the feel of the new gravity. That wasn't to be, instead of walking, it was more like floating. The walk way didn't move, but they did. It took several turns, then ended up at a door way. Where we were meet by a man in a red uniform. He instructed them to get off and introduce him.

Welcome I'm Knightalotastuf. You can call me Knight. I'll be your guide, come along, the council is waiting.

In a few minutes, the four of applicants were standing in front of what David guessed, was called the council. Knight stood behind them.

There were nine strange looking aliens seated behind a long desk. The applicants stood there several minutes, no one spoke. Then they ask the man from China to step into the other room .Knight escorted him out, then returned. Several minutes later they asked the Englishman to step into the other room. Knight escorted him through another door.

The Russian and David just look at each other. It felt like something was going on in their heads. They must be reading their minds. Because the only time they talk was to excuse someone.

Finely after what seem an hour, but in reality was only a few minutes. They excused the Russian, as Knight escorted him out through even another door. The nine members walked through the desk. Not around, through this desk. They came up to David and put there tentacle like arms on his shoulder. Without speaking, he heard all of them, said you will be the one, on Earth to represent the Kula.

David said thank you, then he thought if you can read my thoughts. Thank you I will try to do my best.

The answer came back in his head you are welcome. We were sure you will and yes we are. Now you will have a lot to learn and Knightalotastuf will teach you, listen and learn. We will talk later. They all went out a door in the back.

Before you go what of the others David asked.

One counsel man stopped, they will be sent home with no memory of this. Yet if needed, the one you call the Russian can be reactivated to help you accomplish your task.

Knight came in congratulation, first we need to get you in to the uniform of an ambassador. You will get more respect, than in the uniform of a cargo pilot.

Oh there is a different class of people here.

No were all the same, Knight answered, it is just different jobs have different clothing, not rank all the same in status one person one vote anyone can go before the counsel with an option or complaint.

So you can read minds to David asked.

You mean do I know what people are thinking, then yes. I will teach you how, and how to block out others from reading what you don't want then to hear. Come I will show your living quarters

The living quarters were small. With the slopping bed on one side a couch and bathroom with a sanitizing shower, a toilet, and a sink with no water. Yet when you turned it on, by waving your hand under it, felt like water, all though you could not see anything. In one corner was a desk, with something that looked like a computer on it. You talked to it and it talked back or printed out what you wanted to learn. Later David learned it had an attitude. One time he asked it something, it answered.

David smarted off with, I don't like that answer, so I'm going to ask you one more time.

It answered; I don't care what you don't like. That is the best answer to your question. So take it or leave it, you are not going to get another one.

David spent a lot of time at the desk learning all the ways of these new worlds. Knight was a lot of help teaching him the basic ways of life. Like blocking his thoughts, and thinking his way through solid objects. Once he learned it was fairly easy and really cool. No need to open doors. Of course it had it draw backs. Like reaching for food and putting my hand through the plate then through the table. He was glad Knight didn't see that one. Knight did turned out to be a good teacher. Although his favorite line was (you fool everyone knows how to do that.) Soon David knew what everyone was supposed to know.

What David figured was eight months of learning. When he was called back to the counsel again. Knight waited outside and told him to go through the door, and pay attrition, so he did.

The counsel of nine looked at him for several minutes then spoke. You have learned a lot in your short time here with us. Even your mind block, there are things we cannot read. This is very advance, not many can hide things from us. This is good; people should have thoughts of their own.

David thought that they spoke, when actually; they were not speaking with their voices but with their minds.

Soon you will be ready to go back to your planet and ask then to become a member of the Kula.

What do I tell them that will convince them to become a member of the Kula David asked?

Anything you think is necessary shows them our technology in medicine, space travel; teach them what you have learned here. We see you have not learned fly in a space traveler. We see you know how to fly your air plane it is much like our space traveler.

The next thing David knew Knight came in. He didn't hear them call him. Yet could follow the conversation once he was next to him,

Knightalotastuf you have done well, teaching. The Ambassador, you will make a fine teacher after your probation period. Now you can teach him to fly.

Fly these people fly, David thought

No fly a space traveler, please do not interrupted.

Sorry with everything so advance, I was surprise.

Quite understanding, but you will learn to telaport from one to another. Then and only then, will you be ready to return to your planet, Earth as you call it, now go you have more to learn.

David left and spent the next month learning to fly the space traveler. The transporting was done with a device. The secret to it was, knowing where you wanted to transport to. David could see why you learned to think through thing first, or get stuck in some wall. Or his room door had a problem with that one. One time ended up half in the room and half in the hall, with a door running through him. Lucky you get to see where you were before you pushing final destination. And it warns if you are in midair.

David did see Kit twice going to flight lessons. She would change to flesh color and ask him how he was doing. Then leave with the remark, "let me know when you're up, I'll be sure to stay out of your way, and don't fly into a planet". Then laugh and walk away. David learned that even at warp twelve the computer on the space traveler would miss a planet by thousands of miles.

Finely Knight said I can teach you no more. Anything else you must learn on your own. We will go to the counsel tomorrow morning.

The next morning they stood outside the counsel door. This time David heard the council calls them in. They stood there several minutes. Finely they said to Knight you have done well. We will sign your teacher certificate congratulations. You may leave and celebrate.

Now Mr. Ambassador are you ready to go teach your race what you have learned.

Yes sir's I believe that I'm.

You have learned faster than we expected. We thought another two months, but we see you are ready now. Have you thought of how you will accomplish you tasked?

I have tossed around a few ideals, but mostly just going to play it by ear.

Play it by ear? Oh yes we understand, you will see what it take, then adapt to each situation. You will leave tomorrow a ship will take you and your traveler to the back side of your moon. From there you will be on your own. We will send to your traveler anything you need. Good luck as you would say, zovta as we say it.

The next morning David reported to the space port, where again he meet up with Kit.

Well Mr. Ambassador I get the pleasure of delivery you back home.

Well if you're not going to hit any planets or put me in a black hole. I'll be happy to let you drive.

She looked at him a black hole she question?

It's what you call a cetlacurla.

Oh small worry on that account. The six black holes that we know of, all pilots go a long way around. They are not something to mess with, you have learned well.

Thank you, coming from you I take it as a compliment, David answered.

Well come along your traveler is already loaded. We will leave in ten minutes

As David step on board he felt the gravity lighter. Moments later he was on his way home. It had been almost a year, since he had left. Probably by now everyone would think he was dead, if they had found his bike in the river.

Four days later they were in orbit behind the moon. There was Earth just around the corner.

Kit stops him, come on there something I want to show you, get your space suite on. Once they had then on, she took my hand and transported them to the moon surface. There she pointed to the bright pebbles. Those she said mixed with your fossil fuel on your planet will increases it's poetical a hundred times over. Just something that will help your planet.

Can I touch them, David asked.

Oh yes they are harmless till mixed with your refined fuel. Take a hand full with you. You suite will protect you from any harm you encounter on your planet and protect your identity which might be a good ideal for a while. So your species' will not think you a kook.

You seem to know a lot about my planet, have you been there.

Yes I live there a year, studying you and the others before I picked out the best four to present to the counsel. I was hoping it would be you.

Well you be coming again David asked.

No but I will be monitoring your movement and may be able to help out if really needed. But you know our policies no outside influence, and I would have to have the approval of the counsel. And we would not be here now if we were not afraid that your planet was about to blow itself up. And that would cause a great disturbance in your solar system maybe cause a cetlacurla.

Blow yourself up, what do you mean, David asked.

She then told him the reason why it was important for Earth to join the Kula.

When she had finished, he answered well you know more about why I'm here and how important it is than I do. How come you didn't tell me this before?

I was not authorized to tell you before, only just recently was I told to tell you.

So you're telling me that you can see in the future and this has happen, David asked.

No the future has not happen, there for we cannot see it. We can go in to the past, but only a little ways a cycle or two. Because it has happen, are you following me here?

Yes I think so picking up a few of the bright stones.

Good: let us go back to the ship and get you ready to start on this new adventure.

Chapter 3

A Helping Hand For The Astronauts

David sat in his space traveler as the cargo ship open the cargo doors. And with a little help from the cargo ship was push away. He started his engines, adjusted his gravity, and moving along the ship. He could see Kit waving from the control center. He waved back push the lever up a little. Then he came out from behind the moon. David could see Earth, a green ball floating in space. And the sun shine brightly, instantly the shade visor came up, blocking the bright sun rays. He pushed the power up and steered toward Earth. He figured go slow before popping through the atmosphere, like a bolt of lightning.

He saw the national space station, thought he would make a slow loop around it. Might show them that he was friendly and they would defiantly contact Earth. So people would know he was coming.

After a couple loop around the space station, David headed toward Earth. Unlike the space shuttle, he could control his speed instead of sliding into the atmosphere. He could drop in and not look like a ball of fire.

David had just drop in when he started hearing thing in his head. He strained to listen closer, people were thinking they were going to die up here and about their family members. There were six different thoughts. David was trying to separate them. He did have a communicating device. But did not know the frequency they were on. He powered up and climb back into space. Once Out of the atmosphere, he could hear them clearer.

David figured out it was the space shuttle, when it went by him at seventy thousand miles an hour. David pushed the throttle a head and caught up with them on the third orbit around Earth.

He was thinking hard what frequency the space shuttle ran. All he could think of was at one time they did talk to ham radio operators. But he never got to talk to them. David was thinking what frequency they were running. He was not sure if he remembered it or someone thought of it somehow it came to him 10 meter band. So he slid through the different frequency till he got to the 10 meter band. Finally he heard hello, hello, hello, anyone out there.

Hi David answered nice day for a flight, how you doing over there.

There was a silence except in his head. There were all kinds of strange thoughts; the strongest was, what is it?

Hello David said again. Do you have a problem over there? This is the space traveler next to you. He could see faces in the shuttle port windows

David still had my space suite on so he probably looked strange to them.

Yes we were hit by some space trash, it rupture our fuel tank. We cannot get out of orbit.

Well don't worry, we will think of something. David knew he had a small tractor beam, for picking up space trash, but would it hold a shuttle. If he could save this shuttle it would make a great introduction to the people on Earth, but he didn't want to risk the lives of six men. He asked in the commutator if I can slow you down and drop you in the atmosphere can you land.

Don't know it's never been done before. I don't know how to get back up speed to land probably just drop like a rock And if we got up to speed no way to slow down We would burn up.

Well it's up to you, I'm not sure my tractor beam will hold your shuttle once we hit the earth gravity. I do have room for three or four of you here in my traveler. Do you have a way of getting over here? I could take down three and come back for the rest. It would take me about 2 hours to land and come back, could you hold out that long David asked?

Yes we can hold out for weeks if needed ,does your hatch match up with ours.

No afraid you'll have to walk over David answered. I can hold the tractor beam it will hold us together how will be come out.

Out the bay doors, that the only access to outside. It will be a long walk.

Let me know when you are ready. I can maneuver almost in to your bay to make easier David said.

They open the bay doors. David moved toward their bay, his space traveler larger than there shuttle, it would not go all the way in. David locked in the tractor beam. Soon out of the hatch way came three astronauts in bulky space suites, on a safety line. David drop his cabin pressure and went to open the entrance door, just as the first astronaut arrived, they barley fit through his door in their suite.

David motion to one side then he got the next one in soon all three were in. He shut the door and made my way back up the control center. It was a good thing we did not take four astronauts; it was quite crowed with him and three astronauts in their suites. He moved away from the shuttle and waved. Then said in the commutator don't go away, be back in a couple of hours.

Be looking forward to seeing you, they wave back looking a little worried.

David eases the throttle back and watches the shuttle disappear a head of them. Then looked back at his passenger, smiled and waved welcome. They could not hear him with their helmets on, but waved back. They were still not sure they did the right thing. David pressurizes the cabin and adds gravity. Then motion they could take off their helmets. Reluctant one did testing the air.

Oxygen a little richer than that on earth, but OK to breathe, David said over his shoulder. Where you boys want drop off at the Kennedy Space Center or in Houston.

The cape would probably be best, who are you?

Actually I'm the ambassador from Kula heading for your Earth. What are the radio frequencies for the cape? Better tell them were coming. One of the astronauts gave it to him, and he punched it in to the commutator.

Hello cape, this is Ambassador, David had not thought of that, He could not give them his name at this time.

This is the Ambassador from the Kula. I have three of your astronauts from your space shuttle. I'm Requesting permission to land at Cape Kennedy in forty five minutes.

Permission granted, we have been fallowing your craft and know what is going on.

Thank you, please keep everyone back. I will be taken off as soon as these gentlemen get out and go back and pick up the others.

Request granted Mr. Ambassador you have a clear runway.

Forty three minutes later David was landing on the runway! As he got to the door OK gentleman here your stop please take your entire luggage with you thank you, hope you enjoy the flight. All three laugh and shook David hand and thank him.

When they were out an ambulance came out of a shop, but before it could get to the ship, David had the hatch shut and was back in the control seat taking off. Straight up and then forward, He was at mark four before leaving the atmosphere. It warmed his little space traveler up. I guess I was showing off a little, once in space He thought.

David speed-ed up with no problem; He just had to find the space shuttle. It didn't take long; they called on the cape channel.

We are ten miles above you, coming on fast. Having another little problem, no air in the cockpit we are in our suites, with limited air supply.

OK I'll let you go by then catch up how long is your air supply

Twenty minutes to a half hour.

OK plenty of time coming up. David spotted the shuttle, added power and caught up in just half an orbit. It took the rest of the orbit to get into position. As soon as he was in position the other three came out of the hatch way. David dropped the atmosphere in his traveler and opened the door the astronaut climbed in fast. David closed the door and went to the control and pressurized the cabin. Then told them it was safe to take off their helmets.

All did without hesitation and suck in the clean air. Man, I thank God for you being here, a few more minutes and I'd be talking to him in person the captain said.

Well I'm just glad I happen to be in the neighborhood. Now

commander what should we do about your shuttle craft David asked?

I hate to just leave her floating around and in about ten years it comes falling to Earth, he said.

Well if we had those hatch doors close. We might try to bring it down in one peace, David answered.

They are control by a lever inside the hatchway. The commander answered. No way to shut it then still get out.

Tell me about this lever, David asked?

Black with red on top, push up opens the doors, down closes the doors. There no way to get out in time.

I have an ideal; David moved my traveler away and set the tractor beam. I'll be right back don't touch anything. David thought about the hatchway and pressed what he called the go button and instantly was inside the hatch way. He spotted the lever they had describe and pulled it down. Then thought about his control seat in the traveler and pressed the button again and was back before the doors were half way closed.

How did you do that the commander asked?

David held up the transporter, it called a transported good for short distance. Hell I don't know it might even transport to earth. Don't think I'd want to try it thou. Well shell we see if we can get your ship back to Earth we might lose it when we hit Earth gravity.

Go ahead it will come down sooner or later might as well be when we know it will.

OK here we go, so with the tractor beam lock on. David began slowing down the space traveler. It was slow but their speed was going down, and they were also going down. By the time they hit the atmosphere the shuttle and space traveler started skipping going too fast to enter. David put all the power in to slowing down. The shuttle spring forward then like an elastic band sprung back almost hitting the traveler. But it did slow down, enough to drop them into the atmosphere. David held one hand on the release control just in case. The tractor beam was holding. I'm going to hold it over the ocean, just in case I have to drop your shuttle, he told the commander.

That alright we can retrieve it now if we need to.

They got down to one thousand feet then David push the power forward it stop their decent and contained forward motion. The tractor beam was holding better than David expected. He then contacted the cape, requesting landing instructions.

You can leave it at the end of the runway, oh and thank you for bring it back do you have Commander Roberts, Lt. Hanson, and Lt. Hoffman with you.

Yes they are safe in my craft. David heard a cheer go up over the radio.

Well thank you again you can just throw them out anywhere. Will you be staying with us for a while?

If it is OK with you, I would like to talk to your Ambassador to the United Nation and only him.

OK there is a place at the end of the runway by building B; we will have security set up for you and thanks again for helping out. You say you are the Ambassador from where.

Not where from Kula, it is a federation of planets. David set the shuttle on the runway, releases the tractor beam and moved to where they had mention. It wasn't hard to find security was already set up at lease twenty solders standing around. Before David could open the door for the astronauts, security was in place. The commander was last to leave. He shook David hand, thanked him again, and committed on how nice my space traveler was. Then he asked, if he was coming with them. David informed him he wasn't and he did need to talk to all Nations Ambassador. His business was with all countries of Earth, not just one. This would keep from causing problem. He'd wait here for the United Nations Ambassador.

Chapter 4

The First Device From Space Used On Earth

David had time to think sitting there in his space traveler .while the guys at NASA figured out how to get a hold of the Ambassador to the United Nations. Why not transporter over and see his mother at least let her know he was not dead.

David thought of front lawn of her house and hit the transported button instantly he was there. When he knocked on the door, to his surprise a different lady answered.

Hi I'm looking for Martha Nulls he asked!

She in the hospital the lady answered.

Hospital which one, what happen?

The one in town, in room 231, she had a Heart attack, and she in a coma they don't expect her to last through the night. They are taking her off life support tonight a request by her children.

David thanked her and left and as soon as she closed the door. He transported back to the space traveler. Picked up a few things then transported to the park across from the hospital. He crossed the street and enters the hospital through a side door. Went straight to room 231 there He found his brother and sister with their husband and wife. There was his mother with no tubes attach. They had already disconnected her life support.

They looked surprise when he walked in and even more surprise when he told them to get out. At first they try to protest. David gave them my I'll kill you look and repeated get the hell out now. All four scramble for the door. Leaving him alone with his mother, He took out the mikso (hand doctor) would be a description of it. Started at his mother feet and slowly move it up to her head the red and green lights blinked off and on. As it found and repaired anything that was wrong when all was green. He put the mikso away and walked out in to the waiting room, where his brother and sister were sitting with their families. Well don't except to collect your inherent for another 20 years, she going to be alright, and just to add to their shock David walked through the wall to the next room.

They all just sat there a few minutes. Then they went into their mother's room. Where she sat on the edge of the bed just starting to stand up, David brother went to help her, she brushed him away I can do it on my own. Almost sprang out of the bed. Stretch her arms reaching toward the ceiling and back a few times. I have not felt this good in 20 years. Boy I'm hungry for a chocolate Sunday. Come on let's go to the cafeteria and see if they have any there, as she walked passed everyone, and added a little skip in her step. Then turned and said you know I dreamed I saw David walk out of the room, is he here.

Mon, David been missing for over a year his brother answered.

I know, off on some adventure, but was he here. Oh well we will see him when he decided to show up, He always dose, come on Sundays are on me.

Meanwhile when David walked through the wall, he was in the next room. There was a nurse attending another patient. She looked up and spotted him. Who are you and how did you get in here she asked?

Give me one minute to explain. David took out the mikso and adjusted the switches and starting to run over her patient see he has a broken leg it read then moving up, it read crack rib, moving further up broken collar bone, at the head it read skull fractured. Now watch this David flipping the switch. And running the mikso over him again this time the lights flashed red and green. The red means it found something wrong. Green means it repaired it. By the time David reached the patients head. The man opens his eyes, started moving around, and then smile at the nurse.

Hi, man I feel great any chance I can get something to eat.

The nurse step back tripping over the cart next to her, looking at David, how did you do that?

It's called a mikso a new medical device used for healing. Come, let's check out another patient, and I'll let you try it. They left that room and in to another. The nurse was still skeptic of him, in the next room there was a small boy who had been hit by a car. He was in a coma and in bad shape with broken bones and internal bleeding he would be going into surgery in a half hour. She said

David like that, she had picked out a good one to test on, he turned on the mikso and started at his feet and slowly moved up to his head the lights blinked red and green. A few minutes after he finished the boy set up asked where his mother was and can he go home, as he climbed out of bed.

That put the nurse into a state of wonderment. OK what's the trick? I'm I on camera or something.

No not a trick, just advance science. Come on you do the next one. In the next room they meet a lady whose kidneys had failed and she was on dailies machine.

David handed the nurse, mikso it gave her a light shock she almost drop it, what was that she asked?

That was the mikso adapting to you, now only you can use this machine. David then explained the switches there he pointed only four so it was easy. As she moved it over the ladies body the red and green light flashed. Soon afterwards the lady sat up still hooked to the machine and said she felt fine in fact she had never felt this good in the last ten years.

The nurse looked at David, this thing is amassing, how about cancer.

Yes he answered even on cancer.

Really OK now tell me who are you and why haven't I heard about this machine before.

I think you had better sit down for this. David said leading her to a chair.

As she sat down, David started, you have heard about the space craft that saved the astronauts right.

Yes everyone has the alien craft that came out of nowhere. She Stopped, That was, she hesitated, and you are not from this planet, this mikso you call it. Is not from this world is it. She almost dropped it again.

You are right it's not from this world. It's a present from a civilization far advance than yours. That wants to be friend with your planet. We can teach a lot of things that will improve your world and we mean you no harm. And will not invade your planet like all your movies say we will. What I need for you to do is heal as many people as possible to show your people that I come in peace. I will be giving other country the mikso Tomorrow, you just happen to be the first.

So you look like us. She added

Oh he hadn't thought of that, she could give him away by his description. Not really David said this is like a mask. If you think you can handle it I'll show what we really look like. David hit the button on his space suite, it turning him into a green marshmallow man, hoping that this would work. When he turned off the suite he could see it in her eyes it would.

David stayed with her for a couple more patients then telaported back to his space traveler. He heard later she healed over a hundred people by morning.

Chapter 5

Contact Is Made

After several days the United States, Ambassador to the United Nation contacted David, asking him if they could meet. David told him it would be alright but anything. He had to tell would be to the whole United Nations Assembly. That he was not going to favor any one country.

The United State Ambassador to the United Nations said he under stood, and they were trying to get all the United Nation Ambassador assembled except it would take a week.

A few hours later a privet plane landed at Cape Kennedy, two men got out and walked toward David space traveler. The security stopped them (David was glad to see, that their orders were, no one was to come up toward his ship.) David went out wearing my Ambassador uniform. It looked more like jump suit of green with a blue sash. He took advantage of the changing device. So as not to look like David Nulls, He had added a touch of green to his body. Hell, that what the people of Earth think, that all people from space are green anyways.

David informed the solders it was all right to let them go by.

The ambassador for the United States introduced himself. Then introduced the Ambassador from India, saying he was the only other

United Nation member in town. Would it be alright if he joined us?

David nodded it was OK.

He then motion over to a table and chairs, David had not notice before; they must have been set up a few minutes before because there were three chairs.

As they sat down the Ambassador from the United State ask if he could get me anything, like food or water as he pointed to the bottle on water on the table.

David declined then asked, do you think that I came here on a whim? We have been studying your planet for years. I know who the Ambassadors to the United Nations are and the Ambassador from India. So who are you CIA, FBI, or some other government office? What did you expect to accomplish with this little crusade.

They both gave David that look like they were in shock!

Now don't give me that look, like you are surprise.

David did not want tell them their thoughts were coming through loud and clear.

Well, actually the President of the United States sent us. He would like to personally thank you for saving the Astronaut's.

You tell him no thanks is needed, I'm sure your astronaut's would do the same for me, if it was the other way around. Beside they are the real heroes for trusting a stranger coming from out of nowhere to help them. Now you can tell your President it would be nice if he invited representatives from all countries. Not just members from the United Nations. What I have to say concerns all the people of this world. Now have a good day, and by the way don't drink that water you offered me. You might not wake up till tomorrow. David got up and went back to his space traveler.

As he entered the traveler, he thought shit they have a lot of nerve. I bring them the most advance technology of this century and they want to use trickery. At least I got my point across that I wanted to talk to representatives from every country not just the members of the United Nations.

David spent the next two days bouncing from country to country testing how far he could really transport. He found out he could go anywhere on the planet. This was really cool, he could be seeing the pyramids in Egypt and the next minuet he is on the Great Wall of China. Everywhere he went the talk was about the alien that had landed. It was a little disturbing; that every place he went there was also a picture of him, in his Ambassador uniform and being green. Someone must have taken a picture at the Cape Kennedy when he was talking to the fake United Nation Ambassadors. I'll bet someone got rich off that picture David thought.

Oh what the hell, now he could go to any country, and be known as just a tourist. Who could speak their language? He did surprise some people in Rome, when he just showed up out of nowhere. David just walked off, like he had been there all the time, but made a note to myself to be a little more careful before materializing. Every where he went he would find someone and leave a mikso unit.

After his travels, when he got back to his space traveler. There was a note on the window, for him to contact NASA. He called them on the radio.

The United Nation assembly would meet in three days. That an escort would pick him up the day before and take him there.

David stopped him there; I believe it will be better if I fly to Kennedy International airport, that morning. Your escort can meet me there. David knew the United Nations building had a heliport but it was too small to land his space traveler. And he really didn't want to be that far from his traveler, after the last shenanigan's they had tried to pull.

Yes, we will arrange that they will be expecting you on the assembly floor at noon. It means we will have to leave Kennedy international around ten o'clock, Do you know our time.

Yes I know your time, that's 10 am. eastern time. I will leave at 11: 30 pm. the day before and land at Kennedy international airport at 2:20 am. There is a half hour window when no planes will be landing.

How does he know that? Then a hand must have covered the mike.

I do my homework, as you say on your world, as David answered his question.

OK at 2:20am. Three days from now, we will notify the tower of your arrival. Will you need anything else?

No that will be quite enough, thank you.

Well everything was set only thing to do was to wait.

Finally the big day arrived; David lifted off at 11:30. He could make the flight in twenty minutes, but he found flying the traveler relaxing. Yes he was nerviest, damn he was going to be talking to representative from every nation in the world, and trying to get them to change their way of life.

David had his speech all planed out and rehearsed. He had so much to offer them. How could they refused, And what if they did?

The counsel said they had faith in him, to do the right thing. He just needed faith in himself.

David flew up along the coast, the moon was almost full. He could see the waves glittering, as they broke on the shore line. He was thinking how lucky the people of earth were, and the last year how He had missed the ocean. Yes there was water on other planets, small lake and rivers; they were nothing like the ocean here on Earth.

Chapter 6

The Offer

Lady and gentlemen, of this assembly, I have come to your planet as a representative from the Federation of planets, known as the Kula. My space traveler has no weapons on it; it does have a protection shielding. I assure you no one else will come, uninvited. I come with an invitation for you to join the federation, I will be your representative here, you can send one or as many as you like to represent you at the Kula counsel, but you will be allowed only one vote, the same as all the other planets. We will share with you our technology and the knowledge of over seven hundred planets in the Kula, or as you call it, the coalition of planets. The first of this thing is the healing box. We call Mikso; you have heard of this device, it has healed hundreds of people in the United States, India, China, and the Soviet Union. I will arrange that every country will receive this device even before your decision to join the federation. Some of you have heard of the little stones. David took five of the stones out of my pocket, holding up for everyone to see, and then he places them on the podium in front of him. These stones when added to your fossil fuel will increase the efficient one hundred times over. To the dismay of the OPECT countries he added. An example is a truck that's gets five miles to the gallon, now gets five hundred miles per gallon of fossil fuel. This will reduce the dependent of the country that have no oil. I will show where you can obtain these, at no cost.

We will help you to build a space traveler, a lot bigger than the one I arrived in. It will be an international joint project, and it will travel twelve times the speed of light. We would not want your represents to be late for a Kula council meeting.

Everyone laughed at this; David could see some were courtesy laughs. But it did break the ice, it helped them to see that he was human, even though he had the shield of green on.

David continued, I know you are asking yourself why the federation is offering all this technology. What does it want in return? You are right to be suspicious, I would be.

Let me explain, you have enter the nuclear age. You have enough nuclear bombs to blow your planet into little pieces. Possible turn it into another one of your suns. This would cause the gravitation pull from other suns to collide, causing a black hole to form, sucking all the other planets into it even other stars, and this would destroy other living forms. We have seen this happen several times.

We are not asking you to destroy all your nuclear weapons, only to reduce them by two thirds. We don't care if you want to blow yourself up we just don't want you to blow the whole planet up.

The choice is up to you, reduce your nuclear weapons, and the sky is the limit. Or should I say the sky has no limits. Now I will try to answer your questions.

The place went into an uproar. David raised his hands one at a time please. I believe the Ambassador from China was first.

I hear you talking to me in Chinese. But no one else is translating. Is your language Chinese.

David thought, I just told them to reduce their nuclear weapons by 2/3 and they want to know if I speak their language. He held up his wedding band, and pointed. This device translates my voice into seven thousand different languages. So that you hear me in Chinese, the Ambassador from Japan hears me in Japanese, whiles the Ambassador from England, and hears me in English. I on the other hand hear you in my language. I hope that answers your question.

He answered yes, thank you then sat down.

Next was Mr. Falua, the Ambassador form Iran. Who will decide which country will disarm their nukes?

Not disarm, destroy, and that will be left up to you to discuss. We will have no say in that matter. I can tell you after destroying 2/3 of your nuclear weapons. You will still have enough left for every country to have one or two.

That seemed to answer most of the question, the hand waving drop to just a few.

Next David recognized the Ambassador from Germany.

Who will build this space ship that goes faster than light?

The people of this world will. We will give you a transporter to move parts from Earth to space. I will be an adviser. If approved by all of you we will send a few technicians to help.

OK next Mr. Lane the Ambassador from the United States your question.

Thank you, but what will you do if we turn down your offer.

There it was, the question, David did not want to answer, but he was not going to lie to them.

Well first of all you will lose out on a lot of good technology, and we will systematically place four satellites around your globe that will identifies and destroy any nuclear missile that get over five hundred feet above the ground.

All hands drop, there were no more question. As this went through everyone mind.

David notice that there were no more questions, he straighten up. Now I know you need to talk this over with your individual government. I'll leave and let you discuss our offer.

David felt better, the hard part was over. All of a sudden one of the soldiers fell over, with blood coming out of his head. Three others soldiers jump on David, pushing him to the ground. People were running and screaming everywhere. No one knew where the shot had come from they just knew someone was shot. They brought up the car and David was literally picked up and thrown in, the Sargent climbed in beside him. And they were rush off to the airport.

Seem like someone not too happy about you being here. The Sargent said after they were on the freeway. I believe we need to up your security.

Why me David asked you don't think they were after me.

Well here in America people don't go around shooting soldier. That bullet was most like meant for you.

Why would someone want to kill me? I'm bring them advance technology, space travel, and a better way of life. In return, asking them not to destroy their own planet.

Maybe someone from the oil company's, or even the medical profession, or even some terrorist group. They all have a lot to lose. Hay it might be some religion fanatic. Who knows? But I'll bet a month pay they were not after one of my men.

David sat back thinking, this make thing a lot more difficult. He did not consider all the consequence this new technology would cause.

Chapter 7

The Truth Comes Out

We will set you up some place that is safe. The Sargent said.

Thank you but I need to go to NASA at the Cape and talk to them.

OK will tell them you are coming. He said as David entered the space traveler, and closed the door. The sergeant gave him the thumbs up meaning he could take off. David lifted off and head south. He then contacts NASA on the frequency of the space shuttle. Which caused a little excitement at the cape?

Because there was no shuttle craft in space, And they had to get someone from mission control, is this you Mr. Ambassador.

Yes, I was wondering if I could speak to Commander Roberts. (He was the commander of the shuttle that he had rescued form space.)

I believe he is on base it will take a few minutes to locate him they answered back.

Thank you is there any chance I can land at the Cape.

There was a long pause; David figured he was getting permission.

Permission granted we have cleared the run way. You can park where you were we will have security set up what time will you be here?

About twenty minutes, did you find Commander Roberts?

Yes he will be here shortly.

David was on the downwind approach. Commander Roberts came over the radio. Mr. Ambassador what can I do for you.

How about taken a little ride with me, I need to show you something.

There was a long pause then Commander Roberts came back on. Yes sir it will be all right I'll meet you on the runway.

David stopped the space traveler in the spot at the end of the runway, with the security. Commander Roberts. Met him at the door of the traveler.

Hi Ambassador what have you got in mind.

Call me David; I'd like to show you something on the back side of the moon.

Of the moon, he asked?

Yes the moon about a four hour trip, with a short stop along the way.

Oh what the hell, this will be something to talk about at the next bar-be-Q. But why me I'm sure anyone in this world would give an arm and leg to go to the moon, and really the moon and back four hours.

Yes really there and back in four hours. Come on in and have a seat. David took off; in minutes they were in space.

I notice you don't have seat belts Roberts said.

You don't need them, with the gyros in this craft it counter act the thrust force.

I thought it might be because of your physical make up Commander Roberts stated.

Well this is a good time for your first surprise. David push the button on the belt. And instantly he turned in to David Null.

The commander took a second look, how you do that.

It simple, just touch of a button, it all in this suit David pointing at the button on his belt.

But you're white, not green why!

We got an hour so I'll tell you a story that you cannot repeat. You see a year ago I was abducted. Well I agreed to go. So I spent the last year in a different galaxy learning how to do this job as Ambassador. They don't want to have an alien as an Ambassador. So they pick up four people from this planet and pick one of us. I was the one they selected.

But the green the commander interrupted

That was my ideal, everyone on earth think that aliens are green. Who am I to disappoint them! Remember when I telaported to the shuttle. I can do that all over Earth and if I did it being green I'd stick out like a sore thumb. But as me I can go anywhere.

By the way if you're not an alien how do you do that? Commander asked

It was not easy it taken almost eight months to learn. Now here comes the big surprise, they came around to the back side of the moon.

Holy shit! What is that, the commander asked starring out the window.

That my African friend is a space cargo ship; it is what the Kula are going to give to the people of Earth, so they can build a larger space exploration ship, come on do want to see the inside.

You think they will let us?

Never know till we asked. David turned in the radio and called Kitaracta. David didn't want to give away the secret of using the mental power of talking. Hi captain, this is Ambassador Null. I have an astronaut from Earth. We are Requesting permission to come aboard.

Permission granted Mr. Ambassador, Bay 3 is open.

They landed, when door were closed they step out. Kitaracta was there to meet them she slipped on a bracelet on to the commander arm. How do you do commander, welcome. I'm Captain Kitaracta.

Kit I call her took me four months to lean to pronounce her name David added.

It is nice to meet you Captain, What this bracelet Commander Roberts asked?

It's a translator; it will translate in seven thousand different languages. Without it you would not be able to understand us and we would not understand you.

Now Mr. Ambassador anything we can do for you.

As a matter of fact, do you think you can get can get me about a thousand more of the hand healers the miKso.

I'll get right on it. Do you want to show Mr. Robert's around the ship.

Yes and thank you, Come on Commander There's a lot of interesting things, you are about to see

David gave Commander Roberts the grand tour and saved the recreation room for last. At that door he stops him, Up till now all the crew members look human. I'm sure Captain Kitaracta had ordered it.

Ok Commander now you have meet the whole crew you remember how I used the belt to change to a green person will in this room all crew members will be in what they look like in their natural form.

To David surprise the commander was not surprise as he had expected. Command Roberts even found the engineer and sat down and got into a conversation. David excused himself and as went to find Captain Kitaracta.

Hi Ambassador put your order in should be here in a few days. How is it going down there?

Work out real good saving the astronaut. It made a good introduction.

Yes that was convent a peace of debris hit a fuel tank leaving six men stranded.

You said that like you knew all about it. Did you have anything to do with that David asked?

I also heard someone try to kill you do you know what that was all about.

Waite a minuet you are changing the subject. What do you know about the shuttle David asked again?

I know that it made for a good introduction and that all I'm going to say about it. Now back to this someone was trying to kill you, do you know why?

Hay someone must not like improvement, and still want to live in the Stone Age.

I think you had better be more careful she said.

Hay you are worried about me.

Green people don't worry about white people.

You were worried, come on admit it you were worried.

Alright I was worried; we have to much invest in you, for you to turn up dead.

Chapter 8

A Surprise For The Doctors

Back at the cape, the reporters were all over Commander Roberts, He was true to his word. All he would say was anything he had to say was that he would tell to the United Nations at their next meeting and he told them anything he had learned belong to all Nations.

NASA informed David they had better security, And that he was to park his space traveler in building C. Well that was not going to happen, David thought.

Thank you, but I believe it will be safer in space. I'll be monitoring your frequencies if you have any information for me from the United Nations and he would be taken off shortly David informed them.

That will be fine; we will be keeping a channel open. And you are cleared to take off when you are ready.

A few minutes later David informed them he was leaving. He lifted off and headed toward the cargo ship, behind the moon.

Kit met him at the bay. Well this is a nice surprise, what brings you back.

You know it's your magnet personally, and your beautiful smile. It sound good and was half way true.

I like the half that is true, and the other half. The fact it is safer.

The next two days Kit and David ran around doing the things like kids, when they are in love, holding hands, looking through the telescope at the planets, together taken long walks on the moon. Sorry kids you cannot do that, it's quite Romantic. The rest, He would not go in to details but says it was fantastic.

Two days later, Kit informed David that four large crated had been transported to the cargo bay, with the mikso in them. They were loading one on his space traveler; there was only room for one at a time.

David had forgotten about them. Now he needed a way to distribute them. He had passed out a few when he was bouncing around when he first got there. He thought of the Red Cross, or even the Peace Corp, as he was heading his traveler toward Earth. Then remember something about the medical profession was having a big convention in Belgium that he had heard about while bouncing around the world early. Most likely they were discussing the ones, he had already handed out. But getting invited might be a bit of a problem. Maybe the Surgeon General could get him in, if only I had a way to get a hold of him.

Then he was sitting there thinking about Kit. When she came speaking into my head.

How sweet, thinking about me with all that on your mind she said, why you don't just transport in to his office.

What you can hear me thinking this far away, how far away can you hear my thoughts?

Quite a ways in space there nothing out there to interfere with thought waves she answered.

David told her it just wasn't proper to pop in on someone unexpected, especially a high government official. They would be shot by secret service men. Before they could say, I come in peace

Kit and David talked, well thought for a few minutes. David Then called NASA asked if they could get him in touch with the Surgeon General of the United States.

A few minutes later, NASA called him back on the communicator.

The Surgeon General was at a conference out of the country and it would take a while to connect them up, on a secured line.

David thanked them, and told he would be standing by.

An hour later NASA contacted David. We have Dr. Warner the United States Surgeon General on the line.

Hello Dr. Warner this is the Ambassador from the Kula federation. I know that you are at the medical convention in Belgium. And I would like to address that convention.

I'm sure they would like to hear from you but I don't know if they have the security to do it, I will talk to the others and see what can be arranged. Can I get back with you later today, he asked.

Yes just contact NASA, I will be standing by.

An hour later David was thinking wished he knew what was going on down there.

Why don't you transport down and see, it was Kit in his head again.

That would work just park my space traveler in the parking lot and lock it up and walk in.

Well how about I take you down. Then come back up or just cruse around, in range for you to transport back if there any trouble.

Now that sound like a plan I can live with. I will come over and pick you up David said.

No need I can transport over to you.

Nothing you people do surprise any more David said. As he was finishing his sentence, she materialized in the space traveler.

David blinked; I thought you were not to go to the planet.

Basically I'm not going on the planet.

They traded places, with Kit at the controls she drop into the atmosphere and down to around fifty thousand feet, saying we should be clear of air traffic here, go ahead and transport.

David transported in next to the building as David Nulls as to fit in as one of the conventioneers, and walked into the building. There were all kinds of excitement going on. Most were talking about him and the upcoming meeting.

David talked to several of the doctors, telling them that the spaceman was most likely friendly and just wanted to help and they should hear him out. They all agreed it would best to at least hear what he had to say but would security be able to protect him They had heard about the shooting at the United Nations building.

After an hour of this David, contact Kit OK ready to transport back where you are.

Just think a foot behind me then transport there. David did as she said and hit the transport button, and was again in the space traveler.

A half hour later they got a call from NASA we have Dr. Warner on the line for you.

Hello Doctor Warner this is the Ambassador

Yes Mr. Ambassador we would like for to come to our convention but are worried about security.

I can transport directly in to the convention room. All they need to watch is outside David said.

You can do that, he asked?

Yes I believe there is a large space next to the speaker.

I don't think I want to know how you know that, when do you want to come he answered?

As soon as possible, you can contact me when you are ready.

OK give me an hour to get it arrange.

It was more like an hour and a half before he called David and said they were ready.

David got out three of the mikso to take with him; Kit kissed him that for luck she said.

David switched on his space suite, so I looked like a green marshmallow to protect my identity. Then thought of the space he saw while he was checking thing out, on his first trip to the convention. Pressed the button on the suite and the next minuet he was standing in front of two hundred doctors with faces that had ether a surprise look or just wonderment.

After seeing that no one was going to shoot him, David spoke. Ladies and gentleman I know this looks a little strange .it is for my protection if you will give me a second I'll turn it off. As he said it he pushed another button and became human form only in green.

Doctor Warner came over to David shook his hand, come you are welcome here I believe you have something to tell these doctors.

Thank you and yes I do David held up one of the mikso, this is the device of the future it does not mean to replace you. It is to make your life easier. And to save lives. I will give each one of you one, and another extra one to distribute to the country's that is not represented here. All I ask is that you charge minimal fee for using .and if someone cannot afford it do it free.

A gentleman stood up in the back so you want us to operate free. We will go broke in a week.

Yes free and a minimal charge to those who can afford it. Think back, did you go to medical school to get rich or to help your man kind. I'm sure if you are sitting in this room that you are here to help your fellow man. Well, this device will do just that. Now do you wish for me to give you a demonstration or would you like to ask some more questions?

Let see a demonstration first, I have heard of it but have never seen it work came the answer.

OK. David said a demonstration first I see a gentleman over there in a wheel chair. Would you like to come up here, and be our first example on how well this works?

He nodded and rolled up front and what is your name and can you walk.

My name is Doctor Reagan and most of you know I have not walked in nine years, since the car accident.

Then Sir, David said you are a good one to start with, can I get a couple of you young doctors to help get Doctor Reagan up here on the desk. Several came up and helped Doctor Reagan lay on the desk. David flipped the switches and started at his feet and moved up his body. When he came to the spot in his back, the lite turned red. David stopped and read the screen it says that the nerves are severed between seven and eight vertebra. David moved on up then stop when the lite came on. And read it again. Doctor did you know that you have a leaky heart valve.

Yes I'm to have surgery after this convention. He answered.

David ran the mikso all the way to his head. OK I told everyone now we have diagnosed a separated nerve and a leaky heart valve. Now we will repair both of them. David flip the switches, and started at his feet and moved slowed toward the top of his head the lite turned red at the nerve to be repaired then turned green the same when it passed over his heart.

Once finished David asked the doctor how he felt.

I feel great I can even feel my feet he answered

Then are you ready to walk David asked

Walk hell I feel like running out and get something to eat. As he pushes himself up and sat on the edge of the desk.

David turned to the other members, that is the one side effect they all want something to eat first, it will go away after the first meal.

The whole audience stood up and applauded, David looked behind him and Doctor Reagan was standing testing his lags. Then he walked over to David and shook his hand.

I don't know how you did it, but you have my vote.

Oh by the way you can cancel that leaky heart valve appointment. It fixes that to David added.

Then Doctor Reagan walked over to the wheel chair and kicked it. Good riddance you pile of junk.

Everyone laughed and there were all kinds of question. Most David could answer, will it cure this, and will it cure that. When it came to how does it work. The only answered David had, it diagnose the problem then repairs it. A lot of question were directed toward Doctor Reagan how do you feel any side effect to this he answered I'm hungry.

The last question stopped everyone. When can we get one of those devices you call mikso.

After a quick lesson on how to use the mikso you can walk out of here with one. We can start when everyone is ready. Have a seat and we will begin. Every one sat down.

OK two volunteers please, two men came forward. Which one wants to be the patient? One doctor stepped forward I'll be the patent as he went around the desk and laid down.

OK, David handed the mikso to the other doctor. The shock will be the device aliening itself to you only and only you. It will read in your language. Every one watching, first two switches up next two down. When he did the doctor got the shock. Now it is set up for you three switches up and slowly moves up the body from feet to head. As he moved it up the red lite came on and stays on all the way up at his head the doctor read the device, cancer, all the way up.

Did you know you have cancer of the bone threw out your body? David asked

Yes, they say I have four months to live.

OK back to the demonstration, this gentleman has cancer threw out his body. Now flip all switches up and repeat the scene. This time the lite turned red to green as it passed over the body. When it reached his head it showed both green.

The man sat up, wow no pain. Everyone applauded.

Did everyone understand first two up, activated it all four down turn off. All four up scans and heals. They seemed to understand it was fairly easy considering they were all educated Doctors. Now if we can clear this aria here and everyone move to the wall. David placed the disk Kit had given him. And then mentally contacted Kit to send the crate. Moments later where the device was, there was a stack of mikso not a crate all in little boxes.

David thought of Kit, well you can surprise me.

It came back I'm a female; we always have a surprise for our men.

David smiled hoping that the doctor was thinking it was because of the delivery.

They were all handed out and the extra were given out to be passed on. David told the Surgeon General if he needed more contact the cape they would contact him.

The next day David contacted the Peace Corp and told them the doctors were using them. He then gave them a demonstration and left a crate for then to hand out to their members. The same with the Red Cross soon all the mikso were passed out.

Now it was back to the waiting game again, the best place. Was up with Kit in the cargo space craft behind the moon?

Chapter 9

Well Thats Just Blows Up Everything

Now they are going to believe anything I say. It should help them want to join the Federation. David told Kit that going to be one healthy planet and just for getting rid of a few nukes.

I really don't know what going to happen, the people on your planet are a strange bunch. They will probable want to negotiate something, or have it in writing Kit said.

Yes your right wasn't always that way; a person's word was good. Now you need a lawyer to write up a contract to borrow your Neighbors lawn mower, they both laughed.

A few days later the United Nation chairman contacted David thew NASA. The United Nations Assemble would meet in a week, on Wednesday with an answer. And would it be alright if he came by Thursday, David said it would fine and he would like to bring Commander Roberts along.

There was a long pause, then yes it would be alright, then NASA cut in saying they would have Commander Roberts there. There was a long pause; David thought they were talking with the Chairman.

We will see you then and sign off. Well that was a fast answer. It could be good or it could be bad hard to tell Kit said it's hard to tell your specie's are unpredictable. I think you had better be prepared for anything, and it might be best to transport in. That way you can get out fast if needed.

Hay lady where your faith, you need to think positive.

She reached and patted David hand. That what I like about you, others see a glass half empty you see it half full, in your eyes everything is a bed of roses, and if not you will plant more. But I'll tell you one thing someone took a pot shot at you. You just be careful, it might be best if I stay close.

Wednesday came and went without incidents Thursday came NASA informed David that Commander Roberts would be there and they would be expecting us right after lunch break around 2 o:clock,

Kit insisted on taken David to the meeting and stay at twelve thousand feet, but five miles away. David thought of Commander Roberts then two feet behind him and transported, check out that it was clear then push finial.

Commander Roberts jump a little when David materialize behind him. They were in a separate room.

I don't know how you do that. But I wish you would give some kind of warning. Well what do you think is going to happen today Roberts asked?

It is impossible to figure out what your government is going to do next. Yet alone what a hundred different governments are thinking. Just then a page stuck his head in the door, looked at David in surprise, oh your both here, as he looked around the room to see if there was another door. I'll inform the assembly you're here.

A few minutes letter he came back and escorted David and Commander Roberts into the assembly room. The chairman motions them over to a chair on the right. We thought it best for you to be here for the vote we will have a roll calling the country with the most to the less. Then stepped to the microphone and announced United States of America, how do you vote.

The United State agree to reduce2/3 per cent. Next the Soviet Union they agree to reduc2/3. And so it went china agree2/3 England agree/ India agree /Iran agree.

David was feeling great, he did it. When Kit came screaming in his head. DAVID GET OUT NOW. Without thinking David hit the transporter button and was instantly in the middle of a river swimming toward some rocks. Not making it pushed back into the rapids going down stream. Finely finding a branch to grab on to caught his breath and cleared his head. He had no idea where he was. He pulled myself over to shore, and landed on the shore trying to figure what happen. Then remember Kit had said to get out. So he thought of Kit in the space traveler, and a foot behind her. When pushed the transporter button nothing happen.

What the hell, the damn thing is not waterproof he thought.

Just then Kit voice came in my head, faintly but he could make out what she said. Are you all right, where are you.

David answered back, I have no idea where the hell I'm at and yes I'm alright, but the transporter is not working.

Well stay where you are, this space traveler does not have a locator on it. I'll have to get my ship to find you.

OK but make it fast it's cold down here, David answered shivering.

Well turn on your space suit she said in his head. It will keep you warm.

Well crap he had not thought of that. He pushed the other button and the suite came on, if anyone was looking he was a green marshmallow. Looking around he was sure there was no one around, this was wilderness. The suit was warm, but he was still wet.

An hour later he was thinking. They're never going to find me; maybe he should try finding his way out of there.

No don't move we have located you, you are in Montana. We will be there in a few minutes. Be ready will transport you aboard.

Ten minutes later he was in the cargo ship. With Kit standing there looking at him. David turned off the space suit still wet. What the heck were you thinking when you pushed the transporter.

I don't know must have been thinking about fishing, only I didn't have a pole. I'm sure I was not thinking about swimming.

Well come along the sanitize will dry you off. Then well figure out what to do. It is a mess down there. The two rockets took out half the United Nations building, killing almost half the delegates.

What David asked?

Two of your U.S. made stinger missiles you call them were shot at the

United Nations building. I was afraid that you did not get out of there in time, till I heard you later. After your sanitized will pick up your traveler and see what the Kula will have to say.

We need to figure out how to straighten this out. Do they know who fired the Stinger? What do you mean pick up my traveler?

I left it floating in space and transported to my ship to speed up your rescue after I found you were not in the building, when it exploited. They don't know who fired the rockets, it still in turmoil down there.

David came out of the sanitizer dry thinking about what happen.

Kit answered, came up I can show what happen, by backing up time a couple of hours.

In the control room Kit switch a screen and touch several places then the United Nation building came into focus , she touched a few more places on the screen, then they could see the rocket coming and hitting the building then exploding. Then a second missile comes in doing the real damage.

David stood there watching in disbelieve. I didn't know you were filming this can you back it up and see where the missal came from.

Kit turned to him, this is not a video this is real time. We moved back three hours in time. This is happen right now.

David just stood there letting this sink in. as she touch the screen the scene change back to the building in rubble. She then touches the screen again and it went back to before the missile was fired. We have to go back to current time before going back again, she explained

They all watch the screen, there David pointed that where the first one came from just then a second missal came out. Stop it right there, David said.

Kit looked at him it doesn't work that way we cannot stop anything in the past.

Can we video it David asked.

I don't know it has never been done before. Beside we do not have a video camera.

What, All your technology and you don't have a video camera

Don't need one, just picture it in our minds and pass it on.

Well here on earth we have not developed that technology yet. How about I go and get a video camera.

Where will you get that Kit asked.

It won't be hard on my planet almost everyone has one. If not a regular then they have one on their phone. Where is my space traveler?

We are coming up on it now, you will see it out the window any minuet. She answered his thoughts.

I'll need a new transporter, David thought back.

Yours should work now that it went through the sanitizer, but you might want to try it first before transporting over to your traveler.

That a good ideal David said, thinking of the resting room and pressing the button and making sure he was there before pushing finial. Instantly he was there it works fine. David thought of the control center and was back. Smiling, well works fine wish all my electronic could be fix that easy. OK I'll go down and get a camcorder

How are you going to do that Kit asked.

Oh that right I cannot just walk into Wall-Mart and buy one with no money. I did have some credit cards but I'm not sure they were good any more. Maybe my daughter has one, I'll try there first.

I hope you know what's your doing Kit said looking doubtful.

So do I, as David thought of the pilot seat in the space traveler and pushed the button. And end up in the traveler. As he checks everything out Kit materialized behind him. What are you doing he asked.

Well you're not going to just land in your daughter yard and walk up and ask to borrow her camera. I'll hold the traveler and you can transport down.

I'm glad one of us is thinking, welcome aboard. David took the traveler to one mile above the Pacific Ocean about five miles off shore and turned the controls over to Kit and thought of the lawn in front of his old house, then activated the transporter.

His grandson started shouting grand pa. His daughter came out of the house and hugs him. Have you heard what happen in New York someone killed the alien.

Yes I heard, that is kind of why I'm here, do you have a camcorder.

Yes, why where have you been? They said you were dead. Grandma and I didn't believe it thou.

It's a long story; I'll tell you later right now can I use the camcorder.

Sure I'll go get it, are you staying for dinner.

Maybe next time, David said as she left. Then she came back with the camcorder, and handed it to him.

David step back what you see here you cannot tell anyone. With that he thought two feet behind Kit and vanished. Back in the traveler David thought that should leave her something to think about.

Kit asked who is something to think about.

My daughter I vanished right in front of her. OK got the camcorder. Let's see if we can film the past.

We are already on our way back to my ship. Don't know what you hope to accomplish. We still need to contact the Kula.

Let's just hold off on that for a while. I have a plan in the back of my mine. I'll tell you when I figure it out.

Plan I didn't hear any, I did not think you could block anything from me.

Everyone needs some privacy.

Now you sound like the counsel, can you block them out?

A little I'm still working on it.

Wow, you can surprise me your better than I thought. We are coming up on my ship. She called to open a bay door and they landed.

In the control room Kit went to the screen and touches some spots. How far back do want to go she asked over her shoulder.

At least an hour before it happens, David answered still trying to figure out the camcorder, he should ask his daughter how it works, before he left.

Chapter 10

Back In Time

Kit moved her space ship back in time an hour before the missiles hit the United Nations building.

They watch as history unfolded before our eyes again, only this time David video it making sure he was getting the time the missile was lunched and where they came from. Once he had that they move back to their regular time.

David watch the video several times then turned to Kit, will the protection shields on my space traveler withstand that blast.

Yes no problem, Oh, no way I just figured what you have in mind. There is just not anyway, do you realize the split second timing it would take. It has never been tried before because. We don't know the consequences. You are trying to change history. Anyways your traveler cannot fit between those building.

It can, if there was a good pilot flying it. David looked her straight in the eyes; you are that good I believe.

You are crazy, and I'm crazier to even think it might work.

They worked on the plan using the ship computer the figure out the exact time for Kit flying the traveler to be in the right spot to take the hit from both missiles

The computer gave them a 76% chance of this working. David thought, that is what convinced Kit into doing it.

We should get permission from the Kula before doing this Kit said.

Davids answer was, it is said; it is easier to apologize, than to get permission. Beside it will take too long, to get a message there and back, not to mention the time they will have to study and discuss it. I'll be an old man, by the time we get an answer.

Yes I remember you always were a renegade when I was checking you out before I picked you. All right when do we do this she asked?

The sooner the better before we talk our self out of it. How about an hour from now David said?

An hour later with Kit at the time screen they shifted back in time two hour before the missiles were fried. Kit and David in the space traveler headed toward Earth. David transported in to the United Nations building just as Commander Roberts show up. David recognized the sergeant in his protection group. As soon as they saw him they move around. David motion the Sargent aside and gave him the camcorder with the picture removed after the missiles were fired showing only where they came from.

Don't look at this just push play when the time is right. David told him.

How will I know it's the right time he asked?

Oh you will know when you get a sign in the sky. Another thing when the assembly meets after lunch break, do not be in the building. It should show you where they came from, and that all I can tell you for now.

David left him wondering, he seemed to be a real soldier and believe he would follow orders.

Commander Roberts and David were led to a room off to the side of the assembly hall. A few minutes later the page came by, and announce the chairman would be seeing them in a few minutes.

A few minutes later he came back and escorted David and Commander Roberts into the assembly room. The chairman motions them over to a chair on the right. We thought it best for you to be here for the vote we will have a roll calling the country with the most to the less. Then to the microphone and announced United States of America, how do you vote.

The United State agree to reduce2/3 per cent. Next the Soviet Union they agree to reduc2/3. And so it went china agree2/3 England agree/ India agree /Iran agree.

At that moment David stood up everyone get down. A second later they heard the blast. Then the building shook a little. And David heard Kit in his head damn it pushed me into the building, but we did it. We damn sure did it.

David went over to the microphone is everyone OK. Someone tried to stop you from doing the right thing.

The chairman got up from the floor where he was knocked down to. He came up to the podium. I believe I say this for everyone here, were going to continue the vote tomorrow morning at 10 O'clock. Anyone who wants to stay and ask these men some question may do so as for now this meeting is adjourned.

No one got up to leave but stood up to ask questions. I believe the Ambassador from South Africa was first. Let's give him the floor.

Thank you, what just happen?

Over half the members sat down, that was the question they were all asking. David could see Mr. Lane the Ambassador for the United States, Was on the phone getting information.

From what information I can get from my space traveler. Someone does not want to see it passed that the governments of this planet want to reduce their nuclear weapons and save the planet, and move into the space age, Or their mad at me. I see the Ambassador from the United States Mr. Lane is off the phone I believe he may have more information than I have. Mr. Lang do you want to address this assemble David asked?

Yes thank you, I just got a report that two Russian missiles were fired from some distance away and were headed toward this building and the Ambassador from the space federation using his space ship intercepted them, his space craft bump into this building not causing any damage. Do to the fast work of our army; we have two men in custody. They are not Russian. So thanks to our friend from the planet of Tistana we are all alive and safe.

The whole assembly stood up and applauded. Don't know if it was for David or Mr. Lane. But they were all looking Davids way and Mr. Lane was applauding to. It was really kind of embarrassing.

David stood up thank you Mr. Lane. I was sure you had more information than I did.

The Ambassador from England stood up.

Yes Mr. Cooper you have the floor.

Thank you, your space craft did it receive any damage. And could it have shot down the missiles.

No my space traveler did not receive any damage it has a safety shield. And as I said before it has no weapons.

Next the Ambassador from Israel, the space ship that you say this Kula is giving us will it have this shielding and weapon's.

I will let Mr. Roberts answer that. He has been on the cargo ship and has done a complete tour of it talking with the crew.

Mr. Roberts stood up nodded toward David, Mr. Ambassador Ladies and gentleman of this assumable it is an honor to be here. I have been on our space shuttle and have been to our space station three times. I have had the pleasure of going on the cargo shuttle they talk about, and have had a complete tour of it guided and on my own. Their shuttle is far advance from ours from its shielding to it engines. And I saw no weapons.

Mr. Roberts the Ambassador from France interrupted him where did you see this space craft.

In space many, many, miles from here.

Will the space ship we are to build have weapons on it?

David stood up, I'll answer that one. Yes it will have weapon's on it for protection only because like your planet here there pirates in space. The space craft you will build is for exploration only not for war. The weapons are only for protection of the craft. Space exploration craft are much larger than pirate crafts and are purity much left alone. Now if there are no more questions I will see you all tomorrow thank you.

Commander Roberts and David went to the stand-by room. David told him I'm not sure I'll be here tomorrow. I have to see how much damage those U.S. made stingers missiles did to my space traveler.

How did you know that someone was going to fire missiles at the building? I'm also guessing that camera you gave to the Sargent had something to do with that attack.

If I told all I know about the attack, you would not believe me ever again, David answered. But maybe someday I'll tell you; right now you really don't want to know. With that David said good-by see you soon. Then he thought about Kit and two feet behind her, pressed the transporter button.

Chapter 11

The Counsel Says No

Back in his space traveler, David told Kit that was damn good flying, and your timing was right on, he gave her a hug from behind.

Knock it off; I did not allowed for the force of those rockets. They pushed me in to the building before I caught it. I should have known better.

Hell if it would have been me I'd have knocked over the United Nations building. Then they would think we wanted to kill everyone, you did great.

I was great wasn't I, she answered

Oh now we are going to hear for a week how great you are.

She gave his arm that was still around her a pat and a rub. You want to practice getting us back to my ship, fly boy or shell we float around in space and fool around.

Sound like fun but I think we had better get back in our own time. We have already lost a day.

That right what are they are going to say when you're not there tomorrow.

I told commander Roberts I had to check out the traveler, I kind lead him to believe that I would not be there.

They got back to her cargo ship, and she went to the screen and turned the dials that appeared and even though David didn't feel anything they were back in own time they had only lost one day.

There was a message from the Kula do not change history on the planet.

Opps it came a little late, David told Kit.

What do you mean opps, were in trouble now. I told we should have got permission.

I told you it is easier to apologize than to get permission. I'll send them a message telling them that they said to do whatever it takes, and keeping all the Ambassador alive looked like the best way.

And you think that's going to work.

If I'm sincere about it they will. Turn on the transmitter.

She turned on the transmitter. They were too far away to see anyone in person but the picture of the Counsel came on.

David put on his humble face and step in front of the screen and I'm sorry we didn't get your message in time. You told me to do whatever it takes to get them to join the Kula and I felt that the best way would be to keep all the Ambassador alive. It did help to convince the few none believer's that we mean them no harm. And Kitaracta did a fantastic job of flying nothing was harm. They now know who was trying to stop Earth from joining the Kula. As it was everything turned out alright. It was my ideal and Kitaracta was just following my orders. (I looked at the floor even more humble). Once again I'm sorry I jump to the conclusion that I thought it was best. End of transmission, they would not get the message for a day or two.

Then David turned to Kit smiled how about that?

Damn you should be an actor; I was even feeling sorry for you.

Well it will take a day or two to hear back from them. By then we should have heard from the Assembly and maybe have some good news. Right now I'm so tired I could fall asleep right here.

Well come along will get some sleep. Kit said taken him by the hand, we both can use some. They walked down to the sleeping room. David looked around found two slabs together and laid down the next thing Kit laid down beside him. The next thing David remembers was! Waking up the next morning feeling refreshed. He met up with Kit in the recreation room. Hi honey and kissed her.

Don't give that Hi honey, not after last night.

Did I do something wrong David asked

No! Just you talk Romantic all the way back, and then you fall asleep. I'm lying there ready for a night of love making, and you fall asleep! I laid there for two hours, watching you sleep thinking you well wake and do the thing we talked about. No you just go to sleep.

I'm sorry, hay we can go back and make love all day, David smiled.

NO I'm out of the mood, maybe later. You must have been really tired, (you needed the rest) maybe later we will catch up on what you promised.

Oh what the hell did I promised, David was thinking.

You promised all kinds of things that I've never thought of she answered.

Ah, meant to block that out, David thought back. As he looked around to see how many others had pick up his thoughts. There were several who had pick up his thoughts and were looking at them. David hung his head a little embarrasses. Then thought butt out, this is between Kitaracta and me.

Everyone that was looking at them turned around and looked at their drinks.

Well I guess we had better check and see what happen down on Earth. Will take the traveler down and I'll talk to Commander Roberts. You can hold the traveler out in space.

David and Kit set out and once in orbit around Earth, David thought about three feet behind Commander Roberts. Then check it out before pushing the finial button didn't want him to be leaning on a wall and he reappearing on the other side.

Commander Roberts was in a restroom standing at the urinals.

Hi how it goes David asked?

Commander Roberts jumped back; damn will you quite just popping in like that, and you made me pee on my foot. Where have you been?

Why did you miss me!

No, but the assembly did, they passed the vote to reduce their nukes by 2/3 and want to know what's next.

Well when they get half of the 2/3 dismantle. We Will delivery to them the cargo ship, and start on the explorer ship. But we will not put the engine in till all 2/3 of the nukes are gone.

Sounds fair but you had better tell them that. They have been having meeting for the last two days waiting for you. They are adjourned till this afternoon at one O'clock, are you going to be there.

Yes I'll meet you in the waiting room at12:55.

Chapter 12

Approved By The Assembly

David met Commander Roberts in the waiting room just before the assembly was to meet. The page inform the speaker that they were there, soon he escorted them in. As they entered everyone stood and applauded. David told the speaker, that he was glad they decided to reduce their nuclear weapons.

He said yes that was good, but word had gotten out, how you sacrificed the space traveler to save their lives. That was the main points that sway; the few hold outs to vote to join the federation.

David thought, well I hope they heard that back in Tistana, and the counsel would not be so mad about changing history. David held up my hands and motioned everyone to sit down. When they had, he welcomes them to the Kula federation and how the counsel was pleased that they had decided to save the planet. After all that was the main reason for joining. Then he told them that when they have reduced half of the 2/3 of the nuclear weapons. The Kula would present them with the space cargo ship. And they could start building the space explorer ship, and when all 2/3 were dissembled. The Kula would give them the engines. If it was alright with them, if he started training Commander Roberts on how to pilot, the cargo space ship, And that it would take a crew of twenty people. To run it, and mine the shine stones from the moon, that would cut down on the dependency on fossil fuel. Also it would be better that this crew be made up from different countries.

This brought an up roar in the assembly. Most agreed with the pilot being Commander Roberts. It was what countries the crew would come from.

David held his hands up trying to calm the group. After about ten minutes they calm down. The picking of the crew will be up to you. If I may make a suggestion, put the name of every country in for a drawing and pick out twenty countries. Each country drawn will send only one person, to be the crew on the cargo ship. I'm not saying that is what to do, I'm only an adviser. You do it any way you want. But keep in mind that the space exploratory ship will have someone from each country.

The space explorer will be built in space. This cargo ship will be used for mining the stones and delivering the different parts of the space explorer, from Earth to space to be assembled. Later on it may be used for inter planet treading at that time it will need twenty additional crew members.

While they were discussing this problem Ambassador Lane from the United States stood up. The chairman recognized him.

Who will build these parts to be assembled? He asked?

That will be up to you David said, what you need is the best each country has to offer. Like if Canada has the best steel then send it to Mexico or Japan to be assembled. Or the best copper wire sends it to China to be used in the computers. Even the best seat belts if made in India, let them make it. This will be decided by your best scientist. They will all get together, and should have the final say in who will do what. Even build one part in one country and another part in another. Every country will have the plans to the Space explorer, and have the formula to making the interior and outer structure of the exploratory ship.

Who then will decide who these scientists will be, he asked.

I have a list that I will give you these are some of the best we know of. You will have to approve of or reject them, even add more that you know of. This project is all up to you I will just be an observer. Or maybe a referee to see that all country's get a fair representations.

First of all you will have started reducing your nuclear weapons. David reminded them.

This started another round of yelling and accusation, until the chairman, got them under control. I see that we need to talk with our individual governments and get the information needed. Can I get a motion for a one week recess, he asked several stood up. So called, recess for one week. He banged the gravel down. Then came over to David, I don't know. These nonmembers just don't know how we general do things here.

Well you seem to be doing a great job of controlling it David answered.

Yes, send them home for a week, and let them cool off. Their biggest compliant is the country's with no nuclear weapons, think that the ones, who have them can just snap their fingers and 2/3 will go away. From what I know about nuclear missiles it will take several years to dismantle 2/3 of all of them.

Yes I know but I will be around for the long run, and if I can be of any help please feel free to call me. NASA can reach me anytime.

The chairman walked off shaking his head.

I thinking the only help I could offer would be go home. Take two aspirin's and a double shot of whiskey David said to Commander Roberts.

Oh ya you're answered always was a double shot, but I heard it was of rum, it was Kit coming into David brain. So what do you have planned for the next two years?

I don't know, all I can think about right now is that double shot, and going fishing David thought back.

We can handle the double shot; the fishing is up to you. Are you coming up, or not?

Thinking of the seat, next to her in the traveler, David pressed the button, Oh shit David said when he materialized in the traveler. He had forgotten where he was when he vanished on the floor of the United Nations building. Well if anyone was watching that should give them a surprise.

They went back to the cargo ship and waited for the answer from the Kula.

It came six days later, the monitor came on with the Kula counsel on it. Ambassador Hulls looking at the records we did say to do whatever it takes to accomplish your task. And you were very ingenious and dangerous with your plan. We are pleased that it turns out alright. From now on please notify us of your plans. Like giving the Earth people a five million kunks space cargo ship, which we have approved now.

Captain Kitaracta when time comes you will be given yours. To the Earth people and we will be sending you the ZXX5 it should be arriving there in a few days.

David turned to Kit, I'm sorry he said I didn't know.

Oh you are a sorry ass. Now I have to tell the crew we are getting the newest space cargo ship in the fleet far more advance than this rust bucket. She through her arms around him and with a kiss that damn near sucked his eyes out, thank you, I never dream I'd get one of those.

Captain nice job of flying came from the screen, and then it went blank.

There was all kinds of cheering going threw out the space ship news traveled fast of the new space cargo ship.

David didn't understand the excitement that seem to come from everywhere in the ship. Till two days later when the ZXX5 came floating up next to them. It was like they were in a tug boat and it was a cruise liner.

They called in our heads using mental perception instead of the radio Captain Kitaracta ready to transport you aboard.

OK make that three, all of a sudden Kit. Her second in command and David were standing on the deck of the new ship. One of the crew man steps forward your new crew additional crew members are here to meet you. Twenty allies kind of saluted.

First thing Kit said was, OK knock that off we are not that formal on my ship. This is my second in command, and this is the Ambassador from Earth that is what they call it.

David could have sworn that these aliens broke in to a smile as they step forward and pronounce their names. As kit introduced her second in command he just said, it translated into you are buying the first round then the next he said you are buying the second, and so on down the line. Till he had meet all eighteen, And when he said it they would smile, I think it was hard to tell with this bunch of aliens.

These two will be going back with me. Although it sounds like we had better stay here for the celebration a few days. Just to help your crew get move over of course, the other Captain added.

Of course captain it will be a pleasure having you and your crew with us for a while, Kit answered.

Kit gave orders to her second in command to bring the rest of her crew over. Then turned to David want to see a great ship. She took him on a quick tour then came to a privet cabin. Opening the door she announced and this is the Captain quarters.

Hell it put his apartment on Tistana, look like a shack David thought. With its own sanitizer and a sleep slab twice the size of the ones on the old ship.

Kit laid back and invited him to join her it was like floating on air. Instead of metal walls these seem to have a wood grain that change as you looked at it.

Oh yes as she touch a button on the wall a thought lock out shield, she said no one can hear your thoughts threw this shielding.

Captains kill to have a ship like this. We will be the talk of the fleet. I have only seen one other ZXX4 it was not as nice as this. They have had the plans of this ship forever on the planning board.

She was like a kid in a candy store, playing with the dials and buttons. Then one camera switches to the rec room. Well they have started the party without us, come on lets join in. As David and Kit walked in everyone lifted their glasses. To Captain Kitaracta the best captain in the cosmos a cheer went up.

David knew the crew liked their Captain even before she got a new ship. Now they were really proud of their Captain. One could see it on their faces.

The next day David awoke in the Captain soft bed, he got dressed notice he didn't have a hangover like he thought he would have. He then found Kit standing in the control room looking out into space.

She turned as he entered. Isn't that the most beautiful sight you have ever seen?

David told her seeing her with a background of stars and planets. Was the most beautiful thing he had ever seen?

You could say she blushed, or what we would call blush her green skin on her cheeks turned a darker shade of green.

Her second in command came in, Well Captain Shell we take it out on a shakedown trip.

I was just thinking of that. Warn the crew.

He talked to a screen, attrition crew we are going for a turn around.

Kit touched a screen and the ship began to move. The next minuet they were going by Saturn. David had no idea how fast they were going. But in no time, the bright ball of fire he called the sun was just another star in the sky, planets could not be seen. Soon another sun began to show up.

Proxima Centauri the nearest star to your planet.

David began thinking back to his collage days, and the astronomy class. It was something like, Some 12 light years away. If we were traveling at the speed of light186, 000 miles per second it would take them ten years to get here, they just did it in an hour. That I would need a calculator to figure that one out David told himself.

Around thirty times the speed of light. Kit said turning to David.

Thank you, didn't know I was thinking that loud.

Quite alright I enjoyed watching you think. Not many people on your planet know that Proxima Centauri is your closet star yet alone it would take 12 light years to get there. You do amaze me, sometime. She said. We will loop around her then head back.

As we looped around the sun as Kit called it David could see that it had fourteen planets around it, one even look green like earth.

It is but has very little water. It's called Tibbladexla. That is my home planet Kit said.

You're kidding David asked?

No in a way you can say we are Neighbors.

How long since you have been home?

In your time about thirty years she said.

Well, why don't you stop by and say hi.

I'm kind of an outcast on that planet. I didn't leave anything behind when I left. So there is no reason for me to go back.

David could see sadness in her eyes when she said it. So he dropped the subject.

Kit slows the ZXX5 down so it took about three hours to get back behind the Earth moon and next to the old cargo ship. It did look small in comparison to this new one David thought.

David was back on the United Nation floor thinking about Kit's home planet blocking her out, when someone asked him a question. Commander Roberts gave him a nudged.

I'm sorry I missed the question David apologies.

They say that their astronomers saw something come toward the planet at a very high speed did He know anything about it. Commander Roberts repeated.

David said as I told you I would not lie to you it was a space cargo ship sent by the Kula. Did you also see the smaller ship leave that delivered it? And to your next question yes it is floating up there with no one in it. And commander Roberts will bring it down here. When you have dismantled half of the 2/3 nuclear missiles. We figured it would be best to have Commander Roberts learn to pilot it up there. It is a lot bigger than my space traveler.

Where will you land it when you bring it down? Was the next question?

Probably land in some great big desert with nothing around to hit, the commander answered.

This brought a few laughs from the assembly.

Now I did not hear did you want to have the Kula to send a few technicians to help you. Build your space explorer.

What do you call a few; the question came threw his head from the few who were thinking of it.

I was thinking of four or five technicians and they will leave when you ask them to. This seemed to satisfy everyone.

The chairman called for a vote, it passed with only a handful voting no.

Well if there are no more questions. I will be leaving now. Your chairman knows how to contact me when you have reduced the nuclear missiles to one half of the 2/3 mark.

Commander Roberts may I talk to you for a moment in private.

They walked in to the receiving room, as they entered the room, Commander Roberts turned to David I thought you were not going to lie to this assembly.

I didn't David rebutted his question.

You said that their cargo ship was floating around with no one in it. What about Kitaracta and her crew.

What they saw was another cargo ship that Kit and her crew move onto. Leaving the one to be given to Earth empty for you to learn on I don't want you to kill all of them while you are learning, the least terrifying the hell out of them. Now speaking of learning to fly it, we should start in a month or two. Our estimate it will take about eight months to reach the half way mark. And we need to start rounding up the scientist that are going to be work on the Space Explorer. Here is a list of the ones we know are good. What I need for you to do is find a safe place for them to work. Security will have to be high half of these people are Nobel Prize winners, and the other half are the smartest people on Earth.

So you are just going to pop out of here sit in space and leave me with all this work.

No I was thinking about going fishing. If you need me here is a small transmitter you can call me anytime.

Sound like what I should be doing instead of trying to find a bunch of stranger.

David knew he had picked the right man for the job; call me if you need anything. I might tell you where I'm fishing, as David thought of seat in the traveler and push the button.

Chapter 13

A Secret Is Revealed

Kit had picked the best minds on the planet. Some of these people had more letters behind their name than they had in their first name DR. PHD. IDS. RCN. DDB. BACHLOR, MASTER. PROFSSORS. Some didn't have letters but were known as the best in their field. David added the name David Nulls in the middle.

David had set up a camp site in Colorado on a river away from everyone. Against Kula orders that Kit was not to go the planet, she had slipped away and went fishing with him.

David was out fishing when the deputy sheriff show up and asked if he was David Nulls. When David said he was the deputy pulled out his gun? And told him to drop the fishing pole and get on the ground. David was trying to figure out what was going on. When the deputy told him the FBI was looking for him.

David kind a smiled, well what do they want me for he asked?

Don't know just said pick you up and it was top priority. Now put your hands on the top of your head. He went around behind David and applied the handcuffs to his wrist.

Hay isn't this caring it little too far, If you don't know what they want me for.

Shut up, as he picked David up by one arm and before he could get his feet. He dragged him to the car and put him in the back seat. He made sure David hit the top of the car with his head.

Hay what about my tent and fishing pole David asked?

You won't need them where you are going and I told you to shut up and just sit there. Then after he got in the front seat, he called on the radio. Notified the FBI that he had David Nulls in custody and I'm bring him in, this deputy was really proud of his self. That he had caught FBI number one most wanted.

David really didn't want to bust his bubble and tell him that he was not wanted for any crime. Or the fact that he could vanish out of the back seat of his car at any time he felt like it

At the sheriff office it was the same thing the whole force came out to get David out of the car.

If David wasn't afraid that one of them might shoot him it would have been funny. They really thought they had caught a desperado. So why not have a little fun David thought.

The deputy was telling everyone how he had captured him. And that he was armed and had put up a fight. The deputy was leaving out that David was armed with a fishing pole and two trout.

So David thought hands threw the air and the handcuff fell to the ground, with a clang. David surged his shoulders and brought his hands up in front of him. Then bent down and pick up the handcuff. Holding them out, do these belong to you. Oh I'm sorry I guess you just don't know how to put handcuff on.

All his fellow officers look at him. He took out his gun, and pointed it at David.

You aren't afraid of me now are you; I don't have my fishing pole and those two fish. By the way what did you do with those fish? I hope there not still lying on the ground where I drop them, when you told me to.

This brought laughter from the others.

David had everyone attention now and he was going to play this out. Well are you going to shoot me or take me in and call the FBI? You said they were looking for me. But you didn't say what for. Hay, you don't think it is because I'm the leading scientist, who might know more about this alien than anyone else, or maybe I'm a crazy killer. David walked pass him, handing him his handcuff, and into the sheriff office, Follow by the other officer. and found a chair sat down smiling.

The deputy came in and handcuffed David to the chair.

They would not take the handcuffs off till the FBI agent came in. This took them about an hour and a half, to get there. All the time the deputy keeps watching him.

The FBI agent saw David and order the deputy to take the handcuff off.

Let him take them off him he thinks he' Houdini the deputy replied.

David smiled, stood up and turned his back to them and slip out of the handcuff. It was still clamp on the chair and the other end hanging in the air. As He walked out the door, he stop and turn to the deputy. Well I'm not Houdini, and not a crazy killer. See you around, someday when I come back for my camping gear and fishing pole. As he went out, he said over his shoulder you can have the fish.

Outside the agent asked him, what was that all about?

Long story, now what do you want me for. There no law saying I cannot get away from the rat race for a year. And not tell anyone where I was going.

The Ambassador from Kula wants to see you.

From where, David asked?

The alien from space he answered.

What does he want me for?

Don't know we have been gathering up the top scientist all over the world to build this huge space craft.

It must be something about when I was abducted David said.

You were abducted, he ask looking at David?

No, but it sounds about as dumb as some alien wanting to see me. (David knew if he was going to play both parts, as himself and as an alien he was going have to be careful.)Do you mind telling me where we are going?

To a secured meeting place, I'm not allowed to tell you where.

Oh, a prison, maybe I should have stayed with old deputy dog.

No not a prison, they will tell you more when we get there.

Well how long till we get there, David asked.

About two hours, we will be changing to a plane in Denver.

Did I ever tell you I did not like flying, I think I'm going to be sick. David said holding my belly.

The agent looked at him, a little nervous. We will be on the ground shortly, tried to hold on till then.

David wonder what he would think if he started to turn green. he chuckled. No better not do that, he would probably jump out of the helicopter.

What are you doing, the voice came in David head asked?

David knew it was Kit; I'm going to meet the Ambassador from space. I have just been picked up by the FBI and we are going to some secured place, to meet him.

Hay, in case you forgot you are the Ambassador from space, she said sounding a little shocked.

I know that, I just haven't figured everything out yet. Can you make yourself look like me, in public eye?

I do have that part down for sure. What are you planning?

I'm not really sure but I'm going to meet me in two hours.

Well I just got a call from Commander Roberts you were the last to be picked up and they are all waiting for you and the ambassador to show up.

Alright be ready to transport me the plans for this space Explorer, to my location, when I ask for them. This conversation was all done mentally without anyone else knowing they were doing it.

They landed at Denver and change to a jet plane. David didn't get sick, much of a relief to the FBI agent. They then flew to Kennedy space center, and were shuffle into building B with all the solders around it, and some inside. Yes David thought commander Roberts had pick out a secured place.

Once inside David meet Commander Roberts who looked surprised to see him. But keep it all straight. Mr. Nulls were glad you could make. Is there anything I can get you, and then leaned over closer, like some green paint?

Are there any camera or bugs around David asked.

No the Russian insisted on doing a check so the Americans did a check together.

Good can you get the soldiers out of here?

Commander Roberts went over to the Sargent and talked for a few minutes. Then came back, he said that he had orders they were to stay.

OK give me a minuet I'll see what I can do, as David walked up to the Sargent. Do you still have that camcorder I gave you in New York? David looked him right in the eyes and could tell he was thinking that he did look a little familiar. That right I'm who you're thinking about. Now I like to have only the soldiers in this building you can trust with your life. And will not say anything about what I'm going to reveal to these scientist. Do you understand what I'm saying?

Yes sir, give me a few minutes to clear out only my men, they can be trusted to keep their mouths, and sorry sir but the feds got your camcorder. It helped catch those two who fired the rocket at the U.N. building still don't who hired them.

Thank you Sargent, David said as he walks away. I hope they do find out we will all feel safer.

After a few minutes the Sargent had half the soldiers removed from the room. Then he gave the thumb up sign. David nodded and got up on a chair

Lady and gentleman my name is David Nulls I was born in Seattle Washington June 6 1949. What I'm about to tell you, must not leave this room. A year ago I was asked by the Kula federation to represent them here on this planet. Because they have a strict policy not to interfere in other planets affairs except when it will affect other planets and you might not trust someone from some other planet. For my safety I did not want my identity known that is why I'm wearing this device that can changes my appearance. Commander Roberts already knows this and has been to the space ship that brought me back from a planet called Tistana. Where I spent one year learning about their ways, I know that they only want what is best for the people here on Earth. Now I'm going to use this device and change into what everyone has been calling the Ambassador from the space federation. David touched the button and turned green but it did not change his features. Then it looked like his arms got a little longer and he was a little taller. I repeated what you see must not leave this room. And turned back to David Nulls then went over to the table. And thought OK Kit sends me the plans. Instantly a large set of plans.

Appeared on the desk, these are the plans to your new Space Explorer there is no problem with taking them out to the public because we are going to give them to every government. This is not going to be a big secret. Your job is to figure out what is the best country to assemble the different parts and to coordinate its transport to space and who is to assemble them. As everyone in the room stared David continued, The Kula federation will send five technicians to help us. These technicians will most likely be wearing a device similar to what I have and may look normal they are friendly and very knowledgeable.

Chapter 14

Commander Roberts Learns To Fly

Kit started teaching Commander Roberts on how to fly and land the space cargo ship. It was a good thing they were landing on the moon. Kit said to David He wants to land it like an air plane not like a helicopter. She was telling him that the moon gravity was a lot lighter than Earth and if he landed like that on earth he would make a crater or smash up the ship. That's when David said he would wait back on the ZXX5, besides he would probably make commander Roberts nervous.

Him nervous, what about me, I'm a pilot not a teacher Kit replied. After being on this old tub for twenty years, I'm kind of attach to her and don't want to see her beat up.

After a week Kit figured he had it down well enough to try an Earth landing but thought it best to do a water landing. Then a sand, landing, only then land at Kennedy Space Center if everything went alright.

As they came around to the front side of the moon, Commander Roberts called NASA and informed them of our plans. There was all kind of excitement in the control center. We could see a clear patch of sky over the Atlantic Ocean that had no clouds. OK Kit said for your first landing, but better get used to clouds there not always a clear spot where you want to land, and as that man, Murphy says there never is.

Commander Roberts circle the globe once then headed down toward the blue ocean below. The cargo ship settles down on the water, floating like a ship.

Well that was purity good, David said after holding his breath the last thousand feet.

It was alright but if it would have been on a hard surface we have collapsed the landing legs. But now you know how the gravity pulls, Kit said OK take her up and let's find some soft sand.

Hell I thought it was good wish I had a fishing pole David said.

You and your fishing Kit was in his head again. If we had hit harder they would be fishing us out of the water.

If you're trying to scare me you did, thinking it instead of saying out loud so the commander could not hear him.

The Sahara Desert in Africa has the slowest sand, but the wind blows all the time.

Good kind like your planet Mars. Take her up to fifty thousand feet that will keep us above the airlines.

You been there the commander asked.

Where to Mars, yes several times. There a friendly race. Kit answered.

What David asked?

Oh you thought you are the only inhabitants in this solar system. Half your planets have a life form of some kind. The Martians are more like your worms they live under ground. They are a lot more intelligent than your worms. They have electricity, and phones, as for technology, they are about two hundred years ahead of you.

Come on you are pulling my leg, David said.

Pulling your leg, looking at him, oh yes an expression you use, I never did understand that one.

Means you are telling me a story, David offered.

No I'm telling you the truth they live there. I don't lie OK commander level it off, now watch your speed. That should be it over there. Good just like Mars blowing sand, take her down and watch the gravity pull.

They landed if there was anyone watching they would have never seen us, it was in the middle of a sand storm. Roberts did a good job I didn't even feel us touch down.

That a lot better, now get us out of here we are sinking in the sand, Kit said.

I really think I should have stay in my traveler and missed this trip this David thought.

What are you nervous, Kit asked?

Not if you were at the controls, David thought.

Heck there was a time I landed on Passeon, the whole ship sank out of sight. We couldn't even open the doors to pick up the cargo. I had to hold it a foot off the ground, all the time while they loaded us. Well commander are you ready to hit the payment.

That's not funny David thought

Was to me Kit answered his head.

It's a saying space pilots say when they are going to a port they have never been to, Kit added. Better call NASA and tell then were coming.

Commander Roberts went to the speaker screen. NASA this is the space cargo ship Tamie requesting permission to land at Kennedy Space Center I will need half the runway.

Space cargo ship Tamie you cleared to land whenever you want. Another voice came on, Hay commander do we need to call out the crash trucks.

No Tom but you might move some building back this baby is big, not like those toys you fly. I will be there in ten minutes, over.

What is Tamie David Asked?

French for love, and I love this ship. Beside a captain can call his ship anything he wants. Roberts answered.

I like that; I'll have to find a name for mine. What do you, think of the name of David, kit asked.

Well let's get Tamie on the ground in one piece. And we will discuss it David said looking at the runway coming up.

Commander Robert said no problem as he slid over the runway and set her down, like it was on egg shells.

Now that what I like to see you get a kunk for that as she tossed him a coin. It's customary to get a lucky kunk, on your first real landing. Keep it with you always. Well honey shell we transport out of here. We had left my traveler in space.

Waite you're not staying to meet everyone commander Roberts said.

No Captain this is your party. Ours is up there, David saluted good job. And push the button and telaported to his space traveler.

A few minutes later Kit appeared next to him, she leaned over and gave him a kiss on the cheek. Sure glad that over I think he will take good care of her.

What this a sentimental moment, I didn't get a kunk when I did a perfect landing.

That's because you fly a space traveler not a cargo ship. Cargo pilots do it so they will always have money for one more drink if they crash.

Chapter 15

A Change In Plans

Things were going according to plans the nukes were being dismantled. They had almost reached the goal of 2/3. The Space Explorer was coming along and was over ¾ finished. When trouble began, Captain Roberts had delivered a section that didn't match the plans. There were too many hatch doors. The plans called for two on each side, the assemble part had four on each side two high and two low.

The scientists study the master plans then went to Japan and the plans didn't match Japan had built as their plans showed, with four hatches where the master plans show only two. The problem was the stress points.

David was called in to check it out. As he talked to the aliens who were helping some seem to think there were too many weak points and the other said it should be alright if they just reinforced the girder between. The scientists seem to believe this theory. Rather than take another year to build another one.

David brought over Kit and one of her engineers they study it and agreed reinforces the center beam and there should not be any trouble.

A few months later the haul was completed and pressurized and the hatches were watch closely and a cheer when up when they held.

David was outside watching, when the ship was being pressurized. He was still wondering about who had change the plans.

Another month later the control room was completed. The worker seen more active once the ship was pressurized David check it was the oxygen; it was higher than on Earth it matched the level in his traveler and Kit's ZXX5.

He asked Kit about it.

She explained that in space they usually keep it higher, it keeps everyone sharper they could lower it if they wanted.

She was right about keeping you sharper in his traveler David could always think clearer.

A week later a cargo ship show up, with the engines. The nukes were not completely dismantled but there was only about a hundred left. Kit said the Kula must think that the people of Earth will be doing what they say and decided to reward them. Or something like that, and that she did not order them.

Along with the engines came the specter. It is the device that splits the taings. Kit explained it to David. You have atoms split them you have an atom bomb then there is a nucles split that you have a nuclear bomb then you have a taings it orbits around the nucleon faster than the speed of light. The more of these you split the faster you can go. And that what a specter does, it make the fuel for the engines. What you can hold in your hand will power the Space Explorer for a hundred years. Best of all, that's one of the newer models. That means this ship will go a lot faster than we expected.

I don't know what you did, sweet heart but the Kula is sending us the best of ever thing. Me I get the most advance apace craft the ZXX5, you the new model of the specter, and the engines without asking. So whatever you are doing keep doing it.

She was right we were getting everything we needed to get the Space Explorer up and running, sooner than expected. Still something keep nagging David.

Things were going good the engines installed, when David got a call from Captain Roberts. The United Nations wanted him to come to their next meeting, in two days, at 2 o'clock pm David told him to tell them he would be there, and were you going to be there David asked.

No, they just asked for you, he answered.

Two days later David transported into the waiting room. The page checked in on him as usually five minutes before 2 o'clock, and came back to get him at two sharp.

The chairman met David as he entered, he thank him for coming. The assembly has a few questions to ask you, and you do not have to answer them if you do not want to. The big one is how many crew members are needed on the Space Explorer. David went to the podium and asked Kit about the question then acted like he was counting. Kit came in his head with the answer. There are seventy eight position from the captain to the bar tenders. I'm not saying bar tenders are not just as important as a good captain. There are three shifts. Two hundred and thirty four full time crew members and most are scientist. I can have a list of all the positions tomorrow. Now that is the bare minimum you will need replacements if some are sick or for whatever. You should have at least four hundred. They can always be helpers.

Thank you and the list will help; you say you can have it tomorrow that will be fine the chairman said. The next question is do you think Captain Roberts would make a good Captain of the Space Explorer.

I believe he would be the best candidate for the job. But do you think you can talk him out of the cargo ship, he is just having too much fun, this brought laughter from the assembly, as David said it.

Thank you now can we take some question from the assembly, the chairman asked. And the way he said it. David went on the defense.

Yes that will be alright he said.

The chairman called on Ambassador Lee from china.

Thank you Mr. Chairman, my question is Mr. Ambassador, are you a citizen of the United States of American?

Define citizen, David asked?

Where were you born he answered?

I was born in Seattle Washington U.S.A. A murmur went through the assembly.

And Mr. Ambassador what is your real name.

Sorry but for the safety of my family I cannot tell the whole Assembly. But when this Assembly is recessed, those who swear not to let it leave this room I will tell.

You see there were four people from this planet that were chosen to represent the Kula here on Earth. All four applicants were taken to Tistana. And I was picked to be the one, to be the Ambassador. The Kula feel it is better to have the Ambassador be from the planet they come from, than to have an alien represent the people of a planet. I spent a year in Tistana training for this job. Also if you think I'm not doing a good job you can vote someone else to replace me.

No that is not my intention you are doing a good job, thank you for being honest.

Well thank you for that fine remark, David said when I first came here to this Assembly I told you I would not lie to you.

Are there anymore question I can answer for anyone. No one stood up. None then Ambassadors I will see you after this assembly is dismissed.

Then turned if there is nothing else I will be in the waiting room. David turned and walked out. In the waiting room he breathes a big sigh of relief.

Well that was good you make one hell of an Ambassador, but would never make it as a politician! It was Kit in his head.

You were following that David asked

You were thinking so hard, I could have picked you up on the other side of the solar system.

Twenty minutes later the page came and in and told David to follow him, as he walked in I could see most of the members were still sitting there. All the translators were gone. David went to the podium, Ambassador Lee and members of the assembly, what you are about to learn must not leave this room.

One moment Mr. Ambassador the chairman interrupted. All camera off and shudder closed.

The windows were block off; David walked around in front of the podium. Push the button and became himself with no green on, my name is David Nulls. I was raised here in the United Stated. I'm a widower, I have two kids a son and a daughter and four grandchildren. My citizenship is the planet Earth as long as I'm the Ambassador for the Kula.

David could hear half of them thinking how did he do that? He took the changing box from his belt, and held it up; with this device I can make myself look like an alien. Then pressed the button again and became the green alien. Now Ambassadors I bid you all have a good day and for my safety and the safety of my kids and my grandchildren. Please do not disclose what you have learned these last few minutes.

After David was in the waiting room he transported himself to the secured room at Cape Kennedy, where he knew he would find the Sargent in charge. David didn't know if he sleeps there or what but he was always there when he was. David went up to him and told him what had just happen, and that he was worried about my kids and grand kids.

I will see to it that they will be safe the Sargent assured him. Here is my privet phone number. Have them call me if they even think they are in trouble, He said giving David the phone number.

I thank you; David said then went into the other room. Though of the beach in front of his old house, that he had given to his daughter and her family, and then he was there. David stood there for twenty minutes or so watching the waves rolling on shore. The tide was coming in; it would be a good time to go fishing.

Is that all you ever think about is fishing.

David turned with a jump, it was Kit what are you doing here, he asked?

Just stop by to see if you were alright. Sure is beautiful isn't, she said looking out at the ocean.

It sure is, when their conversation was interrupted with a scream ah a monster. It was David 8 year old grandson Archer. Kit hit her button and the green was gone. David turned around to Archer it's me, grandpa do I look like a monster to you.

Not you grandpa, her he pointing at Kit!

Oh she can be at times but this is my friend Kit. Kit this is my grandson Archer.

How do you do Archer, Kit said holding out her hand.

Archer looked at Kit then her hand, making sure it was not green, and then shook it, nice meeting you. Then he turned and ran into the house. Calling his mother, grandpa here with his girlfriend, that sometime can be a monster.

Kit turned to David, cute kid, what this I can be a monster sometimes.

Just then David daughter came out saving him from having to

explain, that one to her.

David daughter throws her arms around his neck and gave him a big hug. Dad where have you been this time, I been trying to call you for over three months. That worthless son of a bitch son in law of yours wants a divorce and half of the house.

Well that is not going to happen, David told her.

That's what I told him and as soon as you came back, that you would take care of him. He said you were dead and didn't come back and borrow the camcorder by the way where is my camcorder, for some reason in the back of my head I think you stop by and pick it up, and are you going to introduce me to your friend that sometimes can be a monster. I wish you would not scare Archer like that, and telling him all these tales.

This is Kit she a good friend of mine. Kit this is my daughter Mindy. The FBI has your camcorder; I'll get you another one. As for Donald I will defiantly take care of him. There is something I need to talk to you about, and I think we had better go inside, sit down and have some coffee.

What do you mean the FBI has my camcorder? Is this another one of your stories, you lost it, didn't you? She looked at Kit I swear he would loss his head if it wasn't attached.

That is like all men, but I think you had better hear what he has to tell you, and if you think he tell good stories. Waite tells you hear this one. Then she thought so only David could hear her, that's for calling me a monster sometime.

Thank you for that thought, David said to Kit. Now Mindy can you get us a cup of good coffee,as they headed into the house.

I'll have to make some; it will take a few minutes, still want four scoops in it.

Yes a real cup of coffee. David looked at Kit and smiled, now you can taste what real coffee is like. A few minutes later she came back with a tray with three cup of coffee and some cream and sugar.

Help yourself; I didn't know how you liked it. Then she sat down, OK let's hear why the FBI has my camcorder.

Well do you remember when someone tries to blow up the United Nations building?

Yes it was in all the papers how the aliens flying their airplane between them and saved all those people. I think the papers over played it and TV had it on for a week.

Well on your camcorder was a view of where the missile came from and that was how the solders caught those two men. So the FBI keep your camera.

Wow, you were there, and you got it all on my camcorder.

Oh its gets better Kit added.

Will you let me tell this David interrupted; I don't want her to go in frenzy? We were both there. In fact Kit was flying that Space traveler.

They said the alien was flying it.

They were right. Kit is not from this world she from a planet a long way from here.

OK my dad's girl friend is an alien. That does not surprising tome.

It true I'm from Ticbladxia a planet about four light years from here. But it gets better. Your dad is the Ambassador from the Kula federation. He is the alien that everyone is talking about. Only he is not an alien that is only a disguise to protect you and your grandmother, and needs to keep up this until the Space Explorer is built, so that your people can explore space, and visit my people.

OK hold it I get it this is one of my dad's books, it a good story but a little hard to believe.

It is not one of his books and we are just getting to the important part. This is what I look like when not in a disguise, she hit the button on her belt and turned green.

Archer screams from the stairs. I told you she was a monster. Then he ran up the stairs to his room.

Mindy jump back that a good trick. Then she got up to check on Archer. Dad you put her up to this just to scare Archer. This is not funny.

As she went to check on Archer, David said to Kit I told you to let me handle this. I wish I had thought of it couple of years ago.

You mean you did thing to scare your grandson.

Ten minutes later Mindy came down with Archer. OK dad now tell him it was a joke. And not a very funny one at that, I might add.

I would but this is very serious, come here Archer. He sat down beside David, not taken his eyes off of Kit. You have seen the movies where people visit other planets and they are real friendly. Well Kit here is from one of those planets and she here to help build the Space Explorer so we can go in to space and make friend with people from other worlds.

Dad!

Mindy sit down and listen, this is all true. You don't remember how I got your camcorder. Or that I was here a year ago. Don't you think that was really hard to explain. And maybe someday I'll be able to tell you. Right now when the world finds out whom I'm, you and Archer life may be in danger. Just then the phone rang.

Mindy answered it. Then turned to David it's your mother she wants to know if I know where you are. She said there are a bunch of people at her place from the news asking question about you.

Crap, it is already out David said to Kit. How do they know so fast?

I told you it would happen. You and (I have to be honest with them.) Kit said now what?

How did you get here, David asked

I bounced from my ship to yours then to down here.

Archer how would like to see my space ship?

Ooo that would be neat, Archer answered.

OK I'll take Archer and Kit you take Mindy.

Take us where, what do I tell your mother.

Tell her I'm here, because we won't be here. We're going on a little trip to somewhere safe.

She wants to talk to you, holding the phone out to him.

Crap we don't have time for this. Taken the phone, hi Mon, just tell them I'm here at the beach. And you don't know a thing, I'll tell you later. I will call you later, don't worry, it's alright. Bye. And David hung up the phone. Then pulled the number out the Sargent had given him and called him, it's happen. My mother needs help David told him. She is at the lake address.

It will be OK I have men almost there they are coming from the fort just north of there should be there soon. How are you doing?

I'm fine for now I will call you later, thank you.

To make things worse Mindy husband Donald walk in I see your old man came back from the dead. You think he's going to help you.

I'll take care of you later, Kit take Mindy as David pick up Archer, we will be in the back, you take the front.

Kit grab Mindy and vanished, David thought of the back of the space traveler and push the button. Instantly they were in the traveler. David put Archer down in the seat. Mindy was just standing there looking around.

Where are we she finally asked and what just happen?

You are in my Space traveler some six miles above earth. I'm going to take you to a place that is safe from ten thousand news reporters and possible danger.

So what you were telling me is true and that she is an alien. And we have just been abducted.

Well that one way of putting it or you can say we just saved your life. Now what, Kit asked?

The cape I guess, you want to fly while I explain it to Mindy. Archer you want to help Kit fly. You can sit up there with her.

OK she is a friendly alien not a monster, as he moved into the seat next to her.

Mindy looked at David, daddy you have done some craziest things, but if what you have been telling me, this tops them all. You have a girlfriend that an alien. And everyone wants to talk to you. I want to know if she good in bed.

That no way to talk to me David said. They don't even know about her, have you not been listening to me. David pushed the button and his feature changed and turned green. Then change back to his normal self, in time for Archer to say.

Wow, my granddad is an alien to.

Not me this is just a disguise. Kit is the only alien in here.

Then he explained everything that had happen, leaving out the part about going back in time.

By the time David finished. They had landed at Cape Kennedy.

Chapter 16

Mother Problems

With his daughter and grandson safe at Cape Kennedy space center. His mother's house guarded by the army David no longer need a to put in the alien disguise but it also meant he could not go anyplace he wanted to, that someone didn't know him. The tabloids had a picture of him. Mindy ex-husband Donald told every news magazine and newspapers, and anyone who would listen. All kind of storied how Mindy had to be half alien because she did all kinds of strange of things. The more he talked the madder his daughter Mindy got, one day David was at the cape he had stop by to see her and Archer. She asked him if there was anything he could do to stop Donald and the tabloids.

David told her she could problem sue them. But that would take three to ten years. We do have freedom of press here in the United States. Now Donald you can sue him for slander but technically you are not divorce so I don't know what you can do about him.

Sargent Speck who had now become David personal body guard, when he went anywhere on earth, overheard David say this and came over I do have a lot of friends in the FBI and in the Army let me call in a few favor's. I'm sure he might be one of the terrorist who was involved with the attack on the U.N. building. I'm sure when they are threw with him, He will not have anything more to say and will sign your divorce papers.

If you could that I'd appreciate it. Hell I already owe the name of my first born and now you're working on my right arm if there anything I can do for you let me know David told him.

Well now that since you mention it there is one little thing you can do for me. Get me on as a crew member on that space ship they are building.

You know I have no say in who they want for a crew, but I might be able to make a recommendation. I'll see what I can do but no promises.

That is good enough for me. That would a job of a life time, the Sargent said.

You know that twenty years in space is a hundred years back here on earth. It has something to do with time and space travel. Your wife and kids would be a hundred years older if they were still alive.

Oh I'm not married, my mother dead, my father I haven't seen him in five years now.

Well you just might make a good candidate for a crew member.

One of the guards came over. Excuse me Sargent the Ambassadors mother is on the phone asking for him.

How she got this number, Sargent Speck asked.

She is on the military line sir.

OK thank you Marty, we will take it from over here.

David went to the phone and the Sargent handed it to him. Hi Mon, how it going.

I don't know how it going with you I see your name and picture in the paper every day. And I have these solders that won't let me drive out of my own driveway and they will not let any of my friends come over to see me. To top it all off a grand daughter who calls and cannot tell me anything because it is classified.

Are you in the house, David asked?

No I have to come outside and use this nice young man's phone to call my son.

OK I will come over and meet you in the house.

Just when will that will be?

In two minutes, see you soon. David handed the Sargent back the phone. Crap now if I don't have enough problems. I have to go and save some soldier from my mother wrath.

I'm supposed to be with you when you're here the Sargent said.

I don't think we travel the same way, don't worry I have a guardian angel watching over me David assured him. .

That so sweet if you are talking about me. The voice was in David head, it was Kit.

Can I ever get away from you, he thought back.

I have my orders to, keep watch over you and keep you safe. Better than that soldier, because I do travel the same way you do. And I don't have to be hanging on your shirt sleeve all the time.

You have a good point, do you want to meet me at my mothers. I'm sure she would like to meet you.

She already has I'm the nice young man who let her use the phone to call you.

What David said out loud?

Don't worry he will wake up and won't remember a thing, except that he ran into a tree branch and knock himself out for a few seconds. See you soon. I'll be there right behind you.

OK see you soon too.

Are you alright you were just standing there frozen looking into space, and all you said is WHAT like you were talking to someone the Sargent asked?

Yes I'm just fine I was just thinking. I have to go and see mother I'll be back soon. Mindy keep an eye on the Sargent for me. As David said it he realized how dumb that was, he is to watch Mindy and Archer. He thought of my mother's living room and pressed the transport button and was there seconds later Kit was right behind him. Just as my mother walk in the door.

Are you going to tell me how you did that. And who is this young lady with you.

This is my friend Kit; Kit met my mother, Martha Nulls.

It is a pleasure to meet you your son has talked a lot about you. She stuck out her hand to Davids mother.

His mother shook it. So you are the nice alien that sometimes turn green, Archer has been telling me about.

Oh yes we can trust him to keep a secret. David cut in.

Well sit down and tell me all about it. Do you want something to drink; I think I have a soda in the refrigerator. Since the soldiers won't let me go to town without ten of them going with me.

They are here for your protection and to keep all of them damn reporter from knocking on your door.

I know why the soldier are here. I want to hear about you and this young lady. My sources tell me you two are have a thing going on, is it serious.

Your sources you mean Archer. We are just good friends and yes I like her a lot, and yes she is a good cook.

Good, now I did see you in the hospital. Even thou your brother said you were not there.

Yes you were the first person I used the new medical tool on the Mikco. That everyone is talking about. The gift from the people I'm representing, how do you feel?

Twenty years younger. I can even go out and play golf again if I can ever get away from this Army that follows me around. Now what you going to tell those soldiers, so I can see my friends again.

Let me call the Sargent, and see what we can arrange. David took the Sargent phone number out and called, then told him the situation.

I'll send the Sargent in and you explain it to him. You don't want to go outside.

Shortly after Davids call there was a knock at the door. Kit said this will be a problem it might be better if she waited in the other room.

David open the door, come in Sargent he said. The soldier looked at him strangely. Have you met Mrs. Nulls?

Yes several times. When she wanted to leave unescorted, but who are you and how did you get in here.

I'm her son, and how I got here is not important. What is important! My mother feels like a prisoner. I understand the importance of protecting her, when she goes out but I don't think we don't need a whole platoon. Can you just send one to drive and watch out for her, and PROTECT

THE NEWS PEOPLE. If they get in her face she is libel to shoot one of them. She does have a lot of friends come visit her. And we need to let that happen even if it is supervised.

She has a gun the Sargent asked.

Probably my dad had a lot of then and she a good shot, I added. So what do you think, can we work something out.

Yes I will have a few watching the house and have one as a personal body guard. I did not know the situation, and was just following orders.

OK thank you. Now I'll see you to the door.

David cut his mother off there, we will discuss this later. He motion to the Sargent, toward the door. Then out of his mother range I'll talk to her it will be alright, thank you for your time.

No Sir, if you are who I think you are, thank you and it was a pleasure to meet you. He shook David hand and walked out.

When David came back to the living room, his mother started in on him. I don't have a gun, and I don't need a body guard.

I didn't know that and it's better that they think you do. You will have to have a body guard, if for nothing else to keep the reporters away. You cannot talk to anyone about me. It will just get turned around and back in the paper and on TV and be all wrong or different than what you said, you know how they turn around everything to make it sound like it is news.

Now I have to go back to work I will stop by, when I have more time.

Kit came out of the kitchen. Remind me not to play ping with you she was talking in his head.

What is ping David thought back?

It's like your poker game you bluff the others players, for kunks that you have a better zips than they do.

David are you alright? it was his Mother.

Yes Mon just thinking, now you do what they want you to do, just for a little while OK.

OK but I'm not going to have these body guards forever I'm I.

No they will be gone soon. Turning to Kit I'm going to the traveler.

I'll be right behind you. Kit answered.

Mother I will see you later David kissed her, step back and vanished.

Chapter 17

The Real Truth Comes Out

A second cargo ship show up with finial parts. All the workers were back on the planet for Christmas holidays. The aliens were on the space explorer. Putting the final attachment, only these attachments were not part of the plans. David went up to the main control room and found Kitaracta he asked what they were for.

Oh my Earth friend, we are going to take your ocean water back to our planet. It has dried up and the only way to save it is with your water. Like our planet did thousands of years ago. When we used the water from the other planet, the one you call the red planet. It too had water better than you have here. Now it's gone, and .we need yours.

You mean that this whole time your plan was to steal our water. What about the Kula.

Oh there real they just don't care about your little planet any more since we told them that you were not ready to join.

What was the thing about the nukes? Was that just a story?

No you reduced them and the Federation is happy We knew our defense shield could hold off some of your nuclear bombs but not all of them that you had. Since the Kula played right in to our hands. Except they were not going to give you space exploration. It was our ideal to have you build a storage tanks to transport your water for us. Put him in the living Quarters when we flood it we will be rid of this earthling.

I thought we had something special between us?

We did my lover and you were great but my mating season is over. And be sure to hose him down with ocean water

Ocean water why ocean water what so important about it David asked?

It's your ocean water that keeps your kind from using your other half of your brain. That is why your wise men live high in the mountains away from the sea. When we took you away to Tistana you started using the other half, telaporting, mind reading and materializing through solid objects.

As the three aliens lead down David to what would have been the living quarts the room already had a foot of water in it. He didn't know if the ocean water would change his thinking like kit said it would, but he was not taken any chances. He pushes two of the aliens into the water. The third he spun around grab his tentacle and flung him in and went back up the stairs thinking he needs a weapon.

A weapon will not help you; you have nothing that can stop us.

She is reading my mind he must block her out David was thinking. He could not telaport out of the ship, because of the force shield. David thought shut down pump and transported himself to the pump room. Kit must have read my thoughts and was there too. Then things happen he was not expecting.

She flung him across the room and against the wall without touching him, just using her mine.

She could see the look on his face. There things we didn't teach you. As she used her mind and pick him up, pulling David closer to her.

OK bitch, how about this he thought and she drop him and went flying across the room into the wall. Hell, David did even know he could do it to. He then though engine room. Then block her out and thought control room and hit the transporter button and was instantly in the control room. He went to the control panel and flipped all the switches opening all the hatches. When it did millions of ton of water spilled out of the ship sucking in the air, to fill the space. David thought damn good thing, when he open all the hatches that much water going out and not replacing it with would have implode the ship.

David didn't have time to think about it. Before, Kit had figured out where he was. Soon she appeared in the control room. Gasping for air, she looked pale and holding her chest. Then fell to the floor gasping like a fish out of water.

David went to her, and heard her in his head; I cannot breathe your atmosphere oxygen to thin. As her thoughts got weaker, David looked for an oxygen tank, see none. He started thinking of another plans His space traveler was still in the holding bay. He lied on top of Kit with my arms around her thought of the traveler and pushes the button. Instantly they were both in the traveler. He let go of Kit and pressurize the cabin as if He was in space with the rich oxygen. Kit started breathing again. Her color was coming back. David sat her in one of the seats as she gain her strength back. Thinking if she tries anything he would open the space traveler hatch.

Why did you save me, when I was about to kill all the people on your planet to save mine.

That just the way us people on Earth think. We don't take another person life. If we don't have to David added, still keep a safe guard up against her. In fact if you had told us, we might have been able to help you, without you having to steal all of our water.

David figured out later it was not just ocean water that stop people of Earth from developing their mental powers, but also the rich oxygen. And since he did not live his whole life on a high oxygen planet his lungs had not needed the high oxygen and would explain why he always felt better in the space ship and on Tistana.

I remember you saying that you have not been to your planet in thirty years. Was that a lie, and what do you mean your matting session is over. I think you owe me an explanation.

Your right I do owe you that. You can take your hand off the hatch reliever.

Not a chance of that happen, although in your mind I can see you are sincere, I still don't know what you can hide.

I have never met anyone like you. You care for people you don't even know. I have always had to watch my back, from even my own crew.

And it was not a lie about being home in thirty years. My father was a scientist, when I was twelve years old I had a garden and thought if I used some of the chemical in his lab I could get my garden to grow better since water was ration out. I found a bottle of clear liquids so I took it out and put it on planets. Well it killed all my plants and put out a cloud that killed everything it came in contact with. Even the people, hundreds of them died my father put me on a cargo ship. And took the blame for what I had done. They killed him and my mother our name on the planet was a dirty word, that is the only way to describe it. I change my name, and when the Kula said to scrub your mission here. When we change history on the planet that is strictly forbidden that's when I came up with the plan to take your water and restore my father name. I contacted the council on Ticbladxia and told them of my plans. To have you build a ship to take your water and transport it to our planet it is salty and would cause us to lose some of our mental ability. But our planet would survive a few hundred more years. They are the ones who sent the ZXX5, and the engines. I change the plans to fit the pumps that they sent in the ZXX5 and the others that have just arrived. Now you can hit that hatch button and kill me. I'm a dead person anyway this would be better. Than when the council on Ticbladxia finds I failed they will have someone track me down and I don't want to think what that death would be like. One other thing, I did love you and still do.

David was still searching her mine, to see if this was some game she was playing. He even got into the part where she could hide things. And it was all true, he even felt a twinge when she said she love him. If it was an act it was a good one. David took his hand off the button, and reached for her.

She pulled back, how you can be so nice to me after what I have done to you, she had read in his mind that he still had feeling for her to and, would protect her no matter what she had done.

Between the two of use let's get this ship back in space and the pumps out of here we can say it was just a test and we didn't want it to be done with others aboard. What are we going to do with the three crew members that are looking for us?

They will do as I tell them they are the few I do trust, if they are still alive.

Oh hell I forgot about that, I'll go and close the hatches and pressurizes the ship. You stay here till I do. Are you alright and not going to try anything? As she answered he scans her mind. OK I'll be back and thought of the control center and transported there closed the hatches and started pressurizing the ship. Hit his space suite button and touch the screen that steer the ship he felt her rising. Touched the screen again and set it so that it would be back in orbit. He then went to find the three crew man. They were all dead, he felt a pain.

Then Kit came into his head you did not kill them I did. By bring then along. Then he heard her think of the ZXX5 and transport over. Then she was thinking of a gun or weapon. Then she was thinking of killing everyone on the cargo ship that had just arrived bringing the extra pumps.

No don't, he stop her.

They will be trying to kill us if I don't.

Tell them to take the pump off and store them in their cargo hole. That the transporter ship is not ready it leaks.

It's too late they know.

David concentrated on their bay doors and open them. Tell them. If they do not remove the pumps, I will open all their hatches, while they are in space. David could hear all of their thoughts they were putting on space suites. David switch and concentrated on their specter, pulling it lose from its mounts then pulling the connecting rods they came loose. Just as they engage their engines. The whole craft started glowing a bright blue. All thoughts stop coming to him. What did I do he thought.

You just solved all our problems. I did not know you had developed that kind of mental ability. Kit answered in his head.

I killed them, David thought.

No just knock them out, can you turn off the specter.

I don't know how do you turn it off, David said.

Just stop it from spinning there is a lever on the back, it works like a break.

David concentrated on the specter it was bouncing all around. He concentrated on stopping it from moving then on the lever on the back he could see it in my mind but could not hold it and move the lever at the same time.

Concentrated harder you're going to burn a hole in the side of the ship.

David tried to no avail so he pushes his transporter button. The second later he started to materialize his hand was on the lever. He moved it as he felt the shock wave hit. He was momentary stun but not knock out.

He could hear Kit shouting no David, no David, David. Will you stop that you are adding to my headache David thought back.

Your alive, your alive she repeated.

Yes I'm alive but there one person in here that isn't. I thought you said it would only knock them out.

He must have been in direct contact with the connecting rod. As she said rod she materialize next to him. That was really dumb you could be laying there beside him. Are you alright she asked?

Like you are concerned, you would just get in your ZXX5 and fly off.

That's not fair, I care about you.

An hour ago you were going to kill me.

This love hate relationship has got to stop or it will not work out between us.

She throws her arms around giving him a hug. The hate part stops right here and now she said.

He kissed her forehead well. Now how long do we have until this crew will wake up?

Who knows I have never heard of a specter coming off before.

But you said they were knocking out, not dead he answered.

They will be alright, but now what are we going to do with them, I can kill them or just leave them on the moon, when their oxygen runs out they will die.

I told you before, that we don't do that here on Earth. How many can walk threw walls?

Oh probably half she answered.

How many have transporters?

Only a few they are very expensive.

Good lets collect them all and then they can sit in their ship till we figure out what to do with them. I don't like standing here not knowing when they will wake up and come walking threw the wall and jump us.

They found six units Kit used her to find them. It was a trick she said she would teach him later. With them in their hands they telaported back to the Space Explorer David felt better. But he asked Kit what about your crew how many heard what went on over here.

More than half, but they are my crew and will follow me. None are from Tecbladxia, so they will not care as long as we got the ZXX5.

Tell me dose the ZXX5 have any weapons on it. David asked.

She smiled, yes the best made but I still would not try to come up against this Space Explorer. The Explorer shields are better and a better tracking system to aim the canons. But it is built for exploring not for fighting. A battle cruiser could take this ship out in minutes.

Are there any weapons on that other cargo transport we just left that crew on?

Yes they have a two canons small but can be deadly if aimed right. But don't worry they cannot be used without this master switch and their radios will only work a short distance. We had better transport those pumps out of here.

OK put them in your cargo whole, leave one on here the workers will notice the water damage, when they come back,

Chapter 18

The Sommeonnes

The strange phenomenon's that happen that Christmas night, half the people in the world will never know about. Very few people were awake when to ocean drop a foot. But the effect on the eastern coast of North America, That sent a twelve inch tidal wave. Could not be explained and did not cause any damage. But the wave that hit Western Europe was blamed on an earth quake near the surface in the Atlantic Ocean floor, did cause minor damage.

David had gotten the exploratory space ship back up in space saying it was just a test. Then had the pumps moved back into the cargo ship and parked out in space. Kit had promise to help them finish the exploratory ship, As long as David worked on a way to help out her planet. He still kept a close eye on her; make sure she did not get other ideals.

One day when we were sitting in the control center of the ZXX5, He asked her about this taken water from mars and moving it to Ticbladxia.

I don't know it all I can tell you what I do know. About three thousand years ago our oceans started drying up they say it was breaking to oxygen and hydrogen being lighter was pulled into space by our sun gravity that making our oxygen level higher but with no water we would all die. So they sent ship out to find more and we found it on the planet you call Mars. It had the water we needed. We had checked your oceans but they were too salty and the salt would reduce our mantel powers. But on mars the water with it low salt levels. We decided to use it so with all space ship that could hold water we raided the planet well after we had over ¾ of it. The martins dug tunnels and hid the rest underground. Well on the way back to Ticbladxia, when the space ship pulling the water barge, got to the edge of your solar system the barrage blow up, taken the tow ship and one other with it. The scientist figured the martin put a bomb in it or that some pirate thought it was treasure and attract it, either way we never went back to mars till just recently. And found a civilization living under ground. Now that is the way I heard it. There are several other stories. But that is the one I believe to be the best.

Three thousand years ago, you say.

Yes, why you got an ideal. Why do you have a part of your mind blocked, Kit asked?

Because I don't want you to get your hope up, fire this ship up and let's go for a ride.

Where to Kit asked

Oh just around the solar system. Take it to the out skirts.

Kit notified the crew. Ever one to their stations we are going to have a drill. One by one the lights in the control screen came on showing that they were ready. When they all were lit, Kit touched the center light and the ZXX5 started moving faster. You could not feel it but could see the planets go by. Twenty minutes later she touches another lite the ship slowed. Wow this ship is fantastic; she touches another screen and spoke into it. Way to go you took nine seconds off your best time. The first round for everyone is on me. A cheer went up around the ship. Well that cost me about six kunks what are we doing.

See that planet over there we call it xyz; put us in a close orbit around it. She did, now let's go for a walk. Do you have anything to tell what this planet is made up of.

I can do that from here its ice a very small amount of metal.

We touch our suit buttons and instantly we were looking like two green marshmallows David took her hand and transported them to the surfaces of the planet. The gravity was less than the moon but not bad.

OK now what; Kit was talking in David head.

This planet was form three thousand years ago according to our scientist. This is the water you stole from mars. The little bit of metal are the ship that were towing it.

But it is to big Kit answered.

That because this far out any partial that are suck in by the other planet. When the planet moves on the partial will just be hanging there then along comes this ice ball with its gravity sweep it up, growing bigger all the time. It has been building up for three thousand years.

Let's take a sample and go back to the ZXX5.and test it, I'd bet it's the same concentration as that from mars, maybe a few compound add. That would be the ones it picked up over time.

Back on ZXX5 they test the samples David was right. And the major per portion of the extra parcels were oxygen.

How big of a ship would it take to pull this planet over to Ticbladxia, David asked Kit?

There none that I know of she answered.

How about the Space Explorer, you said it had the new engines, and the new model of specter.

Maybe half of the planet, at the most Kit answered.

David was sitting there looking at the planet, with my finger trying to get his ears to pop something to do with the pressure.

Do you have a ringing in your ears too Kit asked.

Yes I thought it was the pressure from the planet. It was stronger down there but it just won't go away, he told her.

That what I noticed to, Kit answered

I want to go back to the surface only in a different place, David said.

OK I'll go with you; I want to know what it is too.

They turned on our space suite and held hands. Kit looked at him and thought you just want to hold my hand I know your plan now.

Always he said as he pushed the transporter button I'm aim to the other side of the planet.

When they materialize the bussing was replace by people thinking.

It's a Martian slang I believe Kit said.

David thought real hard and loud Hello is anyone there.

All the thought went down an octave then one came threw What are you?

We are space travelers,

What do you want here?

Who are you David asked and what do you call this planet.

This is the planet of Sram, where do you come from?

Earth the third planet from the sun. Where are you David asked?

Down here in town.

Can we come down?

Why it asked?

So we can talk. David said.

We are talking now you say you are from the third planet from the sun.

There are stories that we came from the fourth planet have you been there.

Yes Kit answered

Now there a voice that is nice. I'll talk to this one. What did you find on the fourth planet?

People like you and they talk almost like you.

Is that how you learned our language?

No I'm wearing a translator.

You can come down, and bring the other with you. I will turn on the door beacon.

Over there David pointed out for Kit it was small and so was the door. A fury thing appeared at the door.

Sorry I don't think you are going to get in here.

David squatted down on the back of his heels, hi my name is David and this is Kitaracta.

Hello I'm called Rowan I didn't mean to be rude but your voice that comes threw is terrible raspy, much better out here.

Are there other city here, David asked.

No we have burl all the way through the trimbel this is the only population. There are a few out there, a few wap from town but come the cold season they move into town.

How big is your population? David asked.

Over three hundred and all hunters ready to kill. How many on your planet. Is it warm?

There are over four billion inhabitant's on my planet and compared to this it is hot in some places it is a hundred degrees and some places it is cold fifty below freeze.

And the forth planet from the sun how many live there and is it as hot.

Kit answered this one. No it's not as hot highs are around four degree above freezing that what we call it when water turns to trimbel and in the north it gets down to almost one hundred degrees below.

Oh that would be nice. He answered.

We are going back to our ship can we come back and visit later.

Did I offend you in any way I apologize the little man asked.

No not at all I'm just getting cold. I'll warm up and come back.

OK we would like to hear more about our home planet.

See you soon David said and took Kit hand and transported back to her ship.

Once there they turned off their space suites. I came back up here so we could talk and not have them hear us. He told Kit.

I knew it was something because you can adjust the temperature in the suite she answered. OK I hear the wheels turning in your head but cannot figure out what they are saying.

Alright those people can burl through the ice. Say we have them cut the planet in thirds take one third to mars a third to Ticbladxia and leave a third to make more ice for Ticbladxia to use later. That way we are the good guys for getting them home, you the water. And a backup supply.

First we have to make sure they want to go back to Mars. Before we cut up there planet. And how are you going to move 1/3 of a planet.

You said the new Space Explorer can move half. So 1/3 should be easy.

Yes but you are talking about a chunk of ice with people on it, people who have to stay cold.

Come on, quite playing the devil adversary, I'm getting you your water. And I'm going to help these little people out. I'm still working on the snag. That you keep adding. Tell me if we were to expand the shield to cover the ice would it protect the people on the ice.

I have no ideal, but are you going to chance it with these people's lives.

You know I would not do that to even fury worms. I just thought you might know if it would work. So let's think how do we get three hundred Martian home, David said.

Well why don't we just swoop down and open the doors and they jump in.

You got it right almost how about we open the doors in space get the cargo bay cold then hustle them up here, lock on a tractor beam and haul ass to Mars.

That might work, at light speed it would heat up a little but they could survive. And we do have coolers in there.

Well shell we go talk to our little friends but let not say anything till we talk to the Martian they may not want all that water back. Let's take the traveler and land at the door that way we can open the door and invite them in it is more hospital than sitting on the ground.

We will have to keep our space suite on or we will freeze in seconds.

Just before they landed David call Rowan.

My space traveling friends you came back, he answered.

Yes and we came in my space traveler, may we land by your door.

Yes the trimbel is very solid there. I will meet you at the door.

David landed the travel and open the hatch way, as they came out. There to meet them was Rowan and another,

Welcome space travelers I'm called Mike. I'm sorry we cannot invite you in you are much larger than we expected.

That is why we have brought our ship to you, would you like to come in. it will make it much easier to talk to you, if we can sit down.

Thank you but no, we can sit over we have made benches for you.

Well I did not notice them before David answered.

That is because we made them while you were warming up. Come let us talk I have many question about our home planet.

I have question about your planet too. Why is it you were not afraid when we first appeared have you had traveler before David asked.

Oh no you are the first, but our legend tells of you coming and arriving in a big ship and taken us home. I see you only have a small space ship made of metal. Metal is very rear here it must be very expensive space craft. This was Mikie talking in our heads.

No there is a lot of metal on your home planet we call Mars. What you have here is more expensive than metal you have water and trimbel. And this is only our short distance traveler we have a much bigger one up in space. You say your legends, Tell of us coming.

Oh yes one day the Sommonnes will come out of the sky and take us all too where it is warm and we will be very wealthy and happy. We are hoping that you are the Sommonnes.

I don't know if we are the Sommonnes but we might be able to take you back to your home planet. And to arrange you to take back with you this great amount of wealth that you have. The people on your home planet will welcome this much trimbel, and water. There planet is very dry.

Do your legends tell how you ended up out here at the far edge of the solar system, it was Kit asking.

The legends say that our grandparents were very bad and the big metal machines picked them up and left them here till they could prove that we were no longer a menace to the world. We have practice long and hard, not to be a disappointment, to you, and to forgive our grandparents for their evil ways. So when you came, you would see that we are not the bad ones, and that you will deliver us back home.

Well I don't know if we are these sommonnes that you talk about but somehow we will get you back to your home planet. The people on the third planet from the sun, we call Earth, are not going to make you stay out here. For something your grandparents have done a long time ago. I will promise you that. Now that we know that you are here. Before today we thought this was just a big ball of trimbel floating in space. We must go now but I will be back soon.

David motion to Kit toward the hatch way they both got up.

he extend his hand, to shake his paw he reached out with a hand from the fur it was green and shook his hand.

I hope to see you soon you are welcome here Rowan said.

Back in the traveler David switch the heat on and headed toward, ZXX5 when it was warm he switch his suite off. Kit left hers on till they were back in the landing bay, when she did. It looked almost like she had been crying. Are you alright David asked.

She came over and hugged him tight. Those people are being punished for what my ancestors have done, not theirs. I have to make this right, no matter what it takes to do it.

We will, when I tell someone that I'm going to do something. I'll damn sure do it. Come on clean up that sweet face, it does not look good that way. Come on a smile, we will get them home David assured her.

Thank you; I would not want my crew to see me like a sniffling solftie. I'll straighten up and meet you in the control center.

Up in the control center she had composed herself, well what do we do now?

Let go to mars and get the other side of the story. You know this being, the god sommonnes is kind of strange to me, David said.

Don't worry you are only the someone, they got extra letters add in their legend, sommonnes is someone. It could have been anyone who found them, but it was you who is the Sommeonnes.

Well that just busted my bubble. You could have let me baste in the glory for a few minutes at least. On to mars captain, please.

Chapter 19

Earthling Meets A Martian

They landed in front of a large cave. Keep your suite on till we get further underground oxygen is thin even for you and me it would kill as you know.

I know but how do you, survive on Earth, David asked

With this she held up a metal cylinder between her thumb and for finger about an inch long you put it under your tongue and I'm good for twenty four hours. I don't go anywhere without it now. You taught me a good lesion.

I didn't mean to, I was only defending myself I really did not mean to hurt you.

I know that, when you save my life. Kit smiled at David.

I didn't mean to do that either, smiling back at her.

You are a liar, as she winked at him.

You will never know David said.

Yes I do, and that what make me love you even more. Is the fact I do know you. You are the sweetest, kindest person I have ever met.

Stop it you are melting my suite.

As well as mine if I had one, that nice two young people in love. Came pounding through his head. David looked around there behind him stood a Martian. We're not in love he studded.

Oh yes you are, just too blind to see it.

Kit turned around Shelly good to see you.

Well its Kitaracta what junk did you bring to trade to day.

That was all good junk and you know it.

You know I will never admit to that I have a reputation to watch. Now get out of that baggy suite and give me a hug. Where have you these last two years?

Got a new job, I'm showing the new Kula federation Ambassador from Earth around the galaxies.

I heard they were building an Explorer, but it sound to me you're showing him more than just the galaxies. Hello Mr. Ambassador you're the first Earthling here. It's a little different from your planet with all that water. I went on a cruise down there once, sure do like your green and blue.

Well thank you, there is beauty in your landscape to, if you look at it closely as I did coming in.

Oh he's a smooth talker. I can see why you fell in love with him. And good looking too. If Kitaracta ever throw you out, I'll be here to catch you.

Look who the smooth talker now David said.

Well what bring you to our neighborhood?

David saw Kit shaking her head, oh just out visiting the neighboring planets with that good looking guide over there only chance I get to see her. I think I made her blush.

Yes sir you did, now you be sure to stop by and see me before you go.

Hay, you were laying out the crap really thick there. You have nice landscape if you look Kit mantel pass to David.

You were the one who mention Ambassador I was just practicing my Ambassador politic you know kissing baby's foreheads and people's ass David sent back.

Yes your learning, she laughed come on I'll introduce to someone who will not picking your pocket, while she is hugging you.

David reached in his pocket; alright his knife was still there. The wallet he gave up carrying it a long time ago. Hell everyone on earth knew him anyway. The paper and tabloids had picture from when he was three years old, till he was ninety. And he wasn't even that old yet.

They step on the floating walk ways and went into the heart of the city. Up to the mayor palace where Kit said the mayor really did not have any power and that he just inherited the title form his father, who had got it from his father, and so on down the line. The main governing body was a counsel of twenty, one from each district. And it was more like a social club they would meet once a week for lunch. Then twenty minutes of meeting, but the mayor could sit in if he wanted to. Kit informed David we are going to see the mayor wife. She was the one to talk to. As soon as she saw them she came over and shook both of Kit hands.

Kitaracta where have you been, you are looking younger every day. Come let's have some krista and tell me all about it. And who is this young man, with you.

This is the Kula Ambassador to Earth Mr. Nulls.

Oh yes I have heard they join the federation. Are they an open port yet?

Mr. Ambassador this is Samantha the mayor wife. She knows everybody who is anybody. And is the most likely one to talk to.

Oh my, this sound important, here have some Krista and we can talk in the parlor is the way my translator sent it to David. (Basically it was the next room) have a set and tell me what on your mind.

They sat down and Kit started in. We have found three hundred of your people and they want to come home.

What, Samantha asked?

Just jump right in, David told Kit.

Oh you tell her you're the politician she said to David.

When your water disappeared a group of your people went with it. And they have been waiting all this time for you to come and bring them back. They have all this trimbel they call it. Ice we call it.

Yes I know what trimbel is Samantha said.

Good because I didn't know what it was? As I was saying they have enough that if melted they could fill some of your ocean.

Kitaracta, Is he fooling with me Samantha asked.

No he is not, I have seen it and there are three hundred martins living on the planet and they call here their home planet.

The problem is that they have grown calamities they need to live where it is cold. So we were thinking of moving then, to your ice poles.

And you can bring the trimbel with them Samantha asked?

We can in a few months when our Space explorer is finished David added.

I think we need to talk to my husband. She pressed her phone for lack of a name to call it, a red spot on her arm. Honey will you come into the parlor for a minute, NOW she added.

A few second later he materialized in the room. Kitaracta, good to see you, how have you been.

Sit down you can socialize later, she has a problem that you can help with, and it feels more important to her, than the trimbel.

OK I missed something in this conversation he said as he sat down, fill me in please. Turning to David how do you do I'm Rowan.

Kit looked at David and smiled. He knew what she was thinking, as she continued, When your seas disappeared, a group of people were sucked up with it, now three thousand years later, we have found them and they would like us to bring them back here to their home planet.

Well I see no problem in that we will surely welcome them home.

The problem is they want to bring their city with them. And there city is made of trimbel and when melted it will fill your oceans. David added.

Rowan looked at him, is this for real he asked.

Oh yes Kit added only they cannot handle the warm weather they need to live in the ice regions.

There is no problem with that no one else wants to. So when do we meet these people.

We can leave now Kit answered.

Hold on us, I need to sleep this bouncing all over the galaxy I'm tired David spoke up.

Yes Samantha said Kitaracta I can feel that this is important to you but I also feel your need for rest, you will go tomorrow. Come you will rest here for now.

They had the resting slabs Kit took one, and David on the other. It seems like only seconds later he woke up, Kit was still sleeping he went into the other room and found Samantha. She greeted him then offered a cup of krista.

What was that about coffee? She asked.

It is like your krista only it is a little stronger we call it coffee.

Well when Earth becomes an open port. You can bring us some.

What do you mean by an open port David asked?

Some planets are closed by the Kula they are backwards and no one is to interfere with them. You can go there but you have to be discreet, on your visit no contact with the inhabitants. And never remove anything from a closed planet.

Well I did not know that we will just have to get Earth rating change. We do have a lot to share with other worlds. But from my travels we do have a lot to learn.

Maybe not you, but the people of Earth do. I think you started them thinking that they are not the center of the universe. It was Kit behind him.

Nice of you to join us David stood up as she walked in.

Yes this one has manners; I wish he would teach my husband some he would not get off his fat duff if the whole Kula council walked in. speaking of him he should be here any time now. Kitaracta would like some Krista, I hear it is not as good as coffee.

Now don't put words in my mouth, David said it not as strong as coffee he corrected Samantha.

I stand corrected Kitaracta would you like some Krista. We do not have coffee yet. She smiled at David, so he knew she was hinting to bring her some.

I thought that since we are a closed planet I could not remove anything from the planet David said.

You do have a lot to learn, if a person is from the planet then it is alright.

I got it, my next visit I will bring you some. David said.

And what will you trade for whatever you have just talked him out of. You have to be on your guard with this old haggler. It was Rowan, standing the doorway.

Maybe I will trade you, you old fool, where have you been.

I have been out getting a new space suite the old one I have not had on for a hundred cycles. I needed one to impress our guest.

That is short for it didn't fit anymore Samantha added. Well after they have had their Krista you can run along and impress.

A short time later they were back in the ZXX5 heading toward the ball of ice, the Earthlings call xyz. As kit put them in orbit around it Rowan stared at the planet, you say that is all water and our people live there.

David assured him it was.

They loaded into the space traveler and when they were near David thought hard and called Rowen.

The mayor sat back you don't have to yell I'm right here.

I was calling the Rowan on the planet David said.

As the other Rowan came in through our heads, you came back.

Yes and we brought you a surprise, is it OK to land by the door.

Yes currently and I'm feeling someone who is not of your kind, in fact it is one of us.

David landed and Rowan and about ten others were at the door. David Kit and Rowan turned on their space suite and David open the hatch door. The ice martin moved closer, when the mayor step out a cheer went up from the ice people.

Rowan meet mayor Rowan from your home planet. David smiled at Kit.

Been planning that for a while haven't you. She smiled back.

Thank you Sommonnes we still have not expanded the door. And are sorry we cannot invite you in, but we will have it done, now that we know that you will come back. Will it be alright if we invite the mayor in?

Yes my little friend, that is why we brought him, David answered. Kitaracta and I will be waiting in the traveler take all the time you want. I'm sure you have a lot to catch up on. Then motion toward the traveler Kit, and David left

Chapter 20

Martian Meet Martian

In the space traveler David ask Kit, when should we tell them that we want to ship off a third of their planet, to another world to save it.

You're the politician why are you asking me.

That is because I'm running out of ideals, other than telling them the truth.

Will you had better think fast because they are coming out.

They turned on their space suite and open the hatch, and went out to meet them. Well mayor what do you think, David asked.

I think we can defiantly find a place for them on our planet. But this much water will flood the whole planet. So they have agreed to just take part of it. And place it at the cold regions.

That is about what we were thinking. We figured out the Earths Space Explorer, we could only move about 1/3 of the planet. Except we could not move it with the people on it, we are still working on that plan. The only one we have come up with is to transport them over in a cargo bay. It does have chiller but were not sure it can keep it that cold.

We did come up with a plan. That would give them an income and a means of supporting them self. Kitaracta knows of a planet that needs water too. One solar system over you might mention that selling or treading 1/3 could make them very rich. This leaving the last 1/3 in orbit here to keep gathering ice, so they would have a never ending supply they could sell or trade in the future.

Yes that would be a great plan, and here I thought you Earth people were unintelligent. I see now why the Kula has decided to have Earth join. I never have had any contact with your people. It will be a pleasure to sitting down and just talk, there a lot I'd like to know about your planet.

Now that was fast thinking it was Kit in Davids head.

Yes we will have to do that someday. Trying to adore Kit smile. Right now I'm working on getting these people home. Do you want go back and talk to them and see what they think of these plans?

Rowan says he feels bad that they did not make the entrance door larger. Once in the city you and Kitaracta would not have any trouble getting around once inside, it is almost warm in the town maybe just under freezing. And they have a fairly large town. How about we have them meet us out here and you can tell them your plan. It is your and Kitaracta they consider you two as their savors. They call both of you, this Sommonnes the hero in there legions.

David laughed Kitaracta figured it out that is, someone, the extra letters just got add over time.

Oh I see what you mean, still they think you two are something special, and unexpectedly since you came back.

They meet with Rowan outside the entrance. And set on the benches. That they say they dug out of the ice for them. David told them of the plan to get them to Mars and how they could trade 1/3 to the other planet. Everyone agreed it was a good plan. David told them Kit and him would go and talk to the other planet and see if they agreed.

Kit, the mayor, and David all told them that we would be back later as they climbed back into the traveler. They had said they would start dividing the ice ball into thirds by tunnels so it could be broken off and be ready to take them back home.

On the way back to planet Mars David told Kit to swing by Earth, so he could pick up some coffee for Samantha.

Rowan said, so that what that old woman had con you out of, something from a closed world, and by the way what is coffee.

It's like your Krista only stronger and taste better you will have to trust me on that David told him.

Kit put the ZXX5 into orbit and they took the traveler down. While Kit and Mayor Rowan waited outside the air traffic. David telaported to the space center, to see how things were going it was almost finished. Another week to go crews had been assigned and they are doing orientated in France. David asked about Mindy, Archer and the Sargent Speck where were they. The answer made him take step back. They were in France at orientation. That if we saw you, to tell you to be there in twelve days for their wedding.

David thanks them and said he needed two five pounds tins of coffee. Roberts pointed to a case of coffee and said to help himself. He picked up two cans and transported up to the traveler. David told Kit the news and asked how long have we been gone.

Kit answered in space time three days, in Earth time about two weeks.

Well it sounds like we will only have time to drop off the mayor and be back in time for the wedding. Then go to Ticbladxia.

That is the planet with the Erfriens, they sell the meat all over the galaxy. If that's the planet that's need water too. Then you have a good bargaining chip. The mayor said.

Kit put the ZXX5 in orbit and they took the traveler to the space port and transported to the mayor house where they were meet by Samantha. David gave her the coffee.

I like a man who keeps his word.

David told her to use three measuring spoon full. And it makes the same way as she would Krista.

After a lot stronger, good cup of coffee Kit and David headed back to Earth.

David thought of Captain Roberts and tuned in two feet behind and was glad he had learned to check before pushing finial button he was in front of everyone telling them about what they might encounter at different planet. David switches to a spot in the back of the room. That as it turned out was not the best ideal. When he pushed finial and appeared, the lady next to him jump and screamed. That got everyone to stop and look at her and David. He just smiled and waved.

Captain Roberts didn't miss a beat. And that ladies and gentlemen, this is what you can expect. Strange things are bound to happen, this one not that strange. This is David Nulls the Ambassador for the Kula federation here on Earth. Mr. Ambassador would you like to come up and tell the new crew members a few things they might encounter on their travels.

Caught, David said that he would be happy to, as he made my way to the front. Other than the alien you might have met helping build our Space Explorer. They had devices to make then look human as not to frighten everyone. The people in other worlds will look there natural way. For instance one of the first aliens you will meet is our neighbors from mars. And there cousin on the planet we call XYZ the furthest planet from our sun, that is not really a planet it is a ball of ice. They will look like large worms with hands and feet. Don't let that fool you they are very intelligent. The next aliens you will probability meet are on the planet of Ticbladxia in another galaxy, like our own. They are very human like, except they are green. And we are aliens to them. So the best advice I can give you is going out there with an open mind and learn, thank you. David told Captain Roberts he would like to see him whenever he was free.

Be about a half hour, this is not as much fun as flying and I'm a ready for a real adventure, Roberts said.

Oh you will like what I have plan for your shake down trip David smiled, tell you later.

An hour later he ended this part of orientation and came straight over to David. I saw the smile on your face. I heard you got me rope into this being Captain of The Space Explorer. What have you got in your mind for me next? I have already figured out, we are going to meet Marian's at both end of the galaxy.

You can always quite, David said.

Not a chance in hell that will happen, come on what gives

It will just be a little good will and introduction toward our neighboring planet. Then David told about the people on XYZ and how they wanted to go home. When he got to the part about moving 1/3 of a planet for them Captain Roberts stop him.

Are you kidding me move 1/3 of a planet?

No 1/3 of a big ball of ice David corrected, and that just the training run. Then David told him about moving the other 1/3 to another galaxy and that. Kit and he would help him. Kit had moved large object before by using the shields as part of the ship.

Captain Roberts thought about for a minute, it would be a good training for the new crew. And you are right it would establish a good relationship between the two planets. This other planet in another solar system, you say they are our closes planet, with life forms.

No they are the closet one with a form similar to ours. It is the planet that Kitaracta is from! I didn't think he needed to hear the story how they were the ones who had taken the water off of Mars or that they had plan to take the water from Earth's oceans, but did tell him that they had been the ones who sent the engines and the sperter.

I do like your plan; it will establish good repore to start with. Anything else you have plan for us. He asked?

No that is it you will be on your own to go exploring you are the Captain. Your mission is to go where no human has gone before and explore distance planet. I had heard that somewhere, unless you want me to think up something else?

Yes I have heard that somewhere too. And no I think I can find enough to get us in trouble with without your help. On the second thought maybe you can help me. They are planning this wedding on the Space Explorer and the Captain is to perform the wedding. You didn't have anything to do with that do you?

No I just heard about it yesterday. In fact that is why I'm here, where are those two.

I don't know, I think they are avoiding you, they were here a minuet ago, and there they are over there with Archer. Now don't go over and kill my head of security. You can yell at our new school teacher, but I don't think you will be able to talk her out of going.

Catch you later David said walking over to Mindy and the Sargent.

When she saw him headed her way, She meet him part way and came and put her arms around my neck. Oh daddy, I'm glad to see you got the message.

Oh yes I got the message. I thought I was to be the first to know. Not the last after everyone in the world has heard. Then the Sargent came up. And you, you were supposed to watch out for her, not cover her. He stopped and took a step backwards. Then David reaches out his hand, congregation I cannot think of anyone else who could keep her in line. Beside now I can tell everyone my son-in law is head of security on the new Space Explorer.

Thank you sir, I have a feeling you might have had something to do with that.

Chapter 21

It Is A Fair Trade

The wedding went off with a hitch. Captain Roberts came up to David afterwards and asked how he did. David told him he missed his calling he should take up married people. That he did everything just right.

Well you didn't see me sweating bullets. We will give this crew a few weeks of training and we will be ready for your planed shake down adventure.

David told him, that would be fine and that he and Kit would be going to Ticbladxia to set that part up. That first part was already, in motion. And we would be getting back to him. Then David wished the new bride and groom good luck and that he'd see them later, then transported to the ZXX5.

There, he found Kit all stare eyed that the best wedding I have ever seen.

You were there he asked.

Yes I stayed in the back, and watched, and you looked so good all dressed up giving your daughter away.

OK pull yourself together, and let's go to Ticbladxia. We have business to attain to.

I was meaning to talk to you about that. Maybe it would be better if I stayed on the ZXX5 Kit said, and you went down to talk to them. You know, they know about the screw up I did on that attempt to steal the ocean water. I'm sure they have a death warrant out on me by now.

Don't worry about that no one is going to touch you as long as I'm still alive.

That may not be long once you are on the planet, she said.

Oh you of little faith again, if they need the water as bad as you say, they will listen to us.

There you are thinking the glass is half full again, we will see when we get there. I'll trust your gift of gab, or we will die together.

Kit put the ZXX5 in orbit and called in this is ZXX5-016

Captain Kitaracta Irreson requesting permission to land?

There was a long pause. Then they gave them permission to land at space port 15. The furthest one away so when they have to blow us up, it won't stop their space treading Kit told David.

When they landed David told Kit head up like we have nothing to be afraid of.

She did then told the crew to put the shields up as soon as we were out and if told to by her or David to get the hell off of the planet.

Kit and David step out on the platform and were met by an arm guard. The one in charge said to Kit you have a lot of nerve coming here.

Take us to your council and please keep your remarks to yourself, David said. As he started walking without him, when the guard did caught up, follow me this way.

When he turned right, David stop him the counsel is this way.

I have my orders he said.

Well I have just changed them. Now take us to the council.

The guards pointed their weapons at them. Is that what you want to do the counsel said to bring us to them. Your leader here has a different ideal a little accident planed, so the question here is do you want to go against the counsel and shoot us or shoot him for going against the counsel.

They turned their weapons on him. Waite a minute I might have taken the wrong turn. He said yes it is this away as he started walking the right way.

How did you know I didn't hear him thinking? It was kit in Davids head.

Tell you later they are listen, David said out loud. The guard took them up to the world counsel and marched right in. Kind a like they were expected them. David walked right up front Kit stay with me. Greetings I'm David Nulls the Ambassador from Earth in the next solar system over from you. First of all I would like to thank you for the very nice engines that you sent over for Space Explorer. Sorry it did not work out the way you plan. But we like our planet water and sorry that we cannot share it with you. But we do have a planet that has more than it needs and they are willing to trade with you. In fact enough to fill all your lakes and sea, Also this water is not as salty as our ocean water. I have been asked to do the bargaining for them. Now what do you want to trade for your lakes to be filled with this fine water.

Oh my mistake, I now see that you knew nothing about stealing our ocean water. Well if you talk to that man over there you might learn something. Just then the one of the council members made a run for the door. They stop him in his tracks David could feel all the council members holding him in their minds. Then turning him around and force him back in front of them, and then probing his mind. I heard it all how a group had planned to take the water and sell to the counsel for a lot more than he was asked for. When they came to the part about Kitaracta, they turned their attrition on her.

She answered that the ruling came over the communicator as being from the counsel here. And they even gave me a ZXX5 cargo ship. And I didn't think it could have come from anyone else.

She went along with thinking that the counsel had endorsed it, would have succeeded if I had not stopped her David added.

The counsel turned to David would you mind leaving for a short while so we can work this internal problem out, And not in front of an Ambassador from another world.

David told them he would have no problem leaving but Kitaracta was going with him.

Well she is part of this investigation and needs to be here.

Then we have a problem, I told her I would not leave her alone. And she knows I'm a man of my word David said. I will block out your investigation but I will be standing here in this room, watching as long as she is here.

Fair enough a man must keep his word or he has nothing. There is a chair over there pointing toward a side wall; we can get back to your offer as soon as this matter is straightened out. David went over sat down, not taken my eyes off of Kit ready to do whatever, if he saw she was in danger.

David did stand up one time, when she said liar and with a motion of her and thoughts flung the leader of the escort squad against the wall.

Sorry David apologized to the counsel I could not tune that out.

Quite alright we could not stop her either.

If he will not tell the truth I will beat it out of him was the last thing I heard Kit say before David tune her out. From the looks on the counsel faces they believe she could do it and they could not stop her. She must have developed her mental ability more than they thought.

She has, it came through loud and clear, David turned one of the council members that were looking at him. Then gave a small wave to let him know it was him that sent the message.

The next thing David knew was the escorts was escorting the leader out, with weapons pointed at him.

The counsel was motioning David over. He got up and went to stand next to Kit. Were sorry that this incident happens, we have some very rich people who make their money off of the less fortunate. And do not care who they hurt. Now about your offer to fill your lakes and rivers there is a real need for this water. But at the price it would cost another planet we could not do it again as our ancestors did. The actions of these people were not the choice of this counsel. So tell about your water.

David explained about the Martian who were moving back to their home planet from the ice ball and how they would like to trade 1/3 of it for a small heard of your Erfriens and that the people of Earth would deliver the water here as a token of friendship.

The Ticblladxia council decided they need to discuss this in privet, so everyone was removed from the room. And a thought barrier was put up.

Once outside David asked Kit what went on, while he was tune out?

You really tune it out. She asked?

Yes that what I told then I would I did not know if they have a way of checking. But I keep an eye on you if anything started getting strange I would have tune back in, and beside you throwing the man across the room everything seemed normal. Hay you even did that to me.

I was just following orders, she snapped. I wonder what is going on in there. You know we are not out of this mess yet.

A little argument seems two of the council members were in on the stealing of the water. That is probably how they got the message to you David answered.

You can hear them, kit asked? That supposed to be a seal room.

You mean you can't. It is so loud, that it is about giving me a headache. I believe they just killed one of them and are about to kill the other one.

Kit brushed passed David and into the counsel room. Before you kill him I want some answers.

David followed Kit into the room. There was one council members sitting in the chair with blood coming out of his ears. I'm guessing they just blow up his brain with thoughts. That looks like a hell of a way to die. And David was feeling sick.

The counsel stop and looked at her you heard what we were questioning him about?

Yes we did and it take more than those two to pull this kind of shit on me, and I want to know who they are working for.

Well that all we can get out of him, the counsel answered.

Well give us a few minutes with him. Ambassador Nulls can you get pass his blocks.

I will give it a try; David said and turned to the counsel standing up. Say that is a nice try thinking of the wall but we want to go deeper. How about I have Captain Kitaracta bounce you off the wall, one or two times? It worked when he took a second to think about that, he drop his guard and David was in who is Aurther Caningsome, then his mine went blank. And he fell to the floor dead, did I kill him David thought.

No he committed suicide. It was Kit in his head now.

We'll all I got was Aurther Caningsome then all kind of torture and a slow death. Who is Aurther Caningsome?

He would be the one who could afford to pull this off, and it is, Ather Comenson.

Yes that the name I got, but what with the slow death. Waite the slow death wasn't him, it was his family. I believe you had better check on the councilman's family David said.

We will do that, and we thank you Mr. Ambassador we will take it from here the counsel said in Davids head. Would you like to rest now, we will talk about your trade tomorrow.

Your welcome glad I'm could help, but I don't need rest, a glass of wat... David stop myself; a cold drink would be nice.

We do still have drinking water Mr. Ambassador one of the counsel men said.

My apologies David said I did not mean to offend you but I think we will go back to Captain Kitaracta ship. We will be happy to meet with you tomorrow to complete our negotiations at what time would you like for us to come back.

Any time after lunch will be fine. David could feel the relive in the counsel.

Then till tomorrow, may the rest of the day be good. He turned toward Kit. Who had her head held hi and shoulders held back. Is there anything else you want done here?

No it is fine for now. She answered and making sure the counsel heard her.

The security guards meet them outside of the door. We are going to space port 15 and no detours please. David said noticing that they no longer held their weapons on them.

No problem Mr. Ambassador this way.

At the space port David told Kit don't say anything till we are in space.

Once in space what was that all about Kit asked?

I did not get your family will be killed very slowly from the suicide counsel man; it came from one of the counsel man directed toward him. So there is another one involved in the stealing of the ocean water.

So what are we going to do about this she asked?

I have no ideal; I guess we will just have to see how it plays out tomorrow. For now I'm really tired.

But down there you said you weren't Kit questioned.

That because I did not want then to know, how much of a strain that was. You never put all your line in the water, that way if they make a run on you. You can let them think they got away with it. Then they are hook, and then you can pull then in.

What the hell does that mean Kit asked?

It an old fishing trick I use on the smart fish who always steal your bate and gets away.

I might have known it had something to do with fishing. Come on let get some rest.

The next morning they headed down to the planet around noon their time. This time they got spaceport 1 a shorter walk. They were shown to the council chambers, before the counsel men came in. David could feel the tension but could not figure which one it came from.

The spokesman for the counsel addresses him. Now Mr. Ambassador, this water you say will fill our lakes and rivers. What our friends from another solar system asking in return.

Well they are a small population of around three hundred, I feel one Erfrien for each ten, so shell we say thirty, twenty five females, and five bulls David answered.

The counsel seems surprise such a small amount. They drop their guard. David jumped up and grabs one of the councilmen by the suite front. How many more were involved in the stealing of our water, he asked, then pointed at the rest who were about to stand up. Sit down all of you. And learn. Kit was standing at David side. With a weapon pointed at them. David asked again, how many more were involved in taking of the water from Earth.

Maybe twenty all of them are Mr. Comenson people, he choke out.

Any more on this counsel David asked know about it? Don't touch that button. As he was reaching for his transporter I will break your neck before we reach our destination. He moved his hand away from the button. I'm going to ask you again anyone on this counsel involved with the removal of Earths water.

No, he gasps as David was still holding tight to his uniform with his fist pressing on his throat.

Now why did Mr. Comenson give Captain Kitaracta the ZXX5?

I'm not sure, something about he wanted her dead. Because one of his experiments went wrong and he had blame Kitaracta and she might figure it out. He wanted her at ease so he could kill her. The whole planet had all heard how powerful she had become. When David looked at Kit he could see in her face the shade of green coming in, this was not from embarrassment as before, but from anger. David turned loose of the counsel man and turned to her. No you will not do what you are thinking.

No my dear we will defiantly take care of Mr. Comenson. He is much too powerful to take on alone. It was the speaker of the Counsel. We agree to your terms of the trade. We feel you had better leave now for your own safety. I promise you Captain on your return you will have your revenge on Mr. Comenson.

Chapter 22

Kitaracta Gets Her Revenge

They lifted off from the space port, instead of going up into space. Kit keeps the ZXX5 at two thousand feet and headed toward the west of the city.

What are you doing David asked?

Nothing just checking something out, she answered.

Up ahead they crossed a large estate with a huge house in the middle of it. Big enough to be a castle back on earth with the surrounding buildings it could be a fairly large town. In fact if the estate had not, had a wall all around David would have mistaken it for a town.

So this is where the son of a bitch lives. Kit thought.

David pick up the thought, OK now get us out of here they said they would handle it.

Just then a voice came over the speaker. ZXX5-016 you are in restrictive air space leave now, or be incinerated!

Incinerated David looked at Kit who was holding course.

Blasted into small atoms, Kit said not taken her eyes off of the screen.

OK I like my body in one piece, let get out of here now, we got things to do we will handle this matter later. David said.

Kit touched the screen and seconds later they were leaving Ticbladxias atmosphere. Turning to David you heard what they said, because of that bastard down there. My father and mother were killed. I have spent thirty years living with the thought that I killed all of those people. All the while he keeps getting richer and richer. I will kill him, maybe not today but someday.

That right, but not today, we have other things to do. We need to stop by the ice planet. To see how things are going there. David was trying to get her mind off of the revenge she was thinking about.

Four hours later they slid into orbit around the planet XYZ. They spotted the Earths Space Explorer in orbit just ahead of them and up a little over a mile ahead. Kit called over to Captain Roberts who said he had arrived about an hour before they did. And what was the next move.

David told him he'd come over in the space traveler and pick him up and he will take them down to meet Rowan and see how their progress was going on splitting the ice up.

When they had pick up Captain Roberts and gone down to the planet. David mentally called Rowan and asked if it was still alright to land at the entrance. He said it was alright and he would meet them there.

They landed and to their surprise the entrance door was much larger Rowan motion them in. and they got even a bigger surprise. The ceiling of the ice cave was a good forty feet high their houses were small. But there were hundreds of them made out of ice blocks, if they could have painted then they would look like houses on Earth, they even had slope roof when David asked about it, they said it was to let the rain runoff. He was going to question the rain part, Then thought his translator was screwing up when Rowan pick up his though.

The heat melts the ceiling ice and we collect it for our water supplies. Rowan said.

David thanks him for the information, and told him how clever it was. Then asked how the tunneling was going to split the ice ball. And that Captain Roberts was ready to move then back to mars polar cap. Then remember he had not introduced. Captain Roberts. Rowan this is Captain Roberts.

Yes we have met, Kitaracta had introduced them.

Oh leave it to a woman to be formal David thought.

That right, Kit was in his head. We can be polite and wonder at this wonderful city at the same time.

He ignored her and asked again how the tunneling was going.

Rowan proudly announces that it should be completed in two days. And did they want to see the progress they had accomplished walking all over this as small as the planet was it would still take a month to do it.

No not walk we have plans that show how far we are and how far to go. Rowan said, Follow me this way to the main planning room.

In one of the largest building there was an ice table with black drawing on it. It show lines that divided the planet into three separate parts and larger lines to show what had to be done.

What are these dotted lines David asked?

That is the block that holds it together till we want to separate this part. We will leave one man behind to do final separation. We had a lottery to see who it would be. Stephen was the unlucky one we are not sure he will survive. So Mikie, will finish up for him.

Hold it David said you had a lottery on who would die? There must be a better way.

We cannot think of it. So it will be an honor to be the one who will set the rest of us free.

You say you will be ready in two days. That means I have two days to come up with a better way to separate the third from the rest.

Oh Sommonnes Stephen and Mikie would appreciate it, I'm sure of that, Rowan said.

I told you I would get your people back to Mars and that meant everyone. How about showing me one of these supports David asked.

There is one just a short way down this hallway, come I will show you.

They walked for what David figured was about a mile, till we came to one of the supports. It was four foot squared and ten feet tall. David studies it for a while then asked Kit if she had any explosive on her ship. She just shook her head. He looked at Captain Roberts who shrug his shoulders and shook his head, no. He then turned to Rowan I will think of something, how many supports are there?

There are twelve in all one each third he said.

OK I have seen enough let us go back and figure out a way of doing it. You can tell Stephen and Mikie they will be going along with the rest of you to your home planet.

They will be happy to know that, Rowan answered.

Back in the space traveler, after taken Captain Roberts back to the Space explore. Kit said I hope you did not make a promise you cannot keep. It going to take a good plan, to pull this off, without someone getting hurt or worse getting killed.

Do you think you can blast them with your cannons, David asked.

That would take a lot of luck to get that pin point of a shot, maybe one or two .Without blowing the whole planet apart.

David drew out a map of what Rowan had shown him, on the ice table. It was amazing the little details he could remember. This learning to use both side of your mind, had improve his thinking. And control so much he wonder why everyone didn't do it. It wasn't that he was so smart; it was more like he was thinking for two people.

You are smart, a lot smarter than most people; it was kit in his head again.

Oh ya if I'm so smart why I can't I keep you out of my head. David asked.

You can when you want, but you think about me all the time, and you still do not trust me. No matter what I tell you. I do trust you and I'm sure you will come up with something. Why not take a break and meet me in the relaxing room for something cold to drink as you call it.

You know honey maybe you are right if I took my mind off of it for a while, I can think of something, I will meet you there.

Good want to see who can get there the fastest, she added.

You're on David got up and fast walk three doors down to the rec. room, to find Kit already there.

You cheated you were already here David said.

No I telaported from the control room.

That's it; someone could knock off the supports, and teleport to the next one, before the side collapsed in on them. That weapon you had back on Ticbladixa will it blow apart the supports.

Yes it will blow a hole in it big enough to walk through. But you would have to be quick about it. And who do you think would want to try that stunt.

Oh no, oh no I'm not that crazy, beside I would have to know where each one is. I heard what you were thinking.

I wasn't thinking of you I was thinking of me, David said.

That even crazier than me doing it, Kit answered.

By the way where did you get that weapon from in the counsel room?

I always carry it when I'm in a hostel situation, as she pulled it out of her pocket. Just like you carry that knife, not like it would do you any good in a fight. A captain has the right to carry it anytime they want.

Damn, so how does it work David asked.

Touch these three spot and if anyone is in front of it, it will paralyze them for about an hour, touch all four spots at the same time, and if they are in front of you they will be atoms floating in space in seconds.

How many time can you use it till it runs out David asked.

Don't know never had to use it more than twice to get my point across, maybe a hundred times but if you did there would be nothing left around you. That why they are band from every world.

But our guards back on Ticbladxia had some.

No theirs could only paralyze, see the red on the end of this they did not have that.

But that leader was sure afraid of them, David said

That because if hit by three or more it will stop your heart and you will die.

The next morning they went down to the planet and meet with Rowan. David looked at his plans again then telaported to the first and with my knife carved an A on it then to the second one carved a B and so no down the line, till all had a letter on them all the way up to L. something was wrong he should have ended in M. He counted on his fingers. A, b, c, all the way to L it made 12. He slaps his head, you big dummy M is his space traveler. That was how he was to get off the chunk of ice before it collapses on Him. When he telaported back to the main building Captain Roberts had transported down in their shuttle. David laid out the plans when he got to the part, where he would blast the supports.

Kit told them it was a crazy plan and would never work. That he would never get out of there in time.

They all agreed with her. And that someone else should do it.

David insisted that he was the only one fast enough to do it and that was that, end of conversation. Kit try to protest saying she would do it instead. No David told her she was to important doing her job, and if she did it right he would be alright. They finally gave up arguing with him, and agreed. With Kit saying it was still crazy.

The next morning Kit transporter over to the Earths Space Explorer and ran the controls. They open the bay doors in space getting all the cold they could get then dropped to the planet surface holding the Space Explorer bay doors next to the entrance a foot off the ground. When all the ice people were loaded in they closed the doors turned on the atmosphere and cooling units. She took it back up and put on the shields. Then turn on the tractor beam and held it. Only then did she tell David it was alright to go.

David teleported to support A. while he was Standing there looking at it. This is crazy he thought.

Well don't do it, kit was in his head.

David thought back I love you. Then thought of support B and with one hand on the transport button, the other on all four buttons on the weapon he pressed both at the same time and was gone before completely dissolve the support. He was in front of support B, he never took my hand off the buttons and was still firing the weapon so the support started dissolving before he could think of support C. the ice was coming together and the space of ten feet was down to two by the time he teleported to support D at D he caught my breath. His shoulders hurt he reminded himself to hit the four buttons. Then let go before teleporting to the next support. If he had done that between L and M he would have blown a hole in his traveler. He thought E then F and hit the teleported button and was at support E fired the weapon hit the button and was at f before the support started to collapsed. That was it he needed to think of the one after the one he was going to. It work till he got to K it was already collapsing Kit came in his head it 'is going down get out of there now. Without think of L he went right to M and almost hit all four buttons but stop short. He rested for a second to stop shaking.

Kit was screaming in his head are you there and alright?

Yes I'm here and why are you not pulling away he answered.

We are she answered back.

He looked up to see the ice separating. Kit moved back ten mile then moved forward, turning and picking up speed. David took his traveler to the ZXX5 bay when they had closed the doors and then went to the control center Kits second in command had already started toward Mars there was no way Kit could Teleported threw the force shield on the Space Explorer to the ZXX5 so they just follow the best they could. It had been arrange that the second in command would pick David up then He would follow.

At Mars when Kit hit the atmosphere she would take it in a little fast to melt the rough edges off the bottom then slow down. The Martin had agreed to mark a spot at the northern part of the pole they said was the coldest part of the planet.

Kit hit the spot perfectly and set the ice ball down to a softly landing then pulled back a mile reset for a landing one foot off the ground to open the bay doors and let the ice people move back into their homes now back on their home planet after three thousand years. After unloading she took the Space Explorer back into space and turned the control back over to Captain Roberts

He said it was the best flying he had ever seen and he was glad that Kit was doing it and not him.

David told him that it came from thirty years of practice and he would soon be as good someday.

No he said he would never want to try that.

After a day of celebrating with the mayor and the new martins, it was time to go and deliver the other third and pick up the Ebfriens.

They stopped by Earth and picked up some timed exploding devices. David did not want to go through that again, of having to shoot the supports one by one. Back at the ice ball one of the engineer from the Space Explorer set the charges to go off one second after the one ahead of the last right on down the line it took almost a week to get this all ready.

When it did everything came off right. Soon they were on their way to Ticbladxia with another third of the ice ball.

It was going to take three weeks to get there. As Captain Roberts said, he wanted to take it easy but did want to open her and see what the Space Explorer would really do, but keeping the safety of the crew he was keeping to warp six.

Two days from Ticbladxia Captain Roberts, drop out of warp to give time to slow down

That when they met another ship that had just come from Ticbladxia and inform them there was a civil war going on between some big shot land owner named Comenson and the counsel and that Comenson was holding off and it look like he could do it for ever. And it would be best to stay away.

David looked at Kit as they got this message. He could see the darker Green in her face as she thought. That sorry ass just thinks, he going to get away with this .just waited till I get there.

David missed the rest of her thoughts, because Captain Roberts had come up to him asking what he should do. That he did not want to get into the middle of a civil war.

David told him it would be alright because where they were going to put the ball if ice was on another part of the planet.

The next day the planet of Ticbladxia came in sight, Kit was behind Captain Roberts advising him on how to approach the planet. Just before they inter the atmosphere, Kit took the controls and moved the large block of ice to the middle of the planet to where, Comenson army was hole up. With his force shields up and protecting them and keeping anyone from coming on the million Acres estates. Then she turned off the tractor bean, the ice went down melting as it went. By the time it hit the force shield. That was not designed to keep out water. The ice had turned into millions of gallons of water. It floods Comenson entire estate putting it under fifty feet of water. Drowning Comenson Army and disabling his force shield.

Kit had did it so fast she must have had it plan out beforehand. Captain Roberts and David did not have time to react.

As the water ran off in the different rivers toward their almost dry seas, taken party much everything with it. Kit turned to face them with a smile on her face, when she saw the look on their faces.

What is that look for he wanted water, I gave it to him. Gee I hope the sorry bastard can't swim.

They called Ticbladxia space control, who informed them that they did not have a landing big enough for space explore ship to land but they could orbit above the landing port it will remain clear for them. Then came surprise announcements. Congratulation, that's not quite where we expected the water, but it did seem like a better place after all. And that came directly from the counsel. The crew was invited, to a celebration in town tomorrow.

The next day they went to the celebration with Captain Roberts, Kit and David as the guest of honor. The celebration lasted two days so most of the Earth crew got to go and meet their new neighbor, the men and woman from outer space, the Ticbladxians. On the third day they loaded the Erbrien's then transported them up in their space ships, into the cargo hole of the Space Explorer when all was loaded they sent along two people to teach them how to raise and care for the Erfriens. Then they sent one of their own space ship with a load of all kinds of fruit and vegetables.

This time Captain Roberts got to open it up, as he called it. Kit used the ZXX5 to transport the Erfrien's down to the planet Mars.

Chapter 23

In Trouble With The Kula Councel

The space cargo ship arrived two days later. Kit and David went down and explained to the ice people. That the Ticbladxian people sent these good, because they were so grateful for the water, the extra bonus was their way of saying, Thank you.

When they got back to the ZXX5, Kit's first mate informed them that there was a message in the control room screen. David and Kit went into the control room and Kit touch the screen. A picture of the Kula counsel came on. They said that Captain Kitaracta and the Ambassador David Nulls were to come to Tistana. With no stops along the way!

David looked at Kit, what kind of trouble do you think we are in now he asked you don't think they are pissed just because we cut up a planet, do you?

I don't know, but they sure made it clear, no stop on the way. We will know in about three days or maybe less with this new ZXX5 I guess we can really open her up as Captain Roberts calls it. Kit touch the screen again, and informed the crew that they were heading toward Tistana. Then she touched the screen in several places and they started moving, and building up speed. As fast as David was thinking they were going by planets at the edge of the solar system. The stars blurred out. Kit was at the screen touching here and there setting the course.

David could see by the smile on her face she was happy here in the control center.

She turned to him, WOW this baby can move. We should be at Tistana. In two days, at the most. With all this updated computers, sure make a captain's job easy.

She was right in two days they were in orbit above Tistana, Where they were given immediately clearance to land at the space port and to report to the counsel.

David told Kit he would take the blame for whatever they did. Besides what could they do to us?

Well the worse could be ground us, or black ball us from all ports, maybe split us up and vanish us to different deserted planets. Maybe they will reward us for doing such a fine job. I don't see that happening. But you keep thinking positive Kit said.

They landed and there was an escort of one. Who lead them to the counsel building. David thought to Kit it's not an armed guard.

They were escorted right in to the counsel. As they stood there David could feel them shifting through his mind. He could stop them any time he wanted to, but felt it best to let them see what they wanted.

After a few minutes they stopped, and spoke, Let's see if we got this straight. First you change history on Earth, and when we told you to end it .you talked with this Mr. Comenson and got him to finish the job and you got a ZXX5. And Earth got a Space Explorer. Then Mr. Nulls talked the Martins into splitting up there planet, for water for her planet, then Kitaracta, Killed, Mr. Comenson and his army.

Well that's about right David thought.

Kit glared at him, saying this not some joke.

She is right, this is not a joke. And it is not about right.

What is right is you were sent from here to get the Planet to dismantle most of their nuclear weapons at any cost. Now that we have study it, changing history was the only way to do it. Then you find a civilization stranded on a ball of ice, and return them home finding them a way to make a living having their own heard of Erfrien Then you save another planet from drying up. And Kitaracta stops a civil war, with her quick thinking by knowing that a force shield does not stop water.

Someone with this much ability to solve problems, we need here. So if you will resign from the job as Ambassador to Earth. Then take the position of head of the Justice department for the Kula. The duty will be solving the problems between planets. A person of this position must have the right escort. And we plan on having Admiral Kitaracta be the pilot of that escort in her ZXX5. Why don't you take a few days to think about this? And give us your answer the day after tomorrow. In the mean time you both will be the gust of the counsel. There will be a guide to meet you outside and take you to the resort.

Kit and David turned and walked out the door what the hell just happen David asked?

I think they like you and they just offered you a high position on the council.

PART 2

THE AMBASSADOR FOR THE KULA

Chapter 24

The First New Problem

As the new Ambassador, for the Kula Federation, on the planet of Tistana, Life was a lot different, than the life he had riding his motorcycle David Nulls sat in his office not sure what the new job was. The Counsel had said it would be settling wars between planets. They didn't say war; they said monitoring disputes, and being a mediator between the Planets.

With Kinghtalotofstuf his old teacher, when he had been chosen as the Ambassador to Earth. Came in with a message from the Counsel saying, they wanted to see him.

Thank you Knight that is what David called him from the first time they meet many years ago and now he was David's right hand man. When did they say to come?

Right away Knight said, and then added the counsel said it was important!

Well I guess we should not keep them waiting, David said. As he headed toward the door, Looking back to see if Knight was following, Then remember he could walk through the door but could not see through it. Knight appeared a few seconds later.

In the council chambers David and knight stood facing the five counsel man. To an observer they were just looking at each other. When in reality they were talking mentally.

Well Mr. Ambassador this will be your first challenge. The planets of Albar, and Attis, have been fighting over the minerals right of the planet Melbar for years. We have just received word they have started shooting at each other. So would you mind going there and see what can be done to calm it down. Without changing their history, one counsel man added.

David could swear that he saw the counsel man smile, when he said it. Remembering what David had done to get Earth to join the federation. I will be glad to see what I can do. If nothing else at least we will have firsthand knowledge of what is going on, David answered. I will leave right away, anything else I need to know? Before leaving.

No we don't know much more than that, so we are leaving it to your discretion to handle the situation, Zovta (alien for good luck).

At the space port Knight said Zovta at the space Cruiser. David turned to him; Come on you can go too.

I don't think it is a good ideal; my race does not get along with the Albarins very well Knight said.

All the better reason to go, David then added besides you are protected by the Kula federation. As my assistant you can go anywhere I do.

OK but don't say I didn't warn you Knight said.

I'll make a note of it, that you did warn me, David said thinking how could anyone not like Knight, with his bubbly personality and sense of humor.

David sat at the control board of the space cruiser it was much larger than the space traveler he used when saving the Earth's oceans. But the controls were about the same. After leaving the space port, he set the course for the Planet Melbor. Then went and checked out the ships computers, learning what it had about the planets, Albar, Attis, and what was so special about Melber. It would take a day and a half to reach Melber and David wanted to know more, than they were fighting over some minerals.

David found out that Melber had a rich mineral that powered most of the space ships in the two galaxies. And both Albar and Attis were rich planets because of it. But he found out that all the wealth was split up among sixteen families with ten from Albar and the other six from Attis. He also found out that Attis seem to have less poverty, better roads, better schools and higher social activates, with about the same population as Albar.

David asked Knight about this, and it was as he suspected that the ten families from Albar keep most of the wealth to them self and had a bigger army and was better set up for a war than Attis.

Then David asked Knight why the Alberians didn't like his race as he had put it.

Well my home planet is in the same solar system as Alber. About two hundred years ago the president of Alber set out to conquer the solar system, and did a good job of it almost three quarters of it was under their rule. Then they tried to invade my planet of Jsader. That was their down fall; we kick their ass all the way across the universe. And when they got home we put up a barricade for ten years. Till the ruler died then the Reformed Party took over, and signed a pack to stay home. There are still a lot of them that hold the Barricade against us.

Two hundred years is a long time to hold a grudge, David said.

Well they really didn't recover till around fifty years ago when their exploration team found the minerals on Melber, that has several Taings in it, called Zlite. Normally Zlite had only one Taing in it. The new Zlite found with several, when used as fuel for the newer space ship, they can go faster. The problem is that Attis, had found it first and were mining it. They have been arguing over it since then, now it sound like they are threw arguing and decided to fight over it.

Well it sounds like we had better go to Melber first and see what going on then decided what to do. The space traveler have slowed down, must be entering the solar system. David said as he adjusted the control screen toward Melber.

The space cruiser moved into orbit ten miles above Melber. David turned the controls over to manual, and took them down to a half mile above the ground and cursed over the barren land till they came to one of the mining camps. He spotted the space port and calls them.

This is the ambassador for the Kula federation asking permission to land.

The answer came back by the camp sending a missal toward them. Knight hit the button that put a protection shield around the ship. The missal exploded not doing any damage to the space cruiser.

David took the space cruiser up one mile. Then called again, and repeated his call. This is the ambassador for the Kula federation any more response like that, will be taken as an act of war. Identify yourself please.

This is mining camp3 from Alber and you are not authorizing to land.

OK where do we get the authorization from, David asked?

From the corporate office on Alber they answered.

Thank you I will check in with them, David answered.

From this height the space cruiser had a view of another mining camp. Knight pointed at the other mining camp fifty miles away. There is a camp from Attis, he said.

David adjusted the control screen and move over to it with the shields still up. As they got closer they could see the army attacking the camp. David adjusted the control again and took the space cruiser down between them pointing the front of the space cruiser toward the oncoming army.

The army stopped shooting and just stood there. So David moved the space cruiser toward them. Someone must have given an order to retreat, because all of a sudden the whole army turned around and headed back to the way they had come.

David followed for a mile then stopped and watched, making sure they kept going. Then headed back to the camp, calling them on the radio, this is the ambassador for the Kula federation requesting permission to land.

Who did you say you were? They answered, Never mind yes permission granted.

David repeated, this is the Ambassador for the Kula Federation thank you we will be landing shortly.

At the space port David and knight were met by a band of miners caring hand blazers, but not pointing them at the two new visitors from the space cruiser that had just saved them. One of miners came forward and held out his hand. Don't know who sent you but thank you. You just saved our lives. We are just miners; we have no army, or anything that could have stopped them from taken over this whole mine. We have notified the head office. But it will take two days before help will be here.

I will be around till they get here, watching but I need to check on the other mines right now. But do not worry I will have an open frequency you can call me at any time if needed. Do you have any casualties?

Yes five dead and seven injured, he answered.

Do you have a mikso unit David asked?

Yes the doctor is working on the ones who survived.

Good I have to go now I'll see you later David said as he and Knight headed toward the space cruiser.

Back at the space cruiser Knight asks, OK where are we going now?

To that army, I want to talk to their commander and find out who sent them.

Are you out of your mind? That was a good bluff with the cruiser but I don't think it will work if we have to fight our way out.

Someday I'll teacher you a game we call poker, if a bluff works the first time play it till someone catches on, until then keep it up and until they don't think your bluffing then you use what we call an ace in the hole.

So what is our ace in the hole?

Give me one minute, I'll show you David said as he went to the telescreen. David touched the screen and the Kula appeared. Not in person but it meant that he was just talking to them. This is Ambassador David Nulls I would like a battle cruiser just to come by for appearance only. This is not a war yet and can be stop with the knowledge that a battle ship from the Kula is in the aria, Thank you from Ambassador Nulls.

That is a hell of an ace in the hole as you call it, Knight said. You know it will take 36 hours for them to get this message?

I know that but they don't know it. Now let's go see who is in charge of that army.

The space cruiser computer located the main army camp, and David set the landing spot just outside of the camp. The computer did the rest, as they set down David got up and went to the door then looked back Knight was still sitting in the chair. Come on, you are part of this bluff. We need to make this a real shock. Now walk out like you just kick their ass again.

As they walked out, the soldiers all had their weapons pointed at them? David raised both hands and said all weapons to be put down as he lowered his hands; the weapons were lowered as if by command. Now take me to whoever is in charge, of this group.

A tall soldier came forward, that would be me, and who are you he asked, and why are you with this Jsanderlite?

This is Knightalotofstuf and I'm Ambassador Nulls we are here representing the Kula Federation. And would like to know why a group of soldier is attacking a group of miners. And who gave you those orders

David asked?

That is confidential information, the group leader answered.

Yes I'm sure it is, now who in the corporation would give those orders. David had heard the leader thinking.

That I do not know the soldier answered.

Again David heard the man's thoughts. It is probably from the owner of the company, Mr. Domerter, the soldier thought. Well thank you, your orders for now is to stand down. Or we will take these matters into our own hands and there is a Kula battle ship out there in space just waiting, for orders to come down here.

Come Commander Knightalotstuf you need to notify the fleet, that they don't need to come down here, the situation is under control.

Back in the space cruiser, Knight looked at the Ambassador, what was that commander bit? He asked.

Well you said your planet beat them once before. I thought it might be good to let them know you will do it again. Let's check out the rest of the mines, and then we go have a visit with Mr. Dometer.

Oh, you picked that up too, nice of him to give all that information without saying a word, Knight said. As they checked on the other mines, everything was OK. But they did see two army units, set up a few miles away from the mines.

If they attack the mines at the same time, we will not have time to save both, Knight said concerned.

We will take care of that, David went to the commutation screen, and spoke. Open all channels, commander space battle ship Iffia, this is the Kula ambassador. I'm sending you three locations if anyone from these army units moves toward any mine, evaporate the aria for one square mile around the camp. End of commutation, then gave the location of all three army camps.

The screen went blank, as David turned toward Knight. That should stop any advance, leave all channels open to listen, we will see how many were listening. It didn't take long and the bases were talking to each other on a scrambled channel. David told the computer to save, and then unscramble. A few minutes later the computer came back with the conversation. Unscramble, (if there is a Kula battle cruiser up there it could wipe us out with just a push of a button. I'm not moving.

Neither are we, another voice cut in. OK we stay put till we hear from the corporate office. I will contact them but it will take a day for them to get back to us.) That was the end of the message.

Well that should take care of that; we now have a day to see if we can talk to this Mr. Dometer.

Damn I'll bet you are real good at that game you call poker, I thought for sure one of those soldiers would call your bluff, Knight said.

It always better if you have a little back up when you try to bluff that many, there a saying on my planet, you can fool all of the people, some of the time, some of the people all the time. But you cannot fool all the people all the time. David said then strained his thoughts, thinking Kitaracta that is you out there.

Are you talking to Kitaracta Knight asked, I'm not hearing anything?

Hi lover boy you have been practicing. I'm still out side of the solar system. I don't know anyone who can transfer thoughts that far, Kitaracta answered.

Never underestimate your opponent, what brings you into this neighborhood, David thought.

We were just passing by a couple of solar system over, and heard your call for a battle cruiser. And thought we would come by and see what kind of mess you got yourself into, she answered.

That was a secured channel, David shot back.

It is I didn't know that, Kitaracta came back with.

Oh bullshit you know damn well it is. Are you stocking me, hoping I'd fail?

No quite the opposite, just keeping in touch with you, because when you get on the counsel, I want to be in your good grace. Kitaracta said.

That will be a cold day on Polaris, neither of us will live that long, David said.

You don't know do you, if anything happens to any of the council members; you are the next in line? To be the next council member! That is why the battle cruiser National turn around and is headed toward you at full speed. The only one who can change your orders is the Counsel themselves and they won't do it unless you really screw up.

We are coming into your solar system, this is the Jataime, is there anything we can do for you Mr. Ambassador? This part came over the communication screen.

You can back up the Battle ship the Iffia. While we go to Albar, David answered into his communication screen.

The Iffia battle ship, what are you up to? Kitaracta questioned him in his head, not on the screen.

Glad to see you caught on with battle ship instead of battle cruiser David thought back.

What is going on Knight asked, I'm only getting one side of this thought conversation and sounds like you are crazy?

Kitaracta cut him off with her thoughts, is this another one of your stories? No, it is one of your bluffs isn't it?

Well you are getting to know me very well. David thought back. Then turned to Knight, the conversation is not important, Its only that we are having a conversation with someone. They don't know it is Kit in the XZZ5 cargo ship and not another battle cruiser.

Kit you mean Captain Kitaracta, Knight corrected David.

Yes Kitaracta when I first met her I could not pronounce Kitaracta so I called her Kit and the nick name stuck. But I don't think you should call her that.

OK Mr. Ambassador this the Jataime switching over to channel 1 and contacting the Iffia, Kit said over the communication screen, we will be around as back up if needed.

Thank you Jataime we are going to Albar, we will contact you later, David said into his screen.

Chapter 25

Knightalotofstuf Goes Home

A few hours' later knight and David, contacted the space port at Albar, and were directed to platform 1. As they landed they could see a crowd of people and a band standing on the platform.

What the hell is that David asked Knight?

That is your welcoming committee; you're the Kula Ambassador it is a great honor to a planet to have a person of your status to visit. There will be a big banquet tonight, the president or head governor will be there. There will no business done tonight. It will be one big party.

Oh crap I'm not a politician, I'm a problem solver, David said.

It comes with the job; Knight said smiling shell I get your uniform Mr. Ambassador

No I will get it myself David said heading toward his cabin. Coming back a few minutes later in his Ambassador Jump suite, well let's go meet these people, as he headed toward the hatch door.

Mr. Ambassador it will be a lot better if I'm just a servant, not an assistant today, the Albernees still have a feeling against my race remember.

Besides it will get you more respect from the people and I can most likely get more information from the servants than you will from all those big shots.

OK you got a point come on, James stay behind me, and put on your humble face.

James who James knight asked?

Never mind just a joke from my home planet David said as he opened the hatch door and put on his smiling face, and waved to the people. As he stepped out a woman came up and place a ribbon around his neck.

Welcome to Alber, Mr. Ambassador she said then stepped back.

Next the governor stepped up and hugged David then stepped back. Mr. Ambassador had we known you were coming we could have been more prepared. This is a great honor, come we have a room in the hostel for you we will have a dinner banquet for you in two hours you may want to rest for a while before the banquet.

David could feel the welcome was genuine and that his translator had misunderstood hostel for hotel, and he thanked the governor then started walking beside him pausing long enough to motion Knight to follow. Then asked the governor, have you a safe place for my servant? I know of the dislike that the fine people of Albar have for the Jsaderlites, but they are easy to teach for any job. David had to smile even more, knowing his old teacher. Knight was smiling on the inside to, just behind him.

Yes he will be quite safe, with my workers. The governor said as they walked.

That night at the banquet David meet all the upper class people of Alber, but the one that interested him the most was Mr. Stan Dometer a tall man stood a head taller than anyone else, Except David, they were about the same height. As they meet, Mr. Dometer stared into David's eyes trying to read his mind. David kept him blocked out, just smiling. Then letting a little slip out, yes the reason I'm here to see you, We need to meet tomorrow, but tonight we must enjoy this fine party.

The banquet went on into the night finally David excused himself saying it had been a long day and he needed the rest.

Back in his room David meet up with Knightalotofstuf. Well you were with all the wealthy people of Alber. The rest of the people live in poverty. Nine of the ten families that control everything are keeping it all to their self, and have some big army of their own. That Domerter has the biggest army and the rest kind of follow him. The governor is just a figure head; he dose whatever Domerter tells him to do.

There is one mine owner they called Ponchen, he seems to want to take care of the people that live on the other side of the planet, separate from the rest.

That was a good job, just watch your back. David said well, I thought their conversation was all done by thought. One more thing Mr. Domerter has something that blocked out anyone from hearing his thought. It was not done by him it seemed more electronic. Do they make a portable thing like that? I know you can do it to a room, but just a single person?

I have heard of such a device, never seen one, very expensive. Knight said.

Is there any way to get around it, David asked?

None that I know of Knight answered.

Yes, you can jam the frequency; it was Kitaracta speaking in their heads.

Hi I thought you were guarding the mines, David thought back.

Those clowns, they are too scared besides the fact, they don't move till someone here on Alber tells them to, and the National show up. By the way you know other people might be picking up our conversation.

Not me I'm tune to just you, can't you zero in on just me David asked.

No you smart ass I have not learned that yet. Kit shot back.

Where are you at, can I transport up David asked?

Yes we are in orbit above you, come on in, in front of me at the control room.

David thought of the spot in front of her then pushed the transport button, and appeared in the control room of the space ship seconds later.

As soon as David appeared Kit threw her arms around him and gave him a kiss.

Hay calm down David remarked!

Kit whispered in his ear I have to keep up a front with my crew until I dump you. They all think it is great of me having an Ambassador as a boyfriend.

OK you play your game, now about this thought frequencies disrupter David asked?

Oh, you are always all business; I'll call my engineer up. In the meantime how is it going down there? Kit asked?

Well I'm not sure till I meet with this Domerter tomorrow.

I've heard of him, he is not one to be trusted, watch your back. Do you want me down there to help you?

No I think I can handle this David said.

OK but if you do need me just call. Here my engineers now, tell them what you want and we will see what he can come up with.

David explained what he wanted. The engineer said it would take a while to make and he was not sure it would work but he would try. After a few minutes of talking with Kit David Transported back to his room on Alber, Where Knight meet him and ask if everything was alright.

We will know tomorrow, I'll see you in the morning, I think I need some sleep now, hell it is tomorrow, we will be meeting with Mr. Domerter in a couple of hours.

David was awakened, with kit in his head. Good morning Mr. Ambassador, I will be sending those reports you asked for last night. No sooner had she said it and a small black box appeared on the floor ahead of him.

David picked it up and after looking at it and figuring how to turn it on; he put it in his pocket

A half hour later a lady knocked on the door saying a transport ship was waiting for him, David thought it better not to take Knight with him, for the fact Knight did not have a transporter with him, then made a mental note to get him one. Then walked down to get into the transport, and went to see Mr. Domerter, after a short hop the transporter stopped in front of a large house where he was meet by a servant and lead into a large office, and was told, Mr. Domerter would be in soon. David looked around; there was a large desk on a platform a foot higher than the rest of the room. Little man syndrome, David thought, he wants to look down on his pray.

Mr. Domerter came in a few minutes later, apologizing, .Sorry business you know, and here have a seat. David had activated the small box kit had sent and heard Mr. Domerter thoughts.

This pumas old man I wonder how many kunks is it going to take for him to go away.

No thank you, my visit here is short. The Kula federation wants to know your intention of having an army attack the defenseless miners from Attis.

Oh he wants to play big shot, well let's see how far he wants to take this. It was Mr. Domerter thinking. Then he said I intend to own all the mines on Melber. The question here is how much do you want to go your marry way and leave me alone.

I'm sorry you misjudge me, David said but I don't want your kunks. I want you to call all of your armies back. And have them off Melber in two days.

You cannot tell me what to do with my armies. Then this puma's bastard has three battle cruisers watching the damn planet.

Oh but you see I can, tell you what to do I have the backing of the Kula with me. I cannot tell you what to do on your own planet but since you are breaking the interstellar laws, by attacking a planet. I can set up a blockade around your planet and nothing can come in and nothing can leave and your mines can be confiscated. Now that's what I can do. The question is what are you going to do?

I'm going to think about it. Then he thought this little bastard would probably do just that.

Yes this little bastard would do just that. Now if your armies make any move toward any of Attis mines, my battle cruiser will vaporize them. You have two days to get them off of Melber. Before the battle cruiser will be starting target practice and I hope your armies are not in the way. Good day, I will see myself out, Oh no you won't be shooting, a Kula Ambassador in the back as he leaves. As soon as David was in the next room by himself he thought in front of Knight and pressed the transporter button and found him and Knight in a locked room. He took Knights hand and thought of his space cruiser and pressed the button again. Both men appeared in the control room. David went to the control screen and prepared to take off.

Don't take off they are prepared to blast you out of the sky the minuet you take off, it was Kit in his head. Put your shields up and wait.

An hour later the battle cruiser came in to view. Being four times the size of the city, it blocked out the sun light. Then over all the radio frequencies, you could hear YOU HAVE WEPONES POINTED AT THE KULA FEDERALITIONS AMBASSADORS SPACE CRUISER,

WHAT ARE YOUR INTINTIONS.

All the weapons were lowered.

OK Mr. Ambassador I believe it is safe for you to leave now. Is there anything else you want us to do while we are here?

Thank you Captain and as a matter of fact do you have any extra food packs with you?

Yes sir we do, the captain answered.

Would you mind dropping off a few around town.

No would not mind at all. Anything else we can do for you.

No that will be quite enough. And thank you again Captain, David said as he moved his space cruiser out from under the battle cruiser.

Once out in open air David set a course for the other side of the planet. Knight looked at him. I want to talk with Ponchen, you say that he is helping the people over there, David asked Knight.

Yes that is the rumor I heard before they locked me in that room. I was sure glad to see you. But how did you find me?

It's a little trick that I learned from Kitaracta to think of a person and transport near them. But why didn't you just walk out through the door.

I tried but they had some kind of electronic barrier on around it Knight said.

Well remind me to get you a transporter the next time I can get my hands on one. There's the town, contact them and get permission to land.

They landed and a small group of people were there to meet them, and in the middle, a distinguish gentleman stepped forward. Welcome Mr. Ambassador to Tebect. This is a most pleasant surprise. We don't have the luxuries that Domerter has but we do have fine drink made from our grapes. This surprised David; they call their fruit the same as they did on Earth a million light years away.

They sat a table under a shade tree and a waiter brought the vine. This also surprised David it was close to what he called wine. As David tasted the vine he nodded his head, this is very good vine he said.

Now what have we done to deserve the honor of your visit Mr. Ambassador?

You have done nothing wrong. I was on the other side of your planet and heard what a fine thing you are doing for your people. I thought I would come by and just say hi. And now I see you are doing great and have such fine vine, I would like to stop by more often.

Oh Mr. Ambassador you do us a great honor and feel free to come by anytime.

David could read Ponchen mind, he was not putting on a front. Ponchen was sincere about his invitation. David and Ponchen sat around talking for two hours with Ponchen mostly telling of all the things he would like to do with the town.

At the end David shook Ponchen hand and Ponchen hug David. David told him if there was anything he could help him with to better his town he would be glad to help out.

Ponchen gave David a rack of twelve bottles of vine. David thanked him and went back to his space cruiser putting the vine in the storage compartment, with a lot better feeling about the Alber people.

Chapter 26

The Fishing Pole

In orbit above planet of Attis, David told Knight that he thought it might be better if he visited the planet not as an ambassador but as a regular citizen first.

You will need to use the visualizer (the device that can make a person look like rest of the people on the planet.) you might be a little taller than the rest but they do have some tall people on Attis. I don't think you will stick out that much.

David put on the visualizer belt and switch it on he did look like an Attisian. Then thought of a place outside the Ambassador to the Kula office and then pushed the transformer button. Seconds later he was in the yard. More like the alley. He walked around front, and into the office.

To his surprise it was not like he had expected. The receptionist was sitting on the desk talking to some friend on the phone. When David asked about the Ambassador, the receptionist only pointed toward the back room. The glass door was broken and a peace of something like a bamboo Curtain was leaning against the frame. David moved it aside, dust flying off as he did. As he entered he saw three men and a woman sitting around. Not knowing what Ambassador Clinc looked like, David asked politely, Ambassador Cline?

The woman looked up from the card game they were playing and stared at the stranger for a second, then said he's not here, he's out playing koskia(like our golf) with his brother-in -law the President.

When do you expect him in, David asked?

All four of them laughed, and then one of the men said, He is never in. The Kula doesn't even know we excises, and who are you?

Just someone who thinks the Kula should know that the Alberians are attacking our mines on Melber, David answered.

Well there is not a damn thing the Kula is going to do about it, there is a rumor out that the Kula Ambassador is over on Alber, partying with them, and staying in old Domerter guest house.

David wanted to say something about this, but to be safe he just turned and walked out. He was so mad, not only at the Ambassador Cline, but also himself he should have known that where he was invited to stay was Mr. Domerter's. David just wanted to walk a while. When he came on two boys fishing, well it looked more like snakes than fish. You boys know it is illegal to fish here he smiled kidding the kids are you catching anything. Because I love fishing

We caught three already the second boy answered, who are you?

I'm the new sheriff in town, who likes to fish!

No you are not the sheriff, because my dad is the sheriff. And how can you fish if you don't have a fishing pole.

That is because he is making me carry it for him. It was Kitaracta, standing behind him, holding a fishing pole.

First of all what are you doing here, David thought, second where you get the fishing pole.

You gave it to me on the river back on Earth when the deputy picked you up, Kit thought back. Then said out loud here is your fishing pole sir, handing David the pole.

Both boys were looking at the pole. That's a nice fishing pole, one boy said.

You must be rich, the other boy answered.

No he just likes to fish, Kit answered.

Thank you David thought to Kit. Then to the boys well is it OK if I fish with you.

Sure want some of our grams, they make the best bate.

Thank you, David took one of the Grams that looked like a worm and put it on the hook and tossed it out into the creek. Is that the right place he asked the boys? They both nodded, As David sat down. He then asked have you boys heard anything about this war with Alber.

Ya, everyone has if they start anything we will kick their ass, the one boy said.

The one boy who was the sheriff's son said, my dad says it will not be a nice war and it will all be fought in space. That is why I want to be a space pilot.

Well to be a space pilot it takes a lot of schooling. Do you boys go to school?

Yes sir but we are on holiday leave. Hay mister, you got a crepied on bring him in.

David handed his pole to the boy closest to him, here you bring it in and show me how.

The boy's eyes lit up at the thought of using the pole. As he reeled the crepied in the other boy stood by telling him what to do.

I know what to do the boy with the pole told him as the crepied came on shore. Wow mister you got a big one.

David told them they could have it as he retrieved the pole and handed it to kit. Thank you for the good time, I'll see you later, I got to go and see someone.

On second thought he Handed the pole back to the boy, here you two take care of this one and if you do, we will bring you another one. Now you must share OK.

The boys mouth just fell open as they looked at the pole and then at David.

Yes it is alright and we will see about getting another one if you share and take care of this one.

As David and Kit walked away David thought well that was nice of you to give away my fishing pole. You thought about it first but didn't know if I would part with it. I know you will get me another one.

What were you doing in my head while I was fishing? That's just not right.

That is when you let your guard down; your mind was like an open book, when you were not trying to get information out of those boys.

Hay why are you here, are you spying on me? David asked, and how did you know to bring that fishing pole?.

No I'm not spying on you, I'm picking up some Zlite to take back to the planet you call Mars. The ZXX5 is at the space port waiting for clearance. I just thought I'd stop by and say hi, and when I saw those boys fishing, I knew you would be talking to them, so I transported back to my ship for the fishing pole.

Well it was defiantly the ice breaker, those kids could not keep their eyes off the pole, and that was nice of you to give it up. What do you know of this game called Koskia?

When you're too old to chase woman, you hit a ball around and try to hit a flag. And all the young woman chases you around because they think you are rich, Kit said.

You are kidding, David asked?

Of course it is like your golf but only the upper class plays it. Kit smiled at him. Are you going to talk with the President and that lazy Ambassador next?

Yes if I knew where they were, David answered.

They are at the koskia field. Just think Koskia field and transport there.

You have been spying on me. How you know they were playing Koskia.

Because you were thinking about it Kit said.

Do you mind staying out of my head, or do I have to keep a block up at all times.

If I were you I'd keep a block up I'm not the only one hearing these conversations.

OK thank you now you can go back to your ship and let me handle this.

Sure what are you going to do walk up to the President of Attis and say hi I'm a concerned citizen and wonder what you are going to do about Alber.

Oh and you have a better ideal, David asked.

Yes as a captain of a space cargo ship I have a better chance to see him and you can go as my first mate. You have to go green and I think you will pass off just fine. Unless you want to go as the Ambassador

But I do want them to know that the Ambassador is coming.

OK you can be my communication officer with a special message for the President only, how about that.

That sounds better and we will have a better chance of seeing him, David added. Are you ready to transport.

Oh I thought you wanted to stand here and talk for a while. Got the location and grabbed David's hand and transported both of them to the front of a fancy looking building. As she let go of his hand, come on this will make a good show, a commutation officer will not have a transporter. As she walked up to the guard, I'm Captain Irreson from the space ship Jataime my communication officer has an important message for the president from the Kula Ambassador for his ears only.

One moment I'll see if he will see you, are you carrying any weapons.

No other than my thong now get along with you, and tell him we are here.

After he had left, David turned to Kit. Well that was sure diplomatic.

He was trying to read our minds, and yours was about to give us away. I told you keep a block up. This is not Earth a lot of people hear your thoughts, Kit answered.

The guard came back; The President will meet you in the lounge as soon as he finished the next flag.

Thank you David said and Kit just glared at him as they walked by.

In the lounge Kit ordered two glasses of water, then finding a table, with people watching them. After sitting down she said to David. This is good water but don't drink it anywhere else in town unless it is in dispensers.

Fifteen minutes later the president and the Ambassador came in with their body guards, the Ambassador was wearing the uniform of an Ambassador from the planet, David recognized it right off he had had one just like it when he was the ambassador for Earth. Kit and David stood up.

Captain you say you have a message for me. The president asked. No my radio man has received a message for you, and is for you only.

Well speak up these are people I trust the president demanded.

Well sir if you trust these people I guess it will be OK, David said. It is from the Ambassador from the Kula federation it said he will be coming here to hear about the problem on Melber with the Alberians. And will be here in two days.

See Jak I told you that the Kula would not put up with Domerter interference. The Ambassador said to the president. I only hope he gets here in time

Yes, but he is over there budding up with Domerter I hope he will help us before the war starts. I don't want to be known as the president that started this war.

I'm sure he will stop Domerter I have heard good things about this new Ambassador. And he did stop the Domerter army from taking mine three. Then the Ambassador remembered that Kit and David were standing there, oh you two are dismissed and thank you.

Dismissed Hell, the President said, come on over and have some refreshment, and tell us what you think of this new Ambassador from the federation.

Well thank you I believe I will Kit said. Then turned to David do you want to stay awhile.

No Captain I think I'll wait outside David said.

OK I will meet you back at the ship later. Kit said then turned back to the President and the Ambassador, he is not into socializing. Put him in his radio room and he is as happy as a man before he gets married.

They all laughed at that, come along Captain, the President said; tell us about this new Ambassador.

Well he is kind of an odd ball comes from the Birian system some planet call Earth. That is all David heard as he walked out the door. Looked around, seeing the guard went over to talk with him. What do you think of this new war David asked?

If we get into this war, I hope it is all on Melber. And does not go any farther, because we are a peaceful nation, not like Alber they have armies larger than our whole population. Oh we can put up a good fight. But I don't think it will be good for either planet.

No war ever is, David answered. Well have a good day as he walked off around the corner. And thought of his space cruiser and transported to it.

He met Knight in the control room. Well how did it go down there? Up here there have been radio transmissions back and forth between the mine workers on Melbar and their offices here on Attis. The miners want protection and the owners don't want to send it, thinking it might start the war.

Well I guess our next stop is Melbar but first some sleep. It has been a long day David said.

The next day David met Knight in the control room. Don't you ever sleep David asked him.

Yes sir I got a couple hours in. we are now in orbit around Melbar. The national is in orbit on the other side of the planet.

Can you put me in contact with them David asked?

Yes if we move a little either way our transmissions will not go straight threw the planet.

OK let's move and put me in contact with the Captain. I'm going to get a cup of Krista. Wish I had brought more coffee from earth.

Yes your coffee is much better than Krista Knight said. I to wish you had gotten more.

Just then a 5lbs. can of coffee appeared on the control room floor, in front of them.

David thought, well good morning to you Kitaracta. And thank you.

Well good morning Mr. Ambassador and what makes you think it came from me. It could just be a miracle.

Miracle doesn't just happen like that. Beside you are the only one in this galaxy who knows what real coffee is.

Let's just say it is a present from your home planet. Mind if I come over and have a cup with you.

It is your coffee; can I stop you David asked?

You could tell me to go back to my own ship.

David turned around and there was Kitaracta. Hay what happen to asking permission to come aboard. I could have been necked.

Oh I'd like that better Kit said.

Well how about it if Knightalotstuf didn't have any clothes on?

That an image that would scare me for the rest of my life, No offense

Knightalotofstuf.

None taken, I would not want to see the horrible form you keep under that uniform either.

Knight and David laughed and Kit acted insulted. The joking ended, when a voice came over the speaker screen, Ambassador Nulls this is commander Tellas of the battle cruiser The National is there anything I can do for you.

David touched the screen and the image of Commander Tellas appeared. Good morning sir I was wondering if there was any movement down on the planet.

No sir everyone is just setting on their hands awaiting for orders from Albar.

Are we on secured channel David asked?

Yes the only one who can hear you and me, if anyone is listen they are just getting static.

Good commander can you take out one of those land vehicles, from where you are.

Yes, it would be tricky but we could do it only it would take out about a ten foot circle around it, the commander replied

Can you find one that would not cause any casualties? If so switch to an interstellar unsecured channel.

Switching to the interstellar channel now the commander said.

David switches to the interstellar channel. Commander of the battle cruiser National, This is Ambassador Nulls of the Kula federation, the army troops are not preparing to move off of planet Melbar you have permission to start your target practice.

This is commander Tallas of the Battle cruiser National. Mr. Ambassador, orders understood starting target practice now.

David could not see what the National hit but the communication screen came alive with chatter mostly army on their secured channel.

Commander Tallas came on the screen on a secured channel. One land vehicle vaporized and no casualties standing by for further orders.

Nice shooting commander my complements to your crew, no further orders for now, David said, and cleared the screen.

As Knight came in with the tray of coffee, and offered a cup to Kit and then to David, and taken one himself.

Wow Kit said looking at the screen remind me not to piss you off.

Did I miss something Knight asked?

No not much just the Ambassador flexing his muscles, and scaring the hell out of an army unit on the planet down there.

Not flexing any mussels just showing them that I mean business. And letting them know that I'm not the pumas wind bag he thought I was. Now I think I will go down to the Attis mine and assure them that they are safe.

Are you going alone, Kit asked?

Yes but for some reason, I'm sure you are going to be watching over me.

Switching the communication screen over to the mine frequency, Hello down there in Attis mine three, this is Ambassador Nulls from the Kula Federation. I'd like permission to stop by and view your mining operation.

Yes, sure, it is OK; come by anytime it will be good to see you again.

Mr. Ambassador this is commander Tallas I don't feel it is safe for you to go down there without an escort.

Your concern is noted commander but if I don't go alone how else to convince them they are safe from Domerter army.

Well it is your neck you are sticking out, zovta.

Luck will have nothing to do with it. I've got you up here, keeping an eye out for me. David turned off the screen. Then turned to Kit and better yet I have you watching out for me, see you later. Then he sat down his coffee cup and thought of the mine entrance and pressed his transporter button.

At the mine several miners came out to meet him and hurried him into the mine office. He shook hand and returned the quick hug that was customary greeting for the aria, and then asked about the miners that were wounded in the battle early.

They are all fine and have gone home. We are still shorthanded, not many want to come out to the war zone.

Well Domerter army will be leaving soon and they are no threat now that there is a Kula battle cruiser watching over you and they have orders to vaporize any one that comes close.

Was that them that shot the lightning bolt from out of the space that vaporized something over the hill there.

Yes they were just target practicing on a land vehicle, telling the army that they were not going to mess around next time now, how about giving me a tour of your mining operation.

After the tour David thank the mine supervisor, and transported back to the space cruiser.

Kit show up seconds later. I don't know what is in that mine but I lost track of you, no thoughts were coming across. I was worried and was about to come down when you came out.

You know you really need to get a life of your own. And quit following me. But that is good to know I wonder if anyone else knows that, David remarked? Have you ever been in one of the mines they go for miles and you drive small vehicles to get anywhere?

No, I have never been in a mine it is to refining give me the open space above and I'm happy Kit said. Now what kind of trouble do you want to get into?

I was thinking of going over to one of Domerter mines and see what they are doing David said.

Are you out of your mind, you go down in one of his mines and you will never come out Knight said.

Hell it's Domerter that doesn't like me not the miners. Beside I was thinking of taken you with me. It is real interesting how they mine Zlite

Now I draw a line on this job. This is just suicide Knight said.

Come on where your sense of adventure, wouldn't you like to know how they do it. Beside I want to check this mind block and see if it will stop inside a mine or just stop it from coming out.

You are not being fair; you know as a man of science that I would want to know that. Even if it is the last thing I learn before they kill us Knight said. Which one are we going to?

I think the other side of the planet would be best that way they could not radio and tell Domerter until the planet turns that way. And we will be back here when they can communicate with Albar.

This is such a dumb plan, that it might even work, Kit said.

David set the control for the other side of the planet and took the space cruiser in close to the surface so their commutation would not go out all over space. Basia mining camp is this one of Mr. Domerter mines David asked the transmitter screen.

Yes, who is it that wants to know, came the answer.

This is Ambassador Nulls from the Kula Federation. I'd like permission to land and see your mining operation.

One moment please and who did you say you were.

This is ambassador Nulls from the Kula Federation David repeated.

A few minutes later the voice came back on permission to land at the space port Mr. Ambassador.

See that was easy, David told Knight. As he landed the space cruiser at the port, several miners came out to meet them.

Well none of them have weapons Knight thought toward David!

A supervisor came up and shook hands and the usually hug. That David didn't particularly care for but did anyways. What bring the Ambassador to our small mining camp?

I was just in the aria and after talking with Mr. Domerter. I thought I would stop by just to see how this mining was done.

Well you do us a great honor picking us. Come I will show you around. And your guards with the weapon please advise him not to discharge in the mine.

David looked at Knight and frowned.

Knight just smiled. Then said would it be better for me to leave it out here.

No it is quite alright to keep it with you but I assure you there is nothing in the mine that is dangerous. Come this way I will show you around.

They sat in and electric vehicle and went down in the mine for a ways. David tried to contact Kit with thoughts then asked Knight if he was hearing him getting no response David figured out that whatever was in the mine was stopping the mind reading. After an hour they came back to the surface. David and Knight thanked the supervisor and headed toward the space cruiser when the supervisor stop them just a minuet he said and went into the office and came back with a small replica of a drilling rig and handed it to the Ambassador Just a little something to remember us by I build them in my spare time, he said.

David thanked him and not thinking of anything to give in return he remember the vine in the cargo hole and went and got one and handed it to the supervisor, then he and Knight climbed into the space cruiser and headed back into space.

Once in space Knight breathe a big sigh of relief.

What David asked? have you been holding your breath all the time. Even when they said you could keep your weapon. And speaking of the weapon where did you get a weapon from?

From Kitaracta he answered.

Do you even know how to use the weapon David asked?

No but Kitaracta said that you did and I was to give it to you if needed.

David thought Kit come on over here for a minute.

I'm a little busy right now she answered.

David thought again, unless you are flying straight toward a planet; get your ass over here now!

Kit appeared in the control room behind David, I know your tick off at me giving Knight a weapon. It was for your own good.

I'm not mad about the weapon, I'm piss off that you gave it to someone who did not know how to use it. He could have blown us all up or whatever it would have done.

Well when I get a chance I will teach him how to use it. Because you are too crazy to carry one she said. Say that is nice what is it, looking at the replica of a drilling rig. As she touches its control, it put out a small beam of light that hit the door and burned a hole in it.

David fell over and shut the working replica off. Damn the supervisor didn't tell me it worked! I'm glad it was not pointed at the haul of the ship.

He did say it was an exact replica Knight said

Several hours later an image of Mr. Stan Domerter came on the communication screen. This is to the Ambassador for the Kula Federation. You fired on my troops that were on a practice mission and kill over twenty soldiers and seven civilians' observers. This is an act of war. And we will retaliate.

David thought about this for a minuet then turn on the communication screen. You are wrong again Mr. Domerter. Only one land vehicle was destroyed and there were no casualties. And I was only retaliating for kidnapping my assistant. Let this be a lesson and I will forget your useless threats of starting a war you cannot hope to win. Then David turned off the screen.

Well that was diplomatic, if you don't have a war you will have one now. Kit said.

I don't think so Mr. Domerter is a smart man and knows he cannot win a war against the federation. He is just letting off steam. The only way he knows how to is with his mouth. Let go to Attis.

Chapter 27

Share A Bottle Of Wine

David put the space cruiser in orbit above the capital of Attis and told Knight that he was going to sleep. We will have a big day tomorrow they know we are coming and I suppose we will have to put up with their big fan fair. I dislike that part why not just get down to business. And get it over with and we can be on our way.

Well that is just what comes with being a celebrity Knight said I'll see you in the morning.

Before going to sleep David thought of kit.

Her thought came threw loud and clear, in his head oh, how nice to think of me before going off to sleep.

Hay you are always on my mine, only I was thinking about you for another reason.

Yes Mr. Ambassador and I thought you were thinking about me?

Can you go over to Albar and get me a rack of Tebect vine and be back by the time I meet the president? Thank you and you know I'm always thinking about you.

Oh you are such a smooth talker, see you in the morning.

At the space port of Attis it was the same as before people turned out to see the Ambassador from the Kula, David would like to tell them that the President of anything, is more important than he was.

Then as David and Knight walked threw the crowd David spotted a small boy sitting on his father shoulders. The man below the boy had on the uniform of the sheriff. David turned off the main path of people and went up to the boy. And asked what your name is.

Wide eyed, the boy answered Zim sir.

Well Zim do you still have that fishing pole I gave you and your friend, and are you sharing it.

The boys eyes got bigger and his mouth opened no words came out, he just nodded his head. Then said, my dad has it in his office. He thinks it is someone else. And they will want it back.

Is this your dad down here David asked looking at the man holding Zim on his shoulders.

Well dad that a fine young man you have there. And I enjoyed fishing with him and his friend, and you can give the fishing pole to his friend. Then turning to Knightalotofstuf and holding out his hand, Knight pulled out another fishing pole the one David had brought from Earth with him.

David handed it up to Zim, here you go I hope you catch as many fish with this pole as I have.

As the father just stared, Zim nodded his head. And said I'll catch more.

I'll bet you will, see you down by the creek someday.

David and Knight stepped back into the crowed and went up and meet the President and the Ambassador for the planet. Well Mr. President nice to see you, David said reaching out to shake his hand.

The president taking it, and asking, what was that all about? Did that man offend you? What do we owe this special visit from a diplomat of the Kula federation?

No it is quite the opposite, his son and I just shared some fishing stories. We will talk business later, I see you have a fine festival planed.

Yes in your honor.

Oh you knew that I was coming.

Yes we have heard. We have spies over in Albar. Just as we know they have spies over here.

Kit are you out there David was thinking.

Yes Mr. Ambassador ready to send it down when you asked.

The president look at the Ambassador, were you talking to someone else.

Yes one of our cargo pilot, I have a present for you. It is a very fine vine. I found in my travels. I hope you will accept it as a gift from me.

Well of course it will be an honor we will have it at the fiesta to night. Come let me show our city.

That night at the fiesta the president and the ambassador for the planet of Attis comment on the vine. When the president asked where he could fine such a fine vine. David told him that I came from Albar the President pulled away.

David informed him it did not come from Stan Dometer but from Tebect and that he was not at war with then and he would like to set up trade with then, and to establish a friendly relationship. The President mellow out a little. Or the vine had done the trick. We will talk more about it tomorrow but right now I feel in the need to lay down David said, so if you will excuse me till tomorrow good night.

David meet Knight in the room the Attis Ambassador had set up for them.

This place is not safe to talk in, Knight inform him.

David grabbed Knight by the arm and transported both of them to the place by the creek where he had fished with the two boys.

Knight blinked then looks around, seeing that it was safe. Attis is ready to fight if they have to but will not start it.

Just then Kitaracta appeared, if there is a war Attis will lose they will not be able to stand up against Dometer he will destroy Attis in a few cycle. He has already started his own war on the other mine owner and it now in control of most of the planet, his next move is the only hold out Tebect.

Kit what is the situation over there?

Well while Dometer was spending Kunk on weapons Tebect was spending kunks on defense Tebeck has a good force field set up.

Thank you Captain tell the Battle Cruiser to stay on alert if Dometer dose send anything to Melbor or Asttis he has full authority to do whatever it take to stop them but to use physical force only at the last resorts. And will you keep an eye on his movement from a distance. We do not interfere with any planets disputes only if it involved another planet.

Kit can you set up communication that if I send Knight over to Tebect that we can communicate without taken two days you will be a relay between us.

I can ask our engineer she said.

No you tell your engineer to do it. This is very important. And you need to transport Knight over to Tebect

What? Knight looked at David; you remember I told you that they do not like me on Tebect!

I know but what you will tell them they will glad to have you there.

OK but I hope you know what you are doing?

Next the morning Ambassador David met with the President of Attis and the planets Ambassador to the Kula. David started the conversation. Mr. President as you knows I can step in and stop Dometer army from attacking your mining company on Melbar.

Yes he answered and now Dometer has taken over Lanca, Gofree, and Reade mining company, in a since he has taken over all of Albar.

No not quite all of Albar, Tebect is still holding out. But it is not the Kula policy to interfere with inter planet policies. Now you have an abundance of sissy. And Tebect has an abundant of that fine vine if you were to set up trade with Tebect, that would make a interplanetary dispute and the Kula could interfere and stop Dometer from taken over the whole planet.

The part David was not telling him was that if Dometer did try to start war with Attis that the Kula would step in and stop it.

Sound like a good plan but how will we set up this tread agreement.

I have my assistant over in Tebect talking with Poncher the president of Tebect now. If you like we can set up communication now and you two can work out a deal on trade.

Well Mr. Ambassador it sounds good but I would have to talk it over with our counsels.

That would be fine, but remember Dometer Armies are on the move and we don't want to be too late. Why don't you meet with your counsel and contact me later today.

A few sin later the President contacted Ambassador Nulls asking for a meeting right away.

When they meet the president asked if Albar attack Attis the Kula would step in right.

Yes they would but before the Kula ship could get here millions of your people would die. The president was not as dumb as David thought. So he switch to work on his ego, and millions of Albar citizen in Tebect would also be dead, but if you could save them you would look like a hero.

The President eyes look up. He would like the thought of people thinking of him as the hero. Yes we will do it, but how?

OK we will set up communication between you and the president of Tebect Poncher. Then picking up his tellasponder

Knight are you there?

Minutes later Knight replied, yes and president Poncher has been listening and has agreed to the trade agreement. He will send a representative to hash out the fine details.

Good Kitaracta are you listening.

Yes we have all of it,

Good tell Dometer that if he attacks Tebect the Kula will step in and stop him.

That's your orders Mr. Ambassador

Yes David answered back.

A few sin later Kit contacted David. I'm in contact with Mr. Stan Dometer and he said that the Kula has no right to interfere with the planets affairs.

You tell MR. Dometer that he is interfering with inters planet trading and that is a Kula violation and I will have his ass drag up before the Kula counsel. And I will put him on the slowest shuttle going to Tisana.

He says you are bluffing and you have no authority to do anything.

OK that is it, if he does not pull his army back before I get there. He had better have his bags pack.

Signing off, Mr. President you will have to excuse me. I will have to attain to this matter myself. Please keep your people working on the trade agreement, As David transporter to his cruiser and set the control for Albar.

Hours later David put his cruiser in orbit and thought of Stan Dometer and transporter down in front of him in his office. Mr. Dometer your present is request in the Kula counsel to explain why you are interfering with interplanetary trade.

You are about the stupid's Ambassador I have ever met, reaching in to the desk.

If you touch that weapon I will vaporize you. It was kit standing behind him.

Thank you Captain now if you will remove Mr. Dometer transporter and move him to a secured place until he can be transported to Tisana.

Walking out of the office David announced Mr. Stan Dometer is now on his way to Tisana to talk with the Kula counsel. So who is now in charge?

That would be me a young man stepped forward.

And you are David asked?

I'm Dan Dometer you say that my father is under arrest.

Oh no we are just giving him a ride to Tisana to explain why he is interfering with a city that has inter solar trade with another planet.

I warned my father that he was pushing this too far, and spending too much money on an Army. That the citizen of Albar would revolt. I was not expecting the federation to step in.

Well sir when you start messing with interplanetary trading we have to step in as you say. Now what are you going to do about your army and the attack on Tebect.

I will recall the army right away. How long did you say my father will be away?

Ambassador Nulls was hearing the younger Dometer thoughts. I'm sorry that we cannot spare any fast shuttles I'm afraid he will be gone a long time.

Well then I think he will be surprise, what he will find when he dose returns. I have always wanted to talk with the mine owners on Attis about a joint venture and have had some planes for making Albar a better place to live and have been talking with Ponchen.

You are wiser than your years. Do you mind if I stop back later. For a visit and see your changes.

Mr. Ambassador you are welcome here any time and I think even you will be surprise.

I'm sure I will be. Now if you will excuse me .I have some other business to attain to.

Yes and I have to apologies to Mr. Lanca, Mr.Gofree and Mr. Reada and reduce an Army. Today will be the start of the new Dometer Corporation.

Back in his cruiser Ambassador Nulls was feeling proud of himself, when Captain Kitaracta transported in right in front of him. Well you should feel proud that turned out alright for your first assignment but dumb facing Dometer, with no weapons. You are lucky I was there.

Luck had nothing to do with it I knew you would be there. You see I got you figured out purity well.

Chapter 28

Bad News You Need To Move

Back in Tisana Ambassador Nulls was called to the   Kula counsel upon an arrival. When asked why he was having Mr. Domyer transferred to Tisana.

Well back on planet Earth we had a man such as Mr. Domyer who killed millions of people and never fired a bullet. He commanded other people to do it for him, his name was Adolf Hitler, when he disappeared the killing stopped. I could not find anyone Mr. Domyer had killed himself, but I could convict him of interfering with inter solar trade. Now his son is in charge and doing trade with neighboring planet and no longer any threat of war. And that is what I thought you wanted me to do. We have a saying cut off the head of a snake and the snake will die. So basically that is what I did. I told him he could take it up with the counsel and you would decide.

And when will this Mr. Domyer to be here?

Oh in about ten years, it is a rather slow shuttle he is on.

He did stop any war and arrange inter solar trade It was a little unorthodox but it did work I think he did a good job It was one of the coucilemen talking to the other members.

Thank you David said.

Two members of the counsel look at him. You heard our conversation. That was directed between the two of us. We had everyone blocked out.

Sorry but it came threw loud and clear.

No don't be sorry it just means you are developing your mental ability better and stronger than we expected. Would you like to rest before your next assignment?

No I'm fine what do you have in mind? , Just a little play on words David said.

Is this what you call funny what you are doing is a very serious job.

Yes I know, but if you don't have a little humor once in a while, you could go crazy. Life is not all bad you need to stop and smell the flowers and see the good side of things.

You are right in your thinking, but this next assignment is very important and will test you to the best of your abilities. There is a solar system called Gia who's sun will die out in one hundred years and there four inhabited planets that need to be relocated to another solar system three of their Ambassador are here the forth planet is not in the Kula federation. But we need to protect them also. The three Ambassadors from the Gia Solar system are in the next room they have not been told why they were summons here. We are leaving it all up to you; try doing it without changing history or kidnapping someone. Good luck Mr. Ambassador.

David looks at the counsel man who thought this and he was sure that he saw the counsel man smile.

Ambassador Nulls walk to the door but stop before entering. Well this should be good. Hi I'm Ambassador Nulls from the Kula and your sun is dying and you all have to move the Ambassador thought. No David wrong approach, maybe something like hi it's a good day to move to a new solar system.

That not very tactical David heard one of the counsel man say as he turn to see which one said it. All the counsel man were getting up and exiting out through the door behind them.

David decided to just wing it as he walked through the door into the next room. If Ambassador Nulls had not been around different Aliens he might have been surprise with these three Ambassadors. The one from the planet of Hola was almost human form except his arms reach to the floor and his head was leaning to the side. The second one from Spirts looked like a pyramid with three little feet coming out the bottom. The third from Nocab was all different shape body. That keep changing, except for his head that seem to have two mouths and four eyes one on each side of his head he could see all three hundred and sixty degree around him.

They all stood up as he entered, Gentleman please sits down. I don't know if your scientists have told you yet, but our scientists here have notice that your sun is getting dimmer and in one hundred years from now, it will burn out. So we need to come up with a way to save all your people. I hope with all of us coming together we can work out something that will work. After all we do have a little bit of time. The federation has been looking for suitable planets in a different solar system the problem will be transporting an entire civilization to one or more of these planets.

We will not live on the same planet as those thieves on Nocba it was the Ambassador Yamit from spirts.

And we will not share a planet with either the Spirts or the Nocba this came from the Ambassador Sansa from Hola.

Alright every one, stop it David step between them. I know this is a shock to everyone but you were appointed as ambassador of your world because someone thought you would do what is good for your planet. So, what I'm suggesting is that we go out and find four inhabitable planets.

Why four the ambassador from spirts asked?

We also need to find a place for the citizen of Srovalf to move to.

Why they are just a bunch of swrags, he answered

David's translator could not interpret the Ambassador slang David asked, they are what?

Swrags unintelligent animals the Ambassador Homasic from Hola answered.

Maybe so but the federation is not going to stand by and let them vanish from the universe. So gentleman what do you think our first step should be.

All three started talking at one time.

Gentleman, gentleman let's not talk at one time; my translator will not separate your conversation. Mr. Yumit from Spirts I believe you were first.

Let us go out and find our own planet, first come, first to claim it gets it. OK if everyone agrees and the Kula approves it. But we must keep the others Ambassador informed. Is this agreeable with everyone?

But Spirts has much faster space ship than we do. It was the Ambassador from Hola.

This started another round of arguments. Gentleman we all must work together on this David tried to calm the Ambassadors.

We are, Mr. Yumit said I'm leaving now.

As I'm I, stated the Ambassador from Hola.

I myself will inform the people of Nocba to be looking forward to this dooms Day. You say we have a round one hundred years.

Yes that is what our scientist say, David answered.

We have three exploratory ship out I will inform then to be on the lookout for a suitable planet. Mr. Yumit said Thank you for your time.

The planet I come from also has an exploratory ship out; David said, I will contact them, and see if they have found anything suitable for your people. I know your people need a different climate and atmosphere than that of Hola and Spirts. I will send this information to our exploratory ship. Good day and good luck.

After all the Ambassadors had left, Ambassador Nulls thought Knight Can you hear me.

Knight answered back. Yes as if you were in the other room.

Good I need all the information on the Gila solar System. About the planets of Hola, Spirts, Nocba, and Srovalf

It is all in your computer at your desk, but not much on Srovalf, because they are not members of the Kula and are far behind most worlds in technology.

Well then I guess we need to go to Sovalf and do a little fact finding trip our self.

Shell I meet you at the space port, Knight asked.

Yes but I think I will get commander Kitaracta to transport us her ship is much faster. Kit are you there David thought tuning to her brain waves.

Yes my love, I'm on my way will be there in two shakes as you say.

I knew you would be close but in two shakes that more stocking me than being in the neighborhood. And what is this, my love bit.

I just wanted to be around in case you needed help with the counsel. And my love I wanted everyone to know that you are mine. Don't worry we are on a single wave lengths. I don't know how you do it, but no one else can hear us.

It called selective hearing where I come from and usually only men have it.

I think you just made that up, because when I was there I never heard of it.

Well if you meet me at the space port, I will tell you all about it on the way to the Gila solar system. What do you know of the planet Srovelf?

Not a damn thing, been to Hola but just a short delivery. I could look it up on the computer if you would like.

I had Knight do that, there just is not much information on it. So we are going to see for our self. How long do you think it will take us to get there?

Kit laughed about two weeks your time, that means I can have you all to myself.

Well almost Knightalotofstuf will be coming with us.

Ah crap that will take all the fun out of it. So what is the mission?

The mission as if you didn't know already, is telling the people of a primitive planet that their sun is going to go out. And we need to move them to another planet. These people do not even know there are beings living on other planets, or that there are other planets they just know that there are stars out there.

Hay if they are that primitive just go down to the planet do a few of your magic trick and tell then you are their sun god and you are very mad at them and you are going to turn off their sun, and you are only going to take a few good people and start over on another world.

I cannot do that, David said.

Why not Kit asked?

I'm not going to play God and try to fool these people, they are behind other civilization, but they are not stupid.

Chapter 29

The Only To Fight A War

When they entered the orbit of Srovalf. Kit asked, well what have you decided to tell then?

I think I had better go down in disguise and study the situation.

Oh one of your plays it by ear plans?

Well it has worked so far. You never know till you see it firsthand what is really going on David told her.

So disguise as a local, Ambassador Nulls transported down to the planet, there he talked to the people where he learned that General Otash who control the northern Army was planning to attack the southern army in a fight that had been going on for hundreds of years over a valley of less than six thousand Acres

He then transported over to southern camp where the government army, That Commander McCormick controlled was ready to go to war to keep this valley as their territory. That was to start any day now.

David contacted kit by mentally calling her. Can you transport General Otash and Commander McCormick to a location where I can talk to both of them?

Not unless each of them having a transport disk, she answered.

What disk. No just like you transported us when you brought us from Earth to your space ship?

Oh each of you had one of the disks on you.

I don't remember any disk?

That because I putted it on you while you were all sleeping. Then when you were transported aboard I retrieved them yours was in the vest pocket.

So you have kept secret from me?

More than you will ever know she answered.

Well remind me when we are alone and I'll try to see what else you have been hiding from me.

You are not that strong yet, keep practicing you might get there.

We will get to that later tell me more about this disk?

OK it's about the size of what you would call a half dollars and it has to be on whatever you want to transport up.

Can you transport back to a different location with this disk?

Yes as long as it on then, she answered.

OK send me two of them.

In an instance Kit was standing next to David.

The Ambassador jumped at the sight of Kit standing next to him, I asked you to send them to me, he said.

It doesn't work that way, handing him, two round disks.

Thank you now go back and keeps track of me.

Why don't you want me to help you? By the way what have you got planed?

Not sure but if it works I need you back in your ship to do it.

Just wanted to help, she answered

You will but not down here.

OK honey, but if you need help just think of me and I'll be right back. As she vanished, going back to her space cargo ship.

Ambassador Nulls walked over to Commander McCormack tent. He was stop by the two guards. I have important information for the Commander, David told them.

Just a minute one guard said as he walked in to the tent. Coming back minutes later, Commander McCormick will see you now follow me.

Inside the tent Commander McCormick stood up, so what is this information that is so important?

I have heard that General Otash is going to attack you in two days

And where did you hear this information?

It was a very reliable source, David answered.

Well I have learned to rely on very reliable source. Thank you. And if he wants a war he will get one, I'm not give up this valley and all the piya it produces.

Ambassador David reached down on the floor and picking one of the disks Kit had given him that he had palmed, I think you drop this, handing it to the Commander.

Thank you, I don't remember having it, as he stuck it in his pocket. You may leave now and thank you for the information soldier.

Well that was easy David thought as he walked out of the tent. Once out of sight he change uniforms and transported over to General Otash camp, at the Camp. Where he was once again stop by the guards. I have important information for the General about Commander McCormack David told them.

Soon he was escorted into the General quarters.

What is this important information the General Demanded

Commander McCormick says that if you try to take over the valley that there will be great bloodshed and he knows that you are about attack.

I heard it standing outside his tent.

Just how were you inside his camp?

I was visiting a friend and checking out our competition.

And what else have you learned, the general asked?

Just that General, David answered. Reaching down and picking up the other disk .I believe you drop this handing it to the General.

Looking at it, Strange looking but It's not mine, handing it to one of his solider.

Well it was found on your floor, maybe its good luck?

I don't believe in luck he said.

Well maybe you should keep it a token of victory for the upcoming battle.

Yes, taken it back from the guard, and maybe it is a bribe from Commander McCormick not to reclaim our land back from him. Throw this trader in the stockade; I will deal with him later.

Kit voice came in David head. Well that didn't work ready to transport back up here.

No not yet how accurate is your laser weapon, cans you cut a line across the valley about a half mile wide.

What you call a mile wide is impossible but maybe half that distance. My engineer has modified our power laser but don't tell anyone.

Good enough tomorrow morning do it, Split that valley in half.

Alright at sunrise, but you do know anyone in that path will be fried.

I know but if they are in the path they are spying and problem need to be fried.

OK but in the meantime what are you going to do?

Oh problem get some sleep, David answered.

You know you are in jail!

No I'm not, I'm right behind you.

Kit turned and looked and there stood the Ambassador. So you broke out of jail that is strictly against the Kula laws for an Ambassador to break any planet's laws.

Oh but I didn't break any laws, my escort to the stockade let me go but only after they told me they were tired of the silly war, over a small piece of land. That their great grand-father lost over 200 years ago, and they have been fighting over ever since.

So what else did you find out, Kit asked?

That you were right their oxygen rate is low. And even with the booster I had trouble breathing. Now I know how you had trouble breathing on Earth and had to use the booster. We need to find a planet with a lower rating of oxygen lower than Earth for them to move to, before their sun burns out.

So how are you going convince them to move to another planet when they cannot even agree over ten squares of land?

I'm going to stop the feud first, then convince them they need to change planets.

The next morning Kit burned a line about one quarter wide for thirty miles across the entire valley David transported down and was amazed at how accurate she had done it. Then he thought OK kit transport General Otash and Commander McMormick to my location.

Kit at her control board first transported the General and the Commander to the ship, then instantly to the spot in the middle of the burned line across the valley.

Both look surprise at each other. Then reach for their weapons Ambassador Nulls took those away using just mental powers. That is when they noticed the Ambassador. Now General Otash you want a war and Commander McCormick, you are ready to fight. Ambassador Nulls said, but you both have an army to fight for you. But neither of your soldiers wants to die and that is what will happen. Problem a thousand will die on each side. So I have split this valley in half one half to General Otash you get the southern half to Commander McCormick you the north is that agreeable with both of you. If not this war will start and end right here.

Who the hell are you to tell us what to do General Otash asked and Commander McCormick nodded.

Well they both finally agreed on the same thing David thought. I'm the planet referee he told them, and like I said this war is going to start with you Two and will end right here.

Good give me my gun and I will end this right now General Otash said.

That not the way it is going to go, each of you will go get two men One your second and your third in command and will meet back here at high sun.

And who is going to make us, asked Commander McCormick.

Ambassador Nulls just crossed his arms and just looked both ways at the burn line across the valley. Now go and be back at high sun with your second and third in command, he said.

At high sun both returned with two soldiers all armed with weapons.

David disarmed all six by mentally thinking of all the weapons. They literally fly out of their hands and into a pile at his feet as bent twisted metal. He then motion all six to come over to him.

When all of them were around him David explained First General Otast and Commander McCormick will fight to the death. The one who dies his second in command with fight the winner them the winner of this fight will fight with the next in command of the looser. And this fight will go on, one on one until both sides realize that this is a very stupid war. And agree to split the valley. Now you second and thirds move one thousand steps backwards. As they did David pick up two clubs he had made from tree branches each three feet long and four inches round as he handed them to the two opponents'?

The commander looked at his and asked is this some kind of a joke. Where is the Sword of Calvin I always carry?

If you die we will bury it with you, but for now here is your only weapons. David said you wanted to fight now it is fair and the club can be very deadly. Now gentleman the battle field is yours, as David step back several paces.

The General took this moment to strike hitting the commander on the side of his body knocking him to the ground. The commander recovered before the second blow, hitting the general in the legs, causing him to stagger sideways. This giving the commander time to stand up. The fight continued for several minutes some blows connecting with their opponent most just club to club. Finally General had the commander on the ground and was about to apply the finial blows when David step in and asked the commander do you agree to share the valley. The commander agreed. David asked the General do you agree to share the valley.

Hell no I won its mine.

That's not the way this war is going, now go ahead and kill the commander.

There no need he is down and badly beaten the general said.

That not war, we need dead people David said taken a metal object and pointing at the Commander laying on the ground. The Commander burst into flames and disappeared. David motioned the commander second in command and handed him the Commanders club. Let the war continue, he said as he steps back.

In short the Commander second in command had beaten the already tired General down David again step in and asked the General? Do you agree to share the valley?

Yes the General answered.

Turning to the Commander second in command standing over the General since you are now in command do you agree to share the valley.

Like Commander McCormick wanted to?

No I have beaten their General we have won.

That's not the right answered, David said pulling out the metal rod and the General burst into flame and disappeared. Then he motioned over the General choice Second in command and handed him the Generals club. This war will continue till both sides agree to share the valley if it takes a hundred men from both sides. He said this as he step backed. The General second in command soon had his opponent down. David again stepped in and again, asked if he would share the valley. This time he agreed David asked the winner if he agreed or should he call in the other opponent.

No need for that, we can share the valley and work in peace this two hundred year war has gone on far too long.

David brought out the mikso device and started at the fallen soldier feet and moved up to his head as it moved it healed the soldier battle wounds as the General second in command healed he stood up and shook hands with the other second in command. I believe we can make this work you are right this war has gone on too long.

With that Ambassador Nulls touched the transporter on his belt and disappeared from the planet, appeared back in the control center of Captain Kitaracta space cargo cruiser.

Captain Kitaracta looked at him, well that worked out good but what you are going to do with these two pointing over toward General Otash and Commander McCormick.

I'm sure glad you got the message to transport them up here while I put the image of a fire in the minds of the other officers.

You were damn lucky they still had the transport disk in their pocket. You still did not say what you are going to do with them, kit insisted. The Kula insisted no more kidnapping

First of all let's get them back in good condition.

Kit had her medic revive them, and then took them to the medical station. A half hour later they were back in a room wondering what had happen.

When Ambassador Nulls and Captain Kitaracta walked in they stop talking and stared then started asking questions all at the same time. David held up his hand if you all calm down I will explain. First of all back on your planet they all think you are dead. Second of all you two have been selected to do a very important job to save your people of your planet. Our scientists have determined that your sun is about to burn itself out. That means everyone on your planet will die. You two have a lot of influence on your planet. So you two will be working with our exploration team to find another planet in another solar system and then convince your people to move to it.

We do not have an exploratory team. it was Kit's thoughts coming threw David brain.

No but Hola and Spirts do we just need to teach the General and commander about their planet and put one with Hola and one with Sprints.

You make it sound so simple.

Well can you contact Ambassador Yumit on Sprints? He was the only who might help.

Turning to the General and the Commander, there is one thing from now you will be Mr. Otash and Mr. McCormick Scientist from Srovalf. The General and Commander titles are to be dropped.

What if we don't agree to your terms, it was Mr. Otash?

If you do not want to help your own people from Srovalf then there two options, A we can return your burnt dead bodies back to the planet. B we can put you back to sleep and wake you up one day before your sun burns out.

You do not give us much of a choice; it was Mr. McCormick this time.

Basic I didn't think I would have to give you a choice? I thought you would be thrill at the ideal of getting all this knowledge and to be a hero on your planet, a real hero. Not know as a murder of thousands.

I don't about you Mr. Otash I'm more interested in the knowledge and being a hero than being dead.

Well Mr. what is your name, it was Mr. Otash Asking?

This gentleman is Ambassador Nulls from the Kula Federation. It was Kit that answered.

From what Mr. Otash asked?

The Kula Federation the largest organization of the solar systems.

Solar system there is more than one Mr. McCormick asked?

You have a lot to learn there are Hundreds and thousands of planets that are members.

Just then Knight came in, David introduced him to Mr. Otash and Mr. McCormick, Knightalotastuf these are your new students they need to learn a little about their planet.

Mr. Otash and Mr. McCormich this is Knightalotofstuf I call him just Knight, he was my teacher and if you listen to him you can learn what you need to know to save your planet.

Knight thought what do, I need to teach them.

What to look for in a new planet. Their planet now has a lower oxygen percentage than we are used to Kit has then on something that gives them less oxygen.

Mr. Ambassador are you alright it was Mr. Otash?

Yes I was just thinking. David had forgotten that he and knight were talking mentally.

Chapter 30

The Kanee People

Captain Kitaracta move her cargo ship over to the other side of the planet Srovalf and Ambassador Nulls prepared to transport down to the planet surface.

When Mr. McCormick came to him and advised that it would be better, that when he transport down that he pick a spot outside the city. Because they have an alarm system that will notify everyone, that a stranger is present.

David thanks him, then thought of a spot outside the city and pressed the transport button and vanished from the ship and reappeared on the planet surface,

Insanely he heard screaming and shouting strange, stranger, warning, warning, and stranger in our mist. It was a faint but clear. David stood still and looked around, seeing no one. He put his hand up showing everyone he had no weapons. I have come to talk to your leaders and mean no harm to anyone.

Then if that is true, then move your foot, David heard.

David slowly lifted his left foot six inches off the ground and stood there.

Your other foot you dumb oaf.

David started switching to his other foot.

Careful you moron he heard.

David looked down and almost fell over backwards. There were twenty or thirty little people no larger than an ant on his planet. David set his foot down easy making sure he did not step on anyone. And very carefully lifted his other foot, three little people came running out, then another one with his arm around another person struggling to get out from under his foot. Is it safe to put my foot down now he asked?

Yes now stranger what do you want?

I'm sorry I had miss information about your civilization. And I hope that man will recovery from any injures I cause if there is anything I can do to help out. Please ask me I have very advance medical technology to help.

Who are you, and where do you come from, to have this ADVANCE TECHNOGLAGE.

I will not lie to you I come from a planet very far away, yes I'm a space travel and I come in peace with information to save you and all your family and grand kids and all your friends, the whole civilization of Kanee. Yes I understand this sound like someone who has gone crazy. Let me show you reaching down and picking up the man who was helping the man who he had step on.

Thinking sending me a mikso I hope it works on these little people?

It will it's on it way hold out your hand Kit answered.

When she finished telling David, the mikso was in his hand. He told himself to compliment her on her accuracy

No need lover boy I know I'm good; it was Kit in his brain.

I know, now get out of my head.

Stranger who are you talking to?

It was the man in his hand

You can hear my thought, David asked?

That is how we know when stranger are present.

OK then you know this device will heal your friend.

OK but it does not look like he will not make it, it another tragedies from your kind, on my people.

As David ran the mikso over his palm it not only cured the step on man of all his injuries but cured the other man of his lung inflammation.

As the other man took a deep breath and watch his friend stand up. What did you do to us he asked?

I call it a mikso

Can I have one?

I don't know, let me ask my Supervisor, Kit these people are less than one quarter of an inch tall can we make an mikso that will work for then,

Who are you talking to the man in my hand asked?

My supervisor who is up there in space in their space ship, would you like to meet them?

No I think that is something you need to talk to our Queen about.

This took David by surprise as he sat the little people down so they could jump off his hand.

Follow us we will clear the way, but watch where you step some of my people are old and slow.

OK I will follow you, tell me when to step down. As David follow the little man. They came on a town the high rise buildings came to his knees.

Stop here I will bring our Queen to you!

OK, is it OK to sit on this stump?

Give me a minute to clear it. A few minutes later OK it is alright to sit down, he said.

Moments later the Queen came to the top of the high building. Stranger I understand you save one of my citizen and that you are from another planet far in space. You are the first that we have met from another world, although we have always believed that there are other people out there. It is nice to meet one. Now what can we do for you?

Well it is what I can do for your civilization. You see our scientist have learned that in one hundred of your years that your sun will burn out and this will become a dead planet probably suck into what we call a black hole.

Yes our scientists have been studying it they say two hundred years.

Well your scientist have been study it more than we have so they have a better idea than we do. But we all agree that it will burn out. So what we are offering you is to move your whole civilization to a new planet.

Why are you doing for us, she asked?

Because I'm a member of a federation that believe in preserving any civilization from what look like total annhilation.

And what is this federation?

It is the Kula Federation that watches over all planets.

Just what is the Federation plans, to save us?

It's is to find a planet, to move you to that is safe David said,

I will talk it over with my counsel and get back with you tomorrow, and as I understand it you have to talk with your supervisor, in space, in a space ship. You will bring him with you.

Well it is actually her.

OK bring her with you.

With that David said can you clear a place for her over on that tree stump and a place for her feet. We do not want to injure any more of your people.

Yes they say you have a device that will repair any damage you cause.

Yes the mikso will repair many thing wrong with the body. But sorry it is too big for your people. Maybe we can give you the plans that you can build your own, but I'm not promising you that it can be done. I'm saying maybe it can be done.

I like a man who is good to his word and thank you for the maybe. I know you are not sure and not giving us false hope. Thank you for your time, I will see you and your supervisor tomorrow, we will keep both stump as you call them available for you. Until tomorrow good day, as she walked to the small door and disappeared.

Well that went better than I thought; it was the little mam that David had held in his hand.

Can you hear my thoughts David asked?

Oh yes that is how we commualcate a warning. That there is danger it is only good for short distance so we relay it to everyone. But we cannot hear your space ship when they talk back to you.

Well my little friend would you like to see my space ship?

I'm not a little people in my civilization I'm consider tall.

My apologies sir, would you like to see my space ship?

Yes I have permission from the counsel although it dose scare me a little.

I assure you that it will be safe and at any time you wish to come back

I will bring you.

Oh what the hell you only live twice, yes I would like to see your space ship. Give me a minute to tell my wife, it is she I,m scared of, she is not going to believe this.

I could send a note home with you. David laughed.

I don't think she would still believe it, in fact she would tell me to stop drinking acakov and come home.

Well I would not want to get you in trouble at home.

You are kidding pass up a time to go in to a space ship. For a little trouble from her! When do we go?

Right now as David put down his hand and the man step on. David thought of the control room in Kit space ship and pressed the button on his belt.

Moments later back in the control room of Kitaracta space ship David saw Mr. Oash and Mr. McCormick oh hi I'm glad that you said the people of Kanee were a little shorter than me. This is Mr. sorry I didn't get you name.

Yram, please to meet you General Oash and Commander McCormick.

You know them David asked?

Oh yes we do keep up on any news from the other side of Srovalf.

Well your news is slow these men are no longer General and Commander they are Ambassador for Srovalf and are going to find a planet that they can move their people to when your sun dies out. They will also be looking for a planet for you to live on.

You talk to those things McCormick asked?

David realized that Yram was mental talking and he was speaking out loud to him. Yes David said, Kit can you get Mr. McCormick and Mr. Oash a translator.

Kit looked at David they have one!

Oh sorry yes this is Mr. McCormick and Mr. Oash this is Yram.

Well glad to meet you Mr. Yram

Yes glad to meet you Mr. McCormick.

Holly shit they do talk, Mr. Oash said.

Not only that, David said they are more advance than you are. And their scientist has been study the sun for the last two thousand years and knows that your sun will die out. In fact they say two hundred years. Not a hundred years, And I trust their study better than ours.

Turning to Kit with his hand out, with the man standing in it Yram this is Captain Kitaracta this is her space ship.

How do you do sir, welcome aboard my ship.

Wow she is good looking if she was smaller I'd marry her.

Oh Yram she can hear you're thought too.

Oh crap I just made a fool of myself.

Quite the contrary, thank you for the compliment, then saying out load, nice to meet you Mr. Yram and giving him a wink.

Trying to steel my girlfriend Mr. Yram? David thought.

No, No, I'm a married man just wishing. Yram said looking at David.

I know just kidding makes you stay on your toes, so to speak. We have fun on Captain Kitaracta ship during long voyage.

Oh you like her?

Why does everyone keep saying that, David asked? She is just a good friend.

Yes keep telling yourself that, you might one day believe it.

OK enough come let me show you the ship, David cut him off.

In a room out of the control room David said you mind not talk about me and Kit in front of everyone.

Well you do like her, the first thing you looked at when we got here is her, are you sleeping with her.

That none of your business David answered.

OK, you are.

I told you that none of your business come on I'll show you something that you can talk about. This is the rec. room this is what the crew really look like when they are not in disguise, they come from different planets. David figures he surprised Yram and gets him off talking about Kit and his relationship.

Walking in Yram did a little step back when he said .Hay there one my size.

Where David asked?

Over there in the corner, let's go meet him.

David looked and sure enough there was an ant with six legs sitting at a small table eating something he could not make out.

Going over to the corner, and the little man jump down and walk over to the small table and pull up a chair.

David could hear them talking mentally. And decided he would leave them alone and have a drink.

Half way through his drink Kit came in and sat down beside him. Where did your little friend go she asked?

Over in the corner, talking to another little friend.

Kit looked oh I see he meet Erick.

Erick David said!

Yes our Electrician, he is a wisps at tracing down short in the wiring.

Did you know that the people of Kanee were only one centimeter tall?

Yes I read it on the computer.

Why didn't you tell me?

Cause McCormick and Oash were having too much fun, telling you how you were too tall to go in disguise. I did not want to ruin it for them. But don't worry I told them. It was not a nice thing to do, after you transported down.

Oh thank you, you know I damn near killed one of the villagers by step on him.

Yes but it gave you points and introduced you by saving his life. David just shook his head and orders another drink. Then sat back, OK if you can make tools for Erick why can't you make a mikso for these people.

Because it was not sanitation by the Kula to give lower intelligence life forms advance technology.

Well miss smart pants they expect me to show tomorrow with my supervisor and that going to be you.

Yes I heard you thinking about it, and wonder how you would pull that off.

That simple you're going stay on our wave link and I will do the talking, they have telepathic powers so watch what you think.

OK you are the Kula Ambassador and next in line to the counsel, I will do as you say.

I don't know where you get your ideals, but just try to act like a supervisor. But do not act like we are any better than them.

Just then Yram cut in Excuse me captain could you use another crew member, I'm a good welder.

Kit and David looked down to see Erick and Yram standing there. I'm sorry but I have a full crew, but I will keep you in mind if I need one.

David spoke up a welder; I don't know how good you are. But you my friend are the best respective of your people that I know. You have seen the Captain ship, how much better is a person who can tell the story to your people that we mean then no harm and we are only trying to save them. In years to come they will remember your name as the one who save the whole civilization.

Until tomorrow you can hang out with Erick he can show around the ship. Kit said leaning over and talking to the little people. It has been quite a while sense he has had someone his size to visit with. I think you will be surprise how he gets around the ship.

The next morning David met Kit in the control room. We'll have you figured out what you are going to tell them if they turn down your offer to move.

Just then Erick came in on something that could only be described as a flying carpet with Yram sitting on the back. Erick maneuvered the carpet up to the height of David arm extended Yram step over on to David hand.

Well Mr. Ambassador are we ready to talk to my Queen and counsel.

You have learned a lot in your short time here. Turning to Kit, OK Captain are you ready.

Yes I'll be right behind you Kit said.

David pressed the transport button and made sure of where he would land before energizing. When he was sure there was no one there. He energized and appeared down on the planet in front of the stump he sat on before. Moments later captain Kitaracta appeared next to him.

David set Yram down he went into the tall building and several minutes later came out with the Queen.

Well Mr. Ambassador it was very considerate bring your female pilot with you. I 'm not intimidated by males, when it comes to saving my race from extinction. Now you are here to help us. According to one of our citizen there is a planet that we can send some of our people who will survive this disaster that we know will consume our planet.

David took a step backwards. I see that Yarm was more than a visitor to our ship he was more like a forward scout.

Yes, you could call it that, you would not expect us to just jump right in when a tall person come to visit us?

You are right especially if they say they are from outer space. I understand your hesitation.

Yes we have always thought that there was more civilization out there. And we have been mentoring our sun and know that it is weaker over the last four hundred years. But according our scientist it will last two hundred years. I also know that you have a crew member who is the size of us. That lives on a planet and everyone is the same size as us. That will do for us to send the inspection team to.

David not knowing what to call her cut in her conversation. When just then Kit interrupted That might be alright but the people on Erick planet do not have a meat population they raise their specie for food and have sacrifices to feed the upper class. I'm afraid they might attack you for their food.

Mr. Ambassador you can call me the Queen or Elizabeth. I sense that you did not know how to address me and in you're mind you thought of Queen Elizabeth who ever she is. As for Erick people maybe we can introduce our Emal to them as a meat source.

I apology your Majesty I did not know that you have mentality ability.

Yes we can hear your thoughts but not for a long distance such as you have. But only a few have it. One is my son Yram who you have met. And my daughters who will, if I die become the Queen as you call her. Only the female will rule over this civilization.

Maybe it would be best that you meet Erick before you decide to send out this pilgrimage. Captain Kitaracta would you mind going and get Erick and explain to him what is going on before you bring him down here.

Yes sir Mr. Ambassador, Kit said as she transported back to her ship.

After Kit had transported back to ship, the Queen turned to David. I know that you were the one in charge why did you say that you had to talk to your supervisor last time we talked with me.

That I must apologize again, I needed time to think and I'm sorry but I thought that you might like to speak with a female of our species

You male are all like you feel intimated by a woman,

It is something we are born with, the mother brings us into the world, and the mother can take us out.

The Queen laughed, you make a joke as you call it?

Yes, the planet I come from. The woman are just coming in to power they respect the male but know they control the power.

I read it in your mind your female have what you male want and the male will do anything to get it. But the female needs the male just as bad to reproduce so they will not over rule the male.

All right get out of my head. David said.

Just then Kit came back with Erick still on his wave board in her palm. He sails down to the building to next to the Queen. He then bowed. Your majesty they say that you can bring your Emal to our planet. There is a portion of our planet that is uninhabited that your people can live on. And raise your Emal and set up trade with our people. And feel safe I'm not the one to guarantee it. But if the Ambassador talks to them first, we can live in peace.

OK the Queen said we will agree to send a pilgrim party to establish a new civilization, only if you agree to take Erick on Captain Kitaracta ship as a crew member.

What David asked?

Your assignment is to get everyone off these worlds before our sun dies out.

I told you to get out of my head David said.

I got that before you told me to get out, she said,

OK I will give you that, but it is up to Captain Kitaracta who she has as a crew.

Well he said he was a welder I can use him, and Erick could have a friend.

OK, David said we will see how it will work out and we will keep a close eye on their progress just to make sure.

Kit turned to David; you have a inter solar message coming in on the ship.

David turned to the Queen, I'm sorry but I have to get back to our ship. I will get back to you when we can continue this conversation but it sound like we are agreeable on everything.

As David transported to the ship Kit was in the control room expecting it to be the counsel telling what a good job he had done by moving the inhabitants from this solar system to another.

Instead on the screen were Mr. Oush and Mr. McCormick both were saying we found the planet first.

Chapter 31

Who Killed Who

Ah crap David thought, looking at the screen at Mr. Oush and Mr. McCormick. They both looked purity well beat up. The Ambassador almost had to laugh if it wasn't so important for them to get along for the Ambassadors mission to be successful.

When both Mr. Oush and Mr. McCormick saw the Ambassador both men started speaking at once, both claiming that they discovered the planet first.

David held up his hands, Stop! I want to speak to the Captain.

The Captain step up to the screen, Captain Ispep here Mr. Ambassador.

Greeting Captain, David said can you tell me what is going on. I thought the plan was to transport either Mr. Oush or Mr. McCormick to another ship and for each to find their own planet.

Sorry Mr. Ambassador be were on our way to meet up with Captain Serglo in the Nirips Solar system. And had to pass threw Tsaor system and we came across this planet that fit the requirements that these Gentleman were looking for so I stop to check it out. I took both Mr. Oush and Mr. McCormick down to the plant surface to check it out and both decided to claim it.

So what is the name of this planet The David asked?

Doesn't have a name just a number Kd379461.

David knew that it was one of the planets the Kula had discovered and was mapped in their archives because of the number. OK thank you Captain, I'll get back to you in an hour, sign off. Then turning to Captain Kitaracta, Do we have this planet on the computer.

Yes would you like me to put it up on the screen or on your slab?

Screen would be alright, I may need some of your opinion on this. Instantly the planet came up on the screen with all the information about it on the side. As the planet turned on the screen David noticed that there were two continents this would be the answer to our problems. Kit look at the planet then pointed out the number and writing and pointed it out to David.

That is the mark of Ambassador Retaw from Nocba They are claiming this continent remember they are also looking for a place to relocate too looks like they have found this first.

Well crap they are far more advance than anyone from the planet of Srovalf. We can't put them on the same planet it would be like putting Caesar with the Roman army into the twenty first century with the American army David thought.

Who Kit cut into his thoughts?

Never mind David spoke back just some old history from my planet. How about bring up any other planet in that solar system.

Kit did, there is only one that has oxygen levels that's spglt20, as she enlarge the picture on the screen. Looking at it, there is no one that would want to live on that.

It was a barren planet with four continents but it was at least three quarters water.

The ocean must be what is producing the oxygen, Kit said.

Then David heard a voice behind him that is exactly what we are looking for. David turned to see Yram on his air board. Only Yarm was not talking to him but mantel speaking into his mind.

There are no trees or even a bush. I don't think your Queen would approve of it.

We will bring our own forest with us and our city.

That might not be possible David answered.

Sure it is I have seen the cargo hole on this ship. We can reduce the forest. And then after we move it here we can enlarge it.

David thought about it, thinking they would have to bring small plants and trees but it would take hundreds of years for the trees to grow. It might be the right ideal thing to start then when their sun was ready to die out they would have a place to move. OK We will take the ideal up with your Queen Elizabeth as David called her. Right now I have to get back to the problem at hand with Mr. McCormick and Mr. Oush. Kit you want to get them back on the screen.

She called captain Ispep when he came on the screen. He looked a little weary. Mr. Ambassador please tell me that you have good news for these Two before I put them in space lock and inject them both into space.

I do Captain the planet has already been claimed by the citizens of Nocba and neither one can have it. So you can contain on to your rendezvous with Captain Serglo. And

Just then Mr. McCormick came on the screen. That is not right there is no one living on this planet. And I want it for my people.

Mr. Ambassador, McCormick is right there are no people living on this planet and I was first to claim it for my people.

Well David said I'm sorry to tell you this but the Ambassador from Nocba has first claim on the planet and he will be setting up colonies there, before their sun dies out.

Well then they can share with us and McCormick can go look somewhere else.

In the first place Mr. Oush they are far more advance than you are and it would not work out. I'm sure you will find another planet just as nice. There are millions of them out there. These just happen to be the first one you came across after leaving your solar system. Now if you and Mr. McCormick cause Captain Ispep any more trouble or any fighting. I'm authorizing Captain Ispep to lock you in your rooms for the rest of the Journey. Do you both understand, David did not wait for an acknowledgment he just sign off, Standing there looking at the blank screen?

Till Captain Kitaracta interrupt him. Wow where did that come from David I have never seen that side of you.

I cannot believe that I would be babysitting two grown men fight over a planet. Now let see if we can get Yram back home and see if his Queen wants to move to a Barren planet.

You think the Queen will like moving.

I don't know but Yram seems sure they would maybe if they start now they can have some vegetation growing in a few years.

No we will take a whole forest with us when we move.

David and Kit turned to see Yram standing behind them on the flying carpet. Your cargo hole will hold our whole city and the forest around it.

I don't believe it is that big, maybe some of the city and some of the smaller trees that will grow bigger later.

Oh you will see, how soon we will get back to Srovalf

Well if we turn around we should have you home in a day and a half. It will take several hours to slow down enough to turn around.

A day later they were in orbit around Srovalf, David took Yram down to the planet and was hearing a lot of mental talk between Yram and the Queen about the new planet and plans to get ready to move.

Finely Yram came up to David if Captain Kitaracta, will c land her ship on the makeshift landing pad it will not take long to get are people, city and landscape aboard.

David picked up Yram and went back to the ship. Then asked Kitaracate is this alright with you.

Yes I have been listening to their plans; it seems they have been ready for this since we first talked with them. but I do not remember any landing pad near their town?

It will be a cleared aria near town we just cleared it. I have measure your ship and it will be big enough to land.

OK but if I start getting into any trees I'm coming back up here and kicking your little ass.

Well I sure do not want you to try that. There will be plenty of room for you to land, you will see!

Kit took the ship out of orbit and headed down toward the planet. When she was below the atmosphere she could see a large cleared landing spot. Well I don't know how they did it so fast but we can defiantly land there.

Kit made a perfect landing in the clearing. As they step out of the ship with Yram flying beside then. Yarm change into a man over ten feet tall. David and Kit both looked up startled

OK how the hell did you do that David asked?

Just then The Queen pops up about around five feet tall. Forgive him he likes to show off. Yram go back to a regular size.

As she said it Yram shorten back to six feet tall.

That a good trick, but how is it done David asked again?

We can all do it but we stay small as when you first meet us to avoid being notice. But from what Yram tell me we can have a whole planet to our self without any worry of being pursued by others.

David still in amazement, yes we have found a planet with the same atmosphere, but it is barren land only and will take a few years to get vegetation to grow.

If you will take us in your ship we will bring our forest with us. My son Yram says that your cargo hole will carry our whole village and the forest. If you will take us, it will only take a few minutes to be ready.

Isn't this moving a little fast David asked?

No, we have been planning this for years. When our scientist first discovered that our sun soon burn out. And the people who predict the future said that someone from space would come and move us. Yram go get the plate.

A few minutes later Yram came back carefully carrying a six foot round disk, it contain a small village with a forest around it and carried it over to the ship.

Captain Kitaracta ordered the hatch open. Yram place the small village in and sat down next to it then somehow shrank down to the size that he was as small as the little people on the disk.

David and Kit just stared. The Queen just laughed yes we can be any size we want. That is the whole town and the surrounding forest, Shell we go to this new world.

Kit just shook her head and said well just when I thought I had seen everything.

Hay! Said David I'm getting so that nothing surprises me, but I do have to admit that is really amazing shell we go, as he took Kit arm and the Queen arm and walked them toward the ship.

The next day an a half on the way to planet SPGLT20, when David was called to the control room, you have an urgent message from Captain Ispep. When David got to the control room, Captain Ispep was on the video screen looking worried.

Sorry to bother you Mr. Ambassador. But Mr. Oush killed Mr. McCorick last night.

What? how did that happen, David asked?

We found Mr. McCorick this morning in his room. He had been stabbed with a sword. We were going to put Mr. Oush in the air lock and open the outer doors. But figured we had better talk to you first.

Captain put Mr. Oush on the screen David said.

Captain Iapep turn and motion to the two guards. Who came into view dragging Mr. Oush between them?

David looked at the screen a few minutes. Then spoke, Well Mr. Oush do you mind telling me why you killed Mr. McCormick?

I didn't do it he shudders; I was in my room all night I swear.

David study his face for a while, something in the back of his mine was telling him that this man was not lying. Captain don't do anything till we get there in (David looked at Kit who held up three fingers) in three days David said. For now just lock Mr. Oush in his room and put Mr. McCormick on ice till we get there.

The Captain seemed a little disappointed but nodded his head, as you wish Mr. Ambassador, but I don't like having a murder in my ship.

Then the screen went blank. David turned to Kit and shook his head, just when you think things are going good all hell breaks loose. Let's get these people on the planet and I have notice that you have been taking it easy not to shake up the people in the cargo hole. But we need to catch up with Captain Ispep before he sets Mr. Oush into space with no space suite.

I know Captain Ispep he would not do that, after you told him not to, but he would not think twice about it, if you said to do it Kit Said.

Chapter 32

The Sword Of Calven

After dropping off the Kanee people on planet SPGLT20 and a mile in space Captain Kitaracta and Ambassador David watched as Yram People turned twenty thousand square mile continent of barren Desert, into Twenty Thousand square miles of forest with a large city in middle. Then headed off to rendezvous with Captain Ispep.

Two days later Captain Kitaracta had her space cargo ship a hundred yards off the starboard side of Captain Ispep.

Permission to come aboard Captain Ispep, this is Ambassador Nulls calling.

The Kula Ambassador does not need permission to board any Kula ship came back the answer.

Maybe so but I feel it is always better to ask permission, than to get shot for intruding on someone else ship.

Well that a first Mr. Ambassador you are welcome shell we send a shuttle.

No I have a transporter.

We are traveling twice the speed of light are you sure you want to do that?

David didn't answer that he just thought of the control room and push the transport button and reappeared behind Captain Ispep. Before anyone could say anything, yes I'm sure.

Captain Ispep turns around surprised. Damn I've never heard of anyone transporting while traveling this fast.

Well I'm glad you are telling me that now and not before I transported over. Now what is this situation on Mr.Oush.

Well you know the argument He and Mr. McCormick had over the planet the other day. Now McCormick is dead stab threw the heart with a sword. Only Mr. McCormick carry that old relic of a sword, make him feel important. McCormick shooting off his mouth at dinner how the one who carries that sword has control over all the people to the north of that little planet they come from, and how it has been around for thousands of years. Having that control gives Oush a motive to kill his rival and being in the room next to him gave him the opportunity.

So where is Mr. Oush now?

In his room with a guard at the door.

And where is Mr. McCormick?

In the freezer, I didn't want his body stinking up the whole ship.

Understandable, I would like to talk to Mr. Oush first.

Come this way, as the Captain pointed down the hallway, at the door Captain Ispep instructed the guard to stay with David as he entered the room.

That won't be necessary David told them.

He is a dangerous man the Captain insisted.

I'm sure I can handle Mr. Oush but your man can come along as a witness David said.

As they entered to room, Mr. Oush sat up on the bed. I swear Mr. Ambassador I did not kill McCormick

David studied Mr.Oush mind for a minute, I believe you. So why do you think someone on this ship would want to kill him.

I have been thinking about these last few days and have several ideals, one because of his loud mouth and altitude. But I think it was over that damn sword he is always talking about. It is old and worth a lot of money he claims.

Well I'm here to look into it. Have you had anything to eat?

No they think a condemned man doesn't need any food.

David turning to the guard Take Mr. Oush down to the cafeteria and get him something to eat. Captain will you take me to see McCormick body.

Yes follow me turning to the guard do as the Ambassador says and make sure Mr. Oush does not get hurt.

David Follow Captain Ispep to the store room where the Mr. McCormick laid, Captain Do you have a mikso unit on board.

Yes but it was too late for us to revive the Mr. McCormick he had been dead for over eight hours when we found him.

Yes I understand I just want to use it to examine the body.

You really think that Mr. Oust didn't kill him?

If he did he is real good hiding it in his mind. When I scanned it, I didn't get anything back, except that he was truly sorry over McCormick death. And those thought cannot be hidden from me. And to answer your thoughts, yes I think it was one of your crew members. You never stop and now one man is dead. So the killer is still on this ship.

OK I will see about that mikso unit, as the captain turned to go out the door.

Oh Captain let's keep this just between us and put two guards on Mr. Oush I do not want him turning up dead. When the Captain was gone, David turned to the body of Mr. McCormick Well Commander you have die twice I wonder how you will explain this to Saint Peter or whoever you talk to in the afterlife.

I don't think he is going to answer you. It was Kit mentaling talking to him from her ship.

I'm glad you are following me I'm not sure what to do, have you got any ideals.

No but I'm sure Commander McCorick does not have any ideal either.

Oh you're a lot of help, but something does not seem right how about we drop out of warp and transfer Mr. Oush over to your ship for safety reasons.

OK I'll contact Captain Ispep and establish a rendezvous point.

Good and can you send me over a mikso unit, they don't seem to be able to find theirs.

Seconds later the mikso unit was at David's feet. He picked it up and went to the body of Commander McCorick and moves it over him. The scar from the fight on Srovelf was still there and three smaller holes the new cause of death shows up. How come the mikso did not remove the first scare David thought?

Because I left it there to remind him that he could be dead if it wasn't for us, it was kit back in David head with the answered.

I'm glad you did, it show that Mr. Oush sword did not kill him. This last killing was done with a small knife. I need to find McCormicks Sword of Calvin and see if that one did it. It should be around here somewhere? He was persistent to always keep it with him. I think I will check Mr. McCorick room then if I don't find it there, I'll check Mr. Oushs room.

There you go talking to yourself again.

Captain Kitaracta do you mind staying out of my head for a while.

I would but I needed to tell you we would be rendezvous with you in an hour. Then we can transport Mr. Oush over here.

An hour later both ships were sitting in space side by side. Ambassador Nulls and Mr. Oush transfer over to Kit ship David asked kit what she thought about the situation and how could he get more information on what went on.

Why not ask the computer on RX2006.

OK how do I do that?

Easy ask my computer to connect you up with RX2006 computer.

Oh yes that will be easy, just anyone can ask any computer a question and it will answer without a pass word.

You are not just any one; you are the Ambassador to the Kula and next in line for the council. You have access to any Kula Federation computers. And RX2006 is a federation ship.

I don't know where you get this crazy ideal that I will be the next one to sit on the counsel. But I will try to get on the computer. Computer this is Ambassador Nulls of the.

Mr. Ambassador you are connected.

Mr. Ambassador this is Seethe the computer on RX2006 please use voice authorization.

This is Ambassador David Nulls of the Kula Federation.

Voice authorization recognized what can I do for you Mr. Ambassador Nulls.

Do you know what the Sword of Calvin is?

Yes it is a symbol of the people of Srovelf the holder of the Sword is the ruler of the northern district of the planet, once in the hands of a Commander McCorick.

OK computer do you know where the sword is?

NO it was transported off of RX2006 twenty three minutes ago.

Transported off where was it transported to?

To ZXX5.

What that is this ship. Kit said in surprise computer who transported something on to my ship without my permission.

It was transported by Captain Ispep.

Computer why was I not informed?

Captain Ispep said I was not to inform you because it was to be a surprise for you at tonight's celebration.

Computer what celebration?

I don't know he did not say.

Where was the sword transported to?

The engine room.

The engine room, computer there is nothing transported on to my ship without my authorization regardless of the circumstances is that understood.

Yes Captain.

The engine room of all places the most variable part of the ship. Kit said to David a bomb in there and exploded there would not be an atom left of us for anyone to find. I can't even think Captain Ispep would even think of doing that, He know that is prohibited.

OK but let me finish talking to Rx2006 computer Seethe are you still there.

Yes MR. Ambassador.

Seethe do you know who killed Commander McCorick.

NO Mr. Ambassador or who killed Captain Ispep.

What did you say about Captain Ispep.

Captain Ispep life monitor shut down seventeen minutes ago.

You did not report this?

I was told not to mention it to any one, until we rendezvous

Who told you not to mention it?

Captain Ispep.

When did Captain Isprp tell you not to mention it?

Sixteen minutes ago.

Computer if Captain Ispep died seventeen minutes ago how could he tell you not to mention it when he was dead?

That is a question I will have to study something is wrong.

Computer off David said turning to Kit how about you finding that damn sword and putting it here in your Quarters. I'm going to transport over to RX2006 and see what is going on. As David thought of a place in the control room on RX2006 and touched the button on his belt. Millisecond later he was standing in the control room to the surprise of the crew. Who is in charge here he demanded.

I'm second command Lla Rewop sir.

Where is Captain Ispep?

In his quarters resting.

Good then you come with me David again demanded.

We have orders not to disturb him.

And who gave that order?

He did sir.

And when did he give that order?

Just a little while ago.

How much time is a little While?

Ten maybe fifteen minutes

Come with me Commander Lla Rewop, as David headed off toward Captain Ispep quarters. At the door David just opens it and walked in follow by Commander Lla Rewop.

There on the bed laid Captain Ispep with a big blood stain in his shirt where his heart was. David walked over and open the shirt there were three holes the same pattern as the ones in Commander McCormick.

Computer this is Ambassador Null I have some question for you.

Yes I recognized you Mr. Ambassador what are your question.

How long has Captain Ispep life reading been off?

Twenty eight minutes now.

Thank you computer turning to Commander Lla Rewop who was just staring at the Captain and looking like he might get sick. Well commander how did you talk to the Captain fifteen minutes ago when he has been dear for a half hour.

Mr. Ambassador I swear it came over the intercom fifteen minutes ago and it was his voice asks any crew member in the control room. He said he was going to lie down and no one was to disturb him.

Well we have someone who can mimic the Captain voice enough to fool you and the computer.

That is almost impossible to fool the computer.

Well it happen and whoever did it they also killed the Captain and Commander McCormick those are the same holds I saw in Mr. McCormick pointing at Captain Ispep chest. And Mr. Oush was on ZXX5 at the time. That means you have a murder on board and you are now in charge. So how do we find this impostor?

Mr. Ambassador I have live with this crew for over a year and purity much know everyone and I cannot think of anyone who would do this, Captain Ispep was hard at times but it was always for the best interested of the crew and we all like him for it.

Right then Kit materialized behind David. WE are not asking the right question.

Where did you come from asked Commander Lla Rewop?

I'm Captain Kitaracta from Space cargo ship ZXX5 and we are asking the computer the wrong question. Computer has any one or thing transport on to the ship that no one knows about.

I'm sorry but voice recognition is not authorized to communicate with me.

Computer this Ambassador Nulls I'm authorizing you to answer Captain Kitaracta Question.

Yes Mr. Ambassador in answer to your question Captain. There is something that came aboard on the sword of Calvin I was not program to understand at time it can be as small as a speck of dust and the next time it could be as big as man.

He is one of the Kanee people David and kit almost said it at the same time. Computer David asked where is this thing a right now.

In the engine room I believe it is studying the engines.

David headed out the door and toward the engine room with Kit and Commander Lla Rewop behind once in the engine room David asked. Computer where is this thing at.

Ten step ahead of you a little to the left on the floor.

As David took the first step in the direction the computer had given. Suddenly a figure appeared in front of him a claw like hand came trusting toward his chest. David stops the figure with his mind and pushed it to the wall where it stood motionless David holding it with his mind. David walked over to it looking at the claw there it was the same pattern as the holes in both Captain Ispep chest and in Commander McCormick

Hay you, David asked what you are doing here?

The figure did not answer.

Commander Lla Rewop open those inter doors to the space dock, As he did David moved the figure over the lock with his mind all those it was getting harder to control the Kanee. Once David had the Kanee in the space lock and the doors closed. The figure shrunk to a size invisible to the eye. David went to the intercom; I have my hand on a button that will open those outer doors. And unless you can live in a vacuum you will be just one little blood spot in space.

The figure repaired, I was only doing my job.

And what job is that?

Back on Sreglof I was to spy on Mr. McCormick and see if they were going to attack the Kanee people then when you transport me on board your ship I had new orders to study your ship so we could build our own, or even take over the ship. But then you moved Mr. McCormick over to this ship. I learn to control a ship I first had to control the computer. I learned the Captain voice and then Mr. McCormick caught me and I had to get rid of him. And I had learned that whoever had the Sword of Calvin control the people.

So why did you kill our Captain, Lla asked?

I needed him out of the way to take over the ship.

Well you sorry ass bastard take this to your Queen as Lla Rewop reach his hand and hit David's hand opening the outer doors.

The Kanee taken by surprise exploited into a million pieces that were suck out the door.

David tried to react and closed the outer doors it was too late. David turned to Commander Lla Rewop what the hell was that.

That sorry pieces of shit kill our captain and try to take the ship. Where I come from that is called an act of piracy. And pirates get a free ride in space with no suit. The Captain would have done the same.

I agree. But I would have liked to get more information first.

Chapter 33

The Earth Explorer Helping Out

Well that take care of that, let's check up on Ambassador Yumit on Sprits, then Ambassador Modeerf at Hola. We do know that Nocba has already found a planet and claimed it, we will check on them later.

OK it is Sprints Kit said as she went and set the control for the planet of Sprints. Once that done she turned to David will we have two days to kill what would like to do in the meantime.

I was thinking of a nap what did you have in mind, David asked?

I was thinking of a back rub, and then later a nap, Kit said with a smile and a wink.

An hour later in Kit quarters, David lay back on the sleep slab, it's time like this I wish I hadn't given up smoking. And I wonder what it would be like back on Earth in the forest by the river we were camp at, till that deputy arrested me.

Are you saying you didn't enjoy that?

Oh I defiantly enjoyed that. I was just thinking back on times, when everything was just simple, not worlds coming to an end, or people killing people over water.

You sound like you want to give all this up and go back to the old life with no cares riding your bike.

It was a motorcycle, and give up this life of adventure and not knowing what going happen next, hell no, Good night.

Two days later they were in orbit around Sprints. David calls Ambassador Yumit. How are thing going.

Mr. Ambassador this is a surprise I was going to contact you I have a problem here on Sprint. The government does not believe our sun will burn out in a hundred years.

Will it help if I come down and talk to them?

Did you say come down?

Yes Mr. Yumit we are in orbit above your planet as we speak.

I'm sure it would help but we need some time to prepare for your arrival.

There is no need for any formal welcome.

Quite the contrary Mr. Ambassador it is a great privileges to any planet to have the Kula ambassador visit it. And only the proper welcome would be right, can you give us 24 hours to prepare.

24 hour later Ambassador Nulls and Knightalotofstuf step out of the shuttle craft on to the landing pad and was meet by the usually crowd of people cheering. There they were meet by Ambassador Yumit and escorted up to a podium where he introduced David to the crowd as David step forward, when a shoe came flying out of the back.

David reached out and caught it just before it hit him. He then held it up. Well I have received many gifts in my travels but this is the first that I received only half a pair of shoes.

Ambassador Yumit step forward, sorry Mr. Ambassador but there are some who resent the fact that the Kula federation is telling them they have to move off their planet. I see security has caught the man who throws it; he will be punished for his insult.

What? No bring the man up here.

But Mr. Ambassador he may be dangerous.

Yes he might have another shoe. But have him brought here anyways.

As security push the man threw the crowd David could pick up the thoughts of the people some were cheering the man others were against him. When security had the man up on the podium, David instructed them to let the man go. Then he walked over to him and handed him the shoe. I believe this belong to you, it looks to be in good shape. In fact too good to throw away, now what is your name?

Ygerne the poor man answered with a shaky voice.

Well Ygerne I believe there is a misunderstanding of some of the people here on Sprint about the Kula Federation we are not going to force anyone to leave such a nice planet. We are only trying to warn you of a coming danger. We have learned that your sun is dying out and when it does all your civilization will be wipe out. Moving all your people by that time would almost be impossible. So to save your species, we are telling you this ahead of time. What the people of Sprint want to do about it is up to them. The federation will not force anyone to move. Now Ygerne I would like you to go and tell everyone you know that the Kula Federation will not force anyone to leave. But I also want you to tell them that in the first ten years the temperature drop to high 60 degrees, after 20 years your whole world temperature will be freezing, after 30 years the temperatures are at 0 degrees, in 50 years the world is cover with ice. 75 years very few are alive, 100 years nothing is alive. The sun is now out and the gravity is so strong that it pulls all seventeen planets into it and make a black hole at the bottom of this hole is the burn out sun with all the planets and that gravitation pull. Anything for millions of miles will be sucked in. when that time comes hopefully some of your species have started a civilization on another planet. Go now and enjoy the festival.

Ambassador Yumit step forward you want to let this criminal go.

Yes just because a person has a different believes and have a strange way of showing it does not make them a criminal.

But he assaulted you!

No harm was done we just played catch, with his shoe. This brought laughter from the crowd. Now Ambassador Yumit shell we go and enjoy the festival.

Later that evening Ambassador Yumit got David aside I think I know why you let that man go, but do you really think it will help convince the government to decide to move.

I don't know but it save time trying to tell them tomorrow. They will know why I'm here and it will dispel any thought that the Kula will force anyone to leave their home. And that the Kula is only here to give them a warning of what will happen in the near future.

The thing is they don't believe that their sun is dying out.

Will it help to have our scientists come and show you, how about we set up a thermostatically?

What would this thermostatically do?

It could be set up to monitor your sun and it will show the sun is getting weaker.

How long will it take to show this?

It should only take a month; it will show the sun is getting weaker.

Well we can pitch it to the government and see what they say. another thing the people from Nocab have found a planet similar to theirs and it has two separate continent and from my studies their planet is similar to yours since you are on the same orbit around this sun with theirs being on one side and your being directly across on the other side. I was thinking maybe the two worlds could get to gather and start a jointed civilization.

Ha Sprint and Hola have not got along since they discovered there was a world like theirs in the same galaxies and that was over three hundred years ago.

Well maybe it is time to end this dislike for each other, now that they have something in common, the survival of their civilization.

You can try but I don't think it will work.

Well with that I think I will retire for the night, David said. Will the government see me tomorrow?

Oh yes, whenever you want to just name a time.

How about around ten o'clock?

That will be fine I will tell them. They will be in chambers at ten o'clock, good night Mr. Ambassador Nulls.

When David got to his room they had set up for him. He got a message from Knighalotofstuf Mr. Ambassador may I talk to you for a minuet

Yes where are you?

In the next room as he came threw, the door from the connecting room. That was a prize winner speech then letting that hackler go, at the landing ceremony, the man was put up to it, by the government. It seems that the government thinks that if they move to a new world they will lose control over the people.

After Knight Left There was a knock at the door when David answered it, there stood Kit. David thought it was strange that she would knock at the door, when usually she would just pop in. what are you doing out in the hall come in?

I thought you might want some companionship to night.

David didn't notice that she was talking vocal not mental.

Kit appeared on the other side of the room, No you don't bitch now get out of my friends room before I turn you into space dust.

David turned and there was another Commander Kitaracta. David turned looking from one to the other, what the hell is going on?

That thing is a Tariaripea, it can see what you are thinking of and turn itself in to it. Mainly used by wealthy people to entertain their guest in other words a prostitute and it can change itself into any specie's you are thinking of. It looks like you were thinking of me. Tararipea, Kit said turn toward the image that look just like her. Turn back to your normal state and get the hell out of here, if I ever hear you duplicated me again, the only thing you will turn into is a plasma ray.

Just a minute first turn yourself back into your normal self. As it did, holly shit! David said he was used to seeing different aliens but this was something he could not even imagine. Some parts looked almost human like his own race; other parts of the body were a mixture of at least twenty-five other spices he had met. OK turn yourself into Kinghtalotofstuf as David thought about him. As the Tararipea change into a spitting image of Kinghtalotofstuf, David then mentally thought Knight Can you come in here for a minute.

Sure give me a minute, shortly after that Knight appeared to materialize in the connecting door way. He looked at the image of himself standing at the other entrance without batting an eye, oh a Tararipea.

Yes a Tararipea, why have you never told me about one of these?

I didn't think you ever needed one, Knight said smiling at Kitaracta and winking,

They both gave a little laugh.

Oh that was funny, can they pick up our mental thoughts?

Very few can, they only pick up mental images.

Well Tararipea what is your name and how do I get a hold of you. I may have a need of your service.

What Kit asked?

Not that service, I should have said its special talent.

After getting the information, David excused the Tararipea turning back to Kit and Knight, after we meet with the government of Sprint I want to go to Hola and speak with Ambassador Modeerf. How long will it take to get there?

About two days, Kit answered.

Two days, I can cross a whole Galaxies in two days.

That because we cannot jump into warp speed. We have to use thruster power. A light speed jump would just send us pass Hola.

Just then Kit got a call from her ship on their intercom. Captain come quick and bring Ambassador Nulls with you, no sooner was that message received when Captain Kitaracta grab David and hit the transporter button and instantly were transported to the bridge of her space ship.

When David recovered from the temporary shock, what the hell just happen?

Kit went straight to her second in command while saying over her shoulder, I don't know but we got a message in the emergency channel. Harair what going on?

Captain you had better listen to this, as Harair flip on a switch and the radio speaker came on threw out the ship.

I repeat again this Coronal Roberts of the Julies Cesar a space exploration ship from planet Earth in the Milky Way Galaxy. We have come with important information, why are you firing on us? Stop now or we will be force to defend ourselves.

David concentrated Coronal Roberts where are you?

Who are you and why you in my head?

This is David Nulls where are you.

Oh Ambassador Nulls we are in the Gia system we were just about to enter the orbit above Hola we were going to tell them about the planet Venus in our solar system that meet all their requirements for them to live on. When they started attacking us, our shields are holding for now.

David turned to Kit, set the radio to all frequency as she did David step up to the speaker this is the Ambassador Nulls from the Kula Federation stop your attack on the Julius Cesar or we will destroy you. Then thinking to Kitaracta how long will it take us to get there?

Two day she answered back.

You got two hours.

No way, without going right threw the sun and that is not possible.

Can someone transport threw a sun?

Hell no in the first place no one can transport that far, in the second place no one is that crazy enough to even try it.

How long till we can get out far enough to transport without going threw the sun.

I can get you out so you are in a straight line with Hola but that would be moving away from it, we can do that in an hour, but you will be millions miles away there no way you can transport the far.

An hour and half later kit had moved the zxx5 almost out of the solar system using warp speed, they could see both planets. From this distance both look like stars in the sky. Now how long will it take us to get to Hola?

Still two days, jumping to warp to any spot toward space is easy. But jumping from warp toward a planet not even a computer can do that with the possibility of crashing into the planet.

OK head toward Hola as fast as you can go, he told Kit then thought of Coronal Roberts when he had made contact he told him to come out of orbit and head away from the sun, but not to jump into warp.

Four hour later David contacted Coronal Roberts only to find the ship from Hola were still firing at him and following them, he had not fired back but shields were getting weaker. Kit went up to David; you are not really going to do, what you are thinking?

Why not if I use your forward speed to increases the power of the transporter distance

No one has ever transported that distance, they would have to stop, then would have to drop their shields.

David thought of Coronal Roberts again ,Coronal I want you to stop, fire a warning shot, if they stop shooting I want you to drop your shields, and leave them down till I tell you or you have no other choice.

OK we are slowing to a stop now. It will take a few minutes stand by. Ten minutes later Coronal Roberts thought Ambassador are you out there.

Yes David answered back I have been following your progress go ahead and fire a warning shot.

OK they are moving back, dropping shields.

David thought of behind the Coronal and pressed the transport button, as Kit still telling him not to try it, as he vanished. Moments later reappearing behind the Coronal alright put the shields back up.

As Coronal Roberts jump, you son of a bitch, I asked you to stop popping in behind me, all shields up, Ambassador Welcome aboard the Julies Cesar.

Thank you Coronal now open me a radio line to those ships; better yet open a line to all frequencies.

The Coronal Roberts touch the screen then turned to David. You are on it is all yours, and then step back.

David walked up to the screen, This Ambassador Nulls of the Kula Federation I'm on the Earths Exploratory ship the Julies Cesar. Any attack or aggression toward this ship will be taken as an act of war against the Kula Federation. Now we are going to be going in orbit above the planet of Hola. I will be requesting an audience with Ambassador Modeerof of your planet. He then step back but not so far that the screen would not pick up the words spoken Coronal Roberts you now have permission to return and destroy any ship that fire on you. Then with the screen off David turned the Coronal leave all channels open and let me know if you get a response. David then sat down and mentally contact Kitaracta, Kit contact Ambassador Yumit and explain what happen and I will stop by later after we get this mess straighten out.

Are you alright, why didn't you contact me early, I was sure you didn't make and were floating around is space somewhere.

Sorry but I had other thing on my mind when I got here. nice to hear you were worried about me I'm alright ,a little twitch in my eyes and I can't feel my fingers. Just kidding I'm alright but remind me not to do that again it was a bumpy ride.

Just then Mindy came in and gave David a hug, Dad glad to see you.

Coronal Roberts looked at his head of security, Sorry, Sir it's hard to control the wife when she has her mine set on something Sargent Speck said.

It's alright I haven't seen my daughter in three years, David was saying.

When a young man came in from the entry way, It has been four years, Grandpa you still have the sometime green girlfriend I hear.

David turned well Archer, look who has grown up these last FOUR years still afraid of green people.

Not after what I have seen and heard these last four years.

What do you mean seen and heard?

Oh we have heard about you and the hero of Ticbladxia on almost every planet we visited.

If you mean Coronal Kitaracta she should be here in a couple of days.

Mister Ambassador Coronal Roberts interrupted; we have a message coming in from Hola.

David turned to the screen there was Mr. Modeerof, a thousand pardons Ambassador Nulls. We did not know that you were on the exploratory ship when it invaded our space.

David mental thought no you silly bastard you didn't ask you just thought of blowing it apart. Then he spoke to the screen no damage done we are going to come back into orbit. I would like to talk to you and the government of Hola. When we are not on an inter space frequency, say sometime tomorrow?

That will be fine we will have a welcome celebration.

No need for that, this is not a pleasure visit. Coronal Roberts has important information for the people of Hola. David turned from the screen and gave the end of transmission sign to Coronal Roberts.

After the transmission was cut off Coronal Roberts turned to David I think Ambassador Modeerof was still talking.

About their damn celebration I hate those things.

What damn thing, it was kit mentally asking?

Oh have you been following that, David thought back.

Only part of that, something about blowing it up you need help there we are still half way there should be in range tomorrow.

No everything is alright don't come in here guns a blazing. These people are on defense already, I don't need you to start a war. Did you get a hold of Ambassador Yumit on Sprint?

He should be getting the message anytime now, I had to use the radio his mental ability are very limited.

Ambassador are you OK, Roberts asked?

Yes I'm fine just talking to Commander Kitaracta.

Is she here?

No just a couple a light years away, she should be here tomorrow.

Where is your cruiser if you were not with her?

I teleported here from her ship.

Bull shit telaporter are not that strong.

I used the forward motion of her ship to push the signal; it is defiantly something I would not want to do again. Anyway how are thing going with you.

I have no complaints we were exploring Venus when the notification came out and it fit the specs that we were reading and we had the mayor from mars said that there were no inhabits. We thought that the scientist from Hola would like to check it out.

Well sound good why don't you go down with me tomorrow and explain to them.

You do remember they were shooting at us, if they had anything bigger we would have been in trouble.

I think I will spend a little time with my daughter and grandson David said.

OK right I'll catch with you later.

Chapter 34

The Ambassador Mental Battle

The next morning Ambassador Nulls and Commander Roberts took a shuttle down to the planet. Where they meet by an army of soldier's welcome Mr. Ambassador Follow me please, Ambassador Modeerof is Anxious to meet you, as well as the governing counsel.

As David and Commander Roberts follow the soldiers Roberts leaned over to David, I don't think they are taken use to the government office.

I know they are taken us to prison but I need to know where the Ambassador and the other council member are.

As they entered the prison the guards pointed their guns at them and motion toward a cell. You wanted to talk to Ambassador Modeerof he is the one over in the corner then he laughed and pushed David in, Commander Roberts came tumbling behind him.

David picks himself up and went over the Ambassador Modeerof what is going on?

A week ago General Pions over ran the government. He now has control over the planet. He put me down here to be used for a trade for the Kula to leave him alone.

Does he not know that the Kula will not inter into inter planet affairs beside didn't I talk to you yesterday.

No it must have been a hologram I have been down her since the takeover.

OK stay here I'll get Commander Roberts out of here then be right back to get you.

But how?

I have a transporter. David said.

They have some kind of shield around here; I have tried to transporter it did not work.

Well we will just have to shut off their shield do you know where the generator is.

No but it must be in this building because here is the only place transporter don't work.

In that case I'll be right back as David turned and walked threw the bars of the jail.

How did you do that Ambassador Modeerof and Commander Roberts asked at the same time?

Takes months of practices, be back shortly. Just then a guard came in. David catching him off guard grabs his weapon with one hand and his shirt with the other penning him to the wall. Where is the device that stops transporters from working?

I do not know.

It not nice to lie, as David slammed the guard into the wall knocking him out.

Why did you do that he should know?

He did and now I do, it is on one floor up be back shortly, as David turned and seeing the stairs and running up at the top he meet another guard without thinking David brought up the weapon and fired the solider instantly Evaporated. David paused for a second then contained up the stairs. Shortly he found a room with the shielding device he aim the weapon and fired again. The device vanished. David thought of Commander Roberts then pressed the transporter button and was standing behind the Commander Roberts, OK let go.

Shit the Commander jump and said I asked you not to do that.

Sorry, Ambassador I'll take Commander Roberts up to his ship gives us a few second and then transport behind us. Taken the Commander hand thinking of the control room on the Earths space ship and transported up, second later Ambassador Modeerof Show up.

Just then kit came in David head are you alright I have been getting all kinds of chatter in my head something about a transport shield I have never heard of such a thing. I have to see this.

Well you are late I destroyed it.

Why would you do something like that?

Because it was holding Ambassador Modeerof captive, now I need to figure out what to do next, where are you at?

Coming into orbit about a mile above you!

Did you have any trouble coming in from Holas fighters?

No, no trouble at all I did have to fire one warning blast that hit two of their little toys and the rest took off for the other side of Hola.

Was anyone hurt?

I do not think so, both ship were vaporized, I didn't see anyone hurt.

Oh great so you probably started a war.

I can handle that hold on for a minute. Then she turned to her radioman turn on all frequency. People of Hola this is the Kula royal guard your ships attack me and I defended myself. Now you have kidnapped the Ambassador Nulls of the Kula Federation, I demand his imminently release. I'm standing by for your answer and I'm not very patient.

David mentally told Kit I'm alright; I'm here on the Earths Explorer ship.

I know that, but they don't know I know it.

The radio came back on this is General Pions the controller of the planet Hola your Ambassador Nulls is visiting with Ambassador Modeerof and is in no harm and asked use not to disturb them.

Thank you General I will be coming down in an hour and will be looking forward to meeting you.

I will be looking forward to meeting you too Captain, radio off. Turning to the guard standing by the door way. You find those two Ambassadors and have them here in my office in a half hour or I will have your head on my wall, is that clear.

The guard nodded nervously knowing that the General meant it literally he had seen the General do it before. But general they have escaped.

I don't want excuses I want them found and in this office before this Captain gets here.

Back in space Well Mr. Roberts David said I had better transport back to our ship and find out what Captain Kitaracta is up to. Keep Ambassador Modeerof here and you can fill him in on the planet you found that will be suitable for them to move to.

What this you found a planet Modeerof asked?

That was all David heard before he pressed his transport button and show up behind Kit what was that all about?

Oh the lying bastard I've heard of him before, never meet the man but the stories I've heard a tyrant and the government is afraid of him.

Well according to Ambassador Modeerof he has taken over the government but it is the Kula position not to interfere in inters planet policies.

Well they kidnap a Kula Ambassador basically they involved us that give the right to interfere. How about I just go down and vaporize the guy, we would be doing the world a good deed.

That is not what we want; if you insist on going down I go with you.

OK but I go first you can come a few minutes later.

Alright but no vaporizing.

Kit turned on the communication General Pions .This Captain Kitaracta I will be transporting to your office in five minutes.

OK Captain we are looking forward to meet you.

A few minutes later Kit transported down to General Pions office. Once there she was surrounded by five guards with weapons.

The General step forward any weapons you have on you please put them on the floor.

Kit took from her pocket and laid the laser weapon on the flood. one of the soldiers pick it up and gave it to the General.

He pointed it at her now tell me why I should not vaporizer you. You shot and killed two of my explorer teams. And their space craft vaporizer.

First of all the Explorer teams, bull shit they were war craft and they shot at me first.

Secondly that man behind you will scatter your atoms all over this room before you can figure out how to make that laser weapon work, hello Mr. Ambassador Nulls.

Why hello Captain Kitaracta, nice seeing you here now General if you will remove all your guards from the room we will have a friendly talk.

Guards kill both of these invaders.

David use his mind and told the guards to put down their weapon and leave the room, then forcefully took the weapon's out of their hand and float them in the air pointing at it last owner . This did it the guards all turned and left the room in a hurry. While General Pions protested.

All the weapons drop to the floor as David turned his attrition on the General. Now General I want you to get all the government council members up here.

And if I refused?

Oh that would not be a good thing to do, Kit said.

And what is he going to do about it.

Well first he would bounce you off the wall over there. Just then she used her mental power and throw him against the wall, then he would bounce you off that wall, throwing him against the other wall. As the General was picking himself up Kit add I was just saying that is what he might do, and you would be lucky.

Captain you don't give me credit first after bouncing off that wall throwing the General against the wall then that wall again throwing the general then I would bounce him off the ceiling.

No stop the General called out, you two are crazy I will do it. As he crawl over to his desk and spoke into the intercom.

Kit turned to David are you hearing what I'm hearing, he is just a puppet. He just called someone he thinks has better mental powers and will destroy us.

Well it would explain a lot, this guy is such a weakling there is no way he could control a world. No sooner had David said this than a door open not the one the guard had gone out of a much bigger one. And there was this mountain. It literally looked like a mountain, till it changes down to the size as David and Kit and close to their form.

Ambassador Nulls and Captain Kitaracta your escapades are known threw out the galaxy it a pleasure meeting you.

If it is such a pleasure why were you trying to kill us David asked?

That was the stupid general doing; as he turned to the General you can leave us now.

Except for the part about General you can leave us now. Any bystander would think that Kit, David and this new comer were just staring at each other. The conversation up to now was being done all mentally.

One moment I do have a few questions for the General.

Mr. Ambassador any question you have for the General I assure you I can answer. I'm Debar the controller of Hola.

Well then Mr. Debar can you tell me why you had your war ship firing upon the Kula Federation Exploratory ship from Earth.

We thought it to be a war ship from Sprint we had not seen that design before.

And you expect me to believe that line of crap, oh why do you want the warp engines.

Mr. Debar took a step back, looking at David.

Kit cut in what is going on I missed something about warp Engines.

Mr. Debar here was trying to block out his thoughts about why he really wanted to attack the exploratory ship he had order his war ship to only use low power on the laser so as to not destroy the ship with its new super Engines.

I didn't pick any of that up Kit said.

You are very good Mr. Ambassador, I will have to watch myself closer.

Well Mr. Debar now that we have that settled. And you say you are the controller of Hola what are your plans for the planet that in a few years will become a ball of ice and just disappear.

I have been here these last two hundred years and have not notices any change in our sun. I think it is only a rumor so that Sprint can take over our planet for its own.

Why would Sprint want to take over your planet?

Simple theirs is so over populated there is no room to move.

Due to your attacking on the Earths ship I have not been on Sprint. But I can assure you that your sun is dying out and the people of Sprint do not want your planet. Also that Earth ship you were attacking had found a planet that you could move to before your planet here will be destroyed and your civilization extinct. Now I'm not sure they want to help you.

David stood there staring at Mr. Debar, as Debar stared back, several minutes they just looked at each other.

What going on Kit asked?

David took a couple of step backwards, almost like he was pushed. Then Mr. Debar went back against the door he had just come threw without walking, David had used his mind control to move Debar.

Alright what is going on Kit asked again?

Nothing just two guys flexing their muscles. Now Mr. Debar do we sit down and discuss this or do you want to keep playing these games.

David sudden felt a pain in head but when he rubs it there was blood on his hand as he looked at it. Kit appeared in the room with weapon drawn without warning she aimed and second's later Debar head was gone. That was the last thing David saw till he awoke two days later. Looking into Kit face looking down on him, what happen he asked?

Debar was killing you by destroying your brain a little at a time so you would not notice it. It would have worked if I hadn't stopped him.

What happen to commander Roberts and Ambassador Modeerof.

Oh their getting along fine and have reinstated the council and there interested in Commander Roberts information about that planet in your old solar system.

Chapter 35

The Sun Is Dieing

Ambassador Nulls there is a call from Captain LlaRewop.

OK bring it up on screen. David steped up to the screen, there was Captain LlaRewop and Mr Otash good morning to both of you, I hope you have good news.

Yes they said together. Then Captain LlaRewop steped back. Mr Ambassador we have found a planet that has the same atmosphere as Srovlf. It is in the Milky Way galaxy Mr Otash said with a smile.

Yes I know that aria well, I'm sure they will welcome you. Is there any thing I can do to help you moving, both the people from North and south.

That might be a good ideal I'm not sure how the north will take it with Mr McCormick gone.

Oh I think you might be surprised at how the north and south are getting along beside you have that damn sword and if it really means what they say you should not have any trouble. But we will meet you there. Captain LlaRewop very good job now if you will take Mr. Otash to Srovlf we will meet you there.

Thank you Mr. Ambassador I will glad be to, it will take us five or six days to get there.

David looked at Kit she held up three fingers. Turning back to the screen. OK Captain we will meet you there, signing off. Turning back to Kit well I guess that is our new destination.

Already logged in now you have five days to practices what you are going to tell a primitive planet of people how you killed their two leaders, and then brought back one, and they will have to move. I don't remember Mr. Otash saiing which planet they were moving to just it was in our galaxy. I have been to most of the planets in the Milky Way Galaxy and I can not think of any that are livable that didn't have people already on it.

Well we can not ask then till they drop out of hyper drive and they will be there by then David said. I don't want to go down to the planet till Mr. Otash with that damn sword of Calvin get there, I figure that will help convince the people of Srovlf that we are friendly.

There is some thing else you are thinking about, you have it blocked out from me, what else is on your mind? Kit asked.

I was just thinking if tang are the energy and if zline has this much power. And if those little stones you showed me on Earths moon multiply one hundred times will they work on tang.

I don't know no one has ever try it what are you thinking? I'm not picking up any of your thoughts.

That is because I have you block out if you knew you would think me crazy, I need to talk to the computer. Computer can the fuel stones found on Earths moon be mixed with zline?

Insentient information to answer your question.

They are called simmie stones Kit said.

Thank you, computer can simmie stones mix with zline?

It has never been tried, I do not have the information needed to give a correct answer

How about you guess, David asked?

Computer do not guess, if you want the right answer I need to know all the facts.

Thank you computer I'll see if I can get you all the information you need to give me the right answer.

I detected some sarcasm in your voice, I'm sorry I can not give you the information you requested the computer answered back.

What are you doing Kit asked?

Just having a little chat with the computer. These simmie stones are they found any where else.

There are a few planets that have them but none as abundant as Earths moon. Why are you trying to make a space ships go faster Kit asked going over and sitting beside David.

How long will it take us to stop by and pick up a few of those stones then to Melbar.

About two days to Earth and another two to Melbar, it is out of our way.

OK Well Mr. Otash will just have to wait.

Are you going to tell me what you have in mind? Kit asked while getting up and going to the control, and reprogramed a change of course. You know we have to drop out of hyper speed before we can change course.

Your the Captain I'm just a passager telling you where I want to go.

A day and a half later Kitaracata was putting the ZXX5 in orbit behind the Earths moon. As David and Kit were putting on their space suites. David was holding a box he had found on the ship.

Kit asked couldn't find a smaller box?

No I would prefer a bigger one, come on lets go, as David thought of the moon surface and pushed the transport button moments later he was on the surface. As soon as he was there as he started picking up the simmie stones.

Shortly after, Kit appeared going to fill that whole box she asked? as she started picking up the stones and putting them in the box.

Yes I'm going to need a lot.

What ever you have in mind, you are working hard at keeping it hidden from me. When are you going to tell me what is going on.

When I figure out all the details. OK that's enough Lets go.

Back on the ZXX5 David turned to kitaracata. Well lets go to Milburn. But first I want to stop at Ticbadxia.

That my home planet what the hell are you up to, Kitaracata asked?

I need on of those splicer engines can you call ahead and see if we can get one.

Only one Splicer you going to give the people of Srovlf a space ship, I thought at first you were going to move them to another planet that use fossil fuel. I'll check on the Splicer you sure the council will approve of you giving a backward planet a space ship.

No we are not going to give them a space ship. That is why I didn't want you to know what I have in mind. I'm not sure the council would approve what I do have in mind, and this way you won't be the one to blame if it is not going to work.

After stopping at Ticbladxia and after a little negotiations they had a splicer. They headed to Albar Where David contacted Dan Dometer asking permission to to land.

An Kula Ambassador do not need permission to land but we need a few hours to prepare. This is a great honor, And I believe you will be surprise in the changes around here.

Several hour later Dan Dometer called David, Ambassador Nulls you are cleared to land on platform one.

Kitaracata took the ZXX5 down and landed David could see the town looked different, There was a large turn out of people, it was different from his first visit when Dan Dometer father Stan Dometer controled the town.

Ambassador Nulls we are deeply honored to have your return to Albar and you know Poncher from Tebect.

Yes David said extending his hand and getting the traditional hug.

It is a good surprise seeing you again Ambassador Nulls. Things are quite different now, than last time here. But see for your self we have a festival planed.

Oh damn I hate those things David mentally said to kit.

Well that is the down fall for being famous, Mentally she said back. Then turning to Mr. Dometer and Poncher, it is good to see you again and I'm sure we will enjoy your festival Kit said turning and looking at David.

Well come along let the festival began, Mr Dometer said pointing toward the crowed of people

A cheer went up as David steped forward. David mentally called Kitaracata remind me that to kill you after this.

Just getting back at you for not telling me what you have been up to, this last week.

Fair enough but don't turn your back on me David thought back.

Were you talking to me Dan Dometer asked?

No David said just talking to Captain Kitaracata. I thought we had everyone blocked out.

You slip up I got the part of Fair enough but don't turn your back on me. I thought you might be talking about me.

No you are quite safe it is our Captain Kitaracata who must watch out. Is it a joke or are you serious Dometer asked.

Just kidding, I would not want to lose the best pilot in the galaxy.

Well thank you Kit cut in.

That was not for you to hear David thought back.

Are you two married Dometer asked?

No I wish people would quite saying that. We are just good friends.

In that case friends lets enjoy the party, I have a feeling that this visit is for more than just a friendly visit.

You are right but tonight we party and talk business tomorrow David said.

Well let the party began Poncher has brought his very fine vine.

The next morning David contacted Dan Dometer and set up an appointment. At the meeting David began, Mr. Dometer I need a fairly large amount of zline.

OK what do you consider a large amount Dometer asked?

I was thinking around a thousand pounds.

Oh wow that's is a considerable amount but there is no problem you can pick it up at the Basia mine, I will inform them of you request and arrival. I believe you have been there before ,they are still bragging about it to everyone they see.

Yes they were very nice, I will need a container to carry it in too.

We can provided that also Dometer said.

Thank you from what I have seen of your city you have made a major improvement. Now if you will excuse us, we are in a bit of a rush.

I understand I will make the call they will be waiting for you at Basia. Good luck Dometer said as David left.

They were just coming in to Melbar space when Kitaracata called to Basia camp requesting permission to land.

Yes Mr. Ambassador permission granted, happy to have you back again and we have what you need and it is ready to be picked up.

As Kit landed at the space dock Three men came out on something you could only called a fork lift without wheels, on it was a large box. Kit opened the doors to the storage compartment. They floated the box over and place it inside. Then all three came over to the Ambassador.

There you are Mr. Ambassador there is a little over the thousand pound of Zline sir it is an honor you visited us again.

Actually it was Mr. Domete who sent us to your mine David said. He must think very highly of you.

Wow two honors in one day, no one will believe this. Did you like my scale model of the drilling rig?

Yes it was quite impressive. Now we must go and thank you.

Back in space Kit turned to David well Mr. Ambassador where would you like the best pilot in the Galaxy to take you to now.

Oh I knew when I said it that it would go to your head. Lets go meet Captain LlaRewop and Mr. Otash at Srovlf

Yes as you wish my love Captain LlaRewop has called, four times looking for us.

Two days later they were in orbit around Srovlf Kit contacted Captain LlaRewop OK lets transfer Mr. Otash over to our ship Kit told LlaRewop.

With pleasure Captain LlaRewop, said this guy has been a pain in the butt sense he transferred over here. I thought about giving him a tour of the out side of my ship several times.

Well thank you captain the Kula will compensate you for your help and trouble.

OK we are here what are we doing with a thousand pounds Zline, a box of simmie, and a spliter Kit asked?

Well we still need a space ship David added.

A space ship where are you going to get that?

Well Ambassador Yamit, over on Spirts did say if there was anyway they could help with they would be glad to. Besides I did tell them I would bring them a Pyranometer. Do you think your engineer can make one'

I do not know lets ask him Kit said as she went to the main screen and touched it engineer to the control center please.

No sooner had she said it and he appeared in the control center.

I see you made your self a transporter Kit said you think you can make a Pyranometer?

A what he asked?

Something that will monitor the heat from the sun David said stepping forward.

You mean a thermometer? we have them all over the place.

No I need one that will give us the temperature of the surface and the core of a sun.

Hmm he said rubbing his chin don't know what this Pyranometer looks like but I believe I can come up with something. How soon do you need it?

David looked at Kitaracata she held up two fingers again.

Two days again we are just going to another planet in the same system. Oh that right no jumping to hyper speed for this short distance.

Do you mean we are not going to Srovlf? it was MR. Otash who had been standing off to one side. I want to go home and be a hero . I have been gone for almost a year. They will not even know me when I get back.

They may not know you any ways a year in space is like seven years on your planet. Kit said.

What Otash asked?

It is a long story now just sit back, and enjoy the trip Kitaracata told him. As she went to the control and set a course for Spirts. Then turning to David are you going to tell me what you have planed.

OK but not here lets go to your room. Once in the room David told her we need to talk, and I don't want anyone picking up our thought so keep a block up. You can not tell the council about this I'm sure they would not approve it.

This misterious Kit said, OK all block are up lets hear it.

What I want to do is find a space ship to send into the sun with those Zline surrounded by the simmie stones and a splinter in the middle and reaim the splinter at the Zline and the simmie stones just as the ship hit the sun if it works like I plan it will add energy to the sun making it last longer.

And when did you dream up this crazy plan, you are so far out in left field as you say. You are right the council would never approve this, in fact if we do it the council would probable abandon us on some lone planet. This is so hair brain it's...........Hmm it just might work. OK what do we got to do next?

Need a space ship David setting up with a smile.

And this Ambassador Yumit on Spirts is going to just give one. Well you have two days to figure out what to say for a free two million klunk space ship, that will be the deal of the year.

The next day they call Ambassador Yamit and told him they would be stopping by the next day around four o'clock.

Kitaracata look at David when he had sign off we will be there early than that?

And if we get there early we will be at a damn festival all day.

Why you big kill joy these people have a chance for a holiday, a day off from work a chance to have a day to celebrate.

Not to mention the crew here will get to enjoy the festival.

You are leaving out a chance to play catch with a shoe. OK call them back and tell them when we will get there.

Awww what a sweetie, Kit said as she turned and call Ambassador Yamit back then turned to David Ambassador Yamit on the screen for you.

Ambassador Yamit my pilot just informed me we will be there around nine in the morning so we will be seeing you sooner.

That will be great we will be ready.

Nine o:clock I was thinking around noon Kit said after David sign off.

David just smile at her, well you better kick this tub in the butt and get going. If you don't have to stand at the control all day to get us there on time, I'll be in your cabin relaxing if you want to join me for a drink. As David winked then turn and walk out.

Put the ice in the glass, I'll be right there as she turn to the control and adjusted the speed.

The next morning he woke up and Kit was gone David dressed and put on his Ambassador robe. Then went to the control center Kit handed him a cup of Krista, Good morning Mr. Ambassador did you sleep well.

As a matter a fact yes I did, taken a sip of the Krista, then stop and took another. This is real coffee where did you get this?

Oh I will always have a way of surprise you. We will be landing with in the hour.

After landing there was the usual festival that lasted into the night.

The next morning David meet up with Ambassador Yumit.

Mr Ambassador we know that the sun will burn it self out in the next one hundred to two hundred years. We have brought Pyranometer to monitor your sun to convince your people that it is dyeing. Although I have a plan that I want to talk to you about that just might make you the Hero of galaxy. It will increase the life time of your sun. There is a big IF it might not work but according to all the figures it will work. I have got the things needed to do it. But we need a disposable space ship and some of your engineers to work with ours to put it together.

What do you mean disposable he asked?

Well it will have to go the speed of light and a computer, I have the engine to do it. Do you think can you find us a space ship.

It's the disposable part we may have a problems with. Yamit said. But if you think it will work I'll take it up with the government. They still are not convinced the sun is going out.

Well we will get the Pyranometer set up, and I'm sure it will not take long for them to see for them self.

Where are we going to set it up?

The best would be the tallest building around David said looking around. Porbabley that one over there, as he pointed toward a building.

That the government building, it is good right above their heads.

You get permission and I'll get the Pyranometer. Then David thought to himself I hope it is ready?

Yes it is just sitting here in the control center it was Kit in his head.

Thank you and tell your engineer I owe him the first two rounds. OK I'm on my way over.

I can bring to over, No Ambassador Yamit is getting permission first. We don't want then to think we are coming in and trying to take over.

Back at the ZXX5 Kit asked how it going at getting a space ship then smiled at David.

I'm not sure there are still a lot of the people who don't want to believe it or just won't believe it that their sun is dieing. Well Yamit is getting permission to put Pyranometer on the government building. Do you think your engineer can hook up a remote monitor so the government can also see the results.

I don't know as she went to the control, Engineer to control center.

Hi Ephat our Ambassador here has another request.

What it didn't work, I did my best should read surface and core temperature.

No I'm sure it will work and it is just what we needed. I was wondering if you could put something on it so they can monitor it inside a building.

Ephat broke into a smile no problem Mr. Ambassador I do good work?

Yes Ephat you do fantastic work I'm very impressed with your work. I know Captain Kitaracata would be lost with out you.

Thank you Mr. Ambassador, coming from you that is a great honor he said, as he turn to go. Over his shoulder he said, I will have your monitor in the morning.

That was nice saying that to him you are becoming a real politcian. You know he will be up all night making that for you.

Not a politcian, I just tell the truth David said. I'll met Yamit this afternoon we will know more then. Till then I'm hungry, shall we have lunch.

After lunch David met up with Yamit. Well any good news?

Yes the government says it is OK to place your insterments on the roof, and I believe I have found a space ship we can use, as you say it is disposable. Come it is just over here, it is an old fighter ship. It has been decommission for years.

David looked at it.

Decommission it looks more like it was shot down and crashed, it was Kitaracata coming up behind them.

Well with a little work I believe we can make it work David said, patting Ambassador Yamit on the shoulder good job.

Several month's later the fighter ship was looking like it just might fly again David called on Ephat, Kitaracata engineer. I know I have ask you to make a lot of thing but I need you to do one more of your miracles. I need to make a Spilter unit to turn all the energy from pulsation to a different direction and make it fire at the pile of simmie stones. and the second it starts to turn I want start feeding zlite into the spiliter as fast as the spiliter will split them.

Holly shit that will make one hell of an thermonuclear reaction. I would not want to be within a million light years of it when it happen.

Me ether David said that why we need it to be computer controlled.

Well it can be done but it will take me a while to make it

OK you have two days

What no way Ephat said?

Just kidding David remarked smiling, take all the time you need the fighter ship is still quite a way from being ready. Use the new spliter we pick up in Ticbadxia that is in the cargo bay and put it in the space fighter. We will then need to program the computer to turn the propulsion just be before the fighter melts, so we will probable need some thermal units mounded on the ship to tell the spliter to turn.

OK I get where you are going but do you really think this will work. In theory all it will do is blow the sun apart. and it will die out faster.

Well that one theory I hadn't thought about David said. Lets hope that won't happen. I'm only hopeing that it will add a few years maybe twenty or fifty years to the life of the sun. In my theory I figure it will add a hundred years or so.

I hope your theory is better than mine either way we had better be far away when it happens, Ephat said walking away.

Four months later the space fighter was ready. Kitaracata used her ship with the tractor bean and pull it from it's landing bay into space.

Ephat made the finial inspection and said OK you can load the Zlite and the simmie stones. Carefully he over saw the loading when all had been done he told David everything was ready. All control is at the command board and Captain Kitaracata can lunch any time. Y Once you lunched the computer will take over, it will take three minuets to get up to light speed then you have three minuets to abort if not five minuets later it will hit the sun and start to melt I built a shield around the spiter and it will last almost one minuet. It is all in your control. I hope we don't all die he added.

David called back don't worry after this is over you will be a real hero and thank you for all your good work.

You said that like I won't see you again?

Oh my little friend you will see me again I have many more thing for you to built.

OK Kit the second you lunch you have your engines ready and go. I want you out of this solar system when we do this. I'm going to be at the motoring station David said turning toward Kit..

No I'm going I'll be right there with you. And besides why do you have to be the one who watches the monitor.

Because if it turns out Ephat theory is right I don't want to live with the fact that I killed millions of people.

What happen to your theory, the glass is half full and the power of positive thinking.

Oh I have, It is just that I don't want you mess up in my mess if thing go wrong.Honey Kitaracata said I'm in for the long run with you now lunch that space fighter.

No I have to be at the monitoring station with Ambassador Yamit. And you have to lunch from here. So I will call you when we are ready David said as he transported down to the government building. Where he meet up with Ambassador Yamit who had just left a government meeting.

Ambassador Nulls this is a surprise how are things going. I just confirm with the government and they can now see that our sun is dyeing. I have shown how the ice at the poles is moving down.

Well in about ten minuts you might be able to go in and tell them different.

Are you saying we are ready?

Yes do you want to tell them to come out and watch David asked?

No I do not want to get their hopes up if it does not work.

OK Captain Kitaracata you can lunch anytime now David thought.

OK engine is firing the fighter is away. All we have to do is wait. This can from behind Ambassador Nulls and Ambassador Yamit.

Both jump with a start David turned and there was Kit. What the hell you doing here I told you to get out of the Solar system right after you lunched the fighter.

And I told you, we are in this together you are not going to get all the glory. Don't worry if my ship computer thinks something is wrong it is program to get out to a safe distance.

And you?

It will make a great story, Two star cross lover die frozen it time by the greatest screw up in all of history.

What is she talking about are we going to die Ambassador Yamit asked?

I don't believe so but we will know in about thirty seconds David said. He wait what he thought was thirty seconds. Then said it should be happen right about now.

I don't feel anything Ambassador Yamit said.

You wont feel anything for a day but your sun is ninety three millions away and it will take at the speed of light eight minuets for us to see if there is a sun or not.

So we just wait Yamit asked

Wait and pray David replied.

What are we expecting to happen?

A Thermonuclear Reaction in the sun, David replied again. There it is a brighter light and the sun is still there.

It worked the damn thing worked Kitaracata said grabbing David hugging and kissing him.

So when will we know how many years before the sun will burn out Yamit asked?

Not for a couple of days the Pyranometer will let the computer know and then the computer will calculate and let us know. So again we wait.

Two days later David contacted Ambassador Yamit. We need to talk I have good news but I would like to tell it to your face can we meet.

Yes if it is good news lets meet at the government building in say ten minuets.

OK I will meet you there. Ten minuets later David transported down with Kit and Ephat. Meeting Yamit at the government building. Well Mr. Ambassador Yamit you can go tell your government that thanks to the hard work of Mr. Ephat here and the plans from the Kula federation that your sun energy is back up to temperature of 5,700 Kelvins that is almost what it was a thousand years ago.

That is great but would you mind coming in and telling them Yamit asked?

As Ambassador Yamit led the way David, Kit and Ephat follow as they entered the government chambers everyone stood up and applauded After David explained everything giving Ephat credit for his engineering and David didn't come right out and say it but made the people believe that it was the Kula ideal to try and recharge their sun.

Back on the ship Kit asked why didn't you tell them it was your ideal?

I thought it was better that they believe it came from some intelligent person on the counsel and not just one of my hair brain ideals.

So now when I go back to Srovlf and become a hero, it was Mr. Otash who all this time had been asking and pestering everyone.

That might be a problem Otash you see now that the sun is going to last at lest a thousand years. and what you have learned in the last year we can not let you go back . One reason Your have been gone for seven years in your planet time, something to do with space travel. and with as primitive as the people are in Srovlf they would think you were some kind of a nut. Telling them you have spent all this time in space and meeting all different kind of aliens.

But I have the sword of Calvin Mr. Otash replied.

Yes and they saw you fighting Mr. McCormick then vanished. Think about it they will be thinking that you killed Mr. McCormick for it. And what do you think they will do to you. You being this nut with wild story of space travel and now you have the sword.

But you will be there to tell them about what happen.

Sorry but no we can not do that it is forbidden by the kula to interfere in underdeveloped planets.

Well what am I suppose to do?

We could talk to Ambassador Yamit and he can find something here on Spirts for you to do I'm sure with your expirance in handling people you can help out here.

But I'm nothing here on Spirts Otash said.

You may not be in charge here but back on Srovlf you are dead.

You are right about all things maybe it is better for me to stay here. I believe I will talk to Ambassador Yamit.

Good we will set up a meeting tomorrow David said   A f t e r Ambassador David and Kitaracata stop by Nacba and told Ambassador Homasic that theie sun was now going to last another thousand years. Then on to Hola and contacted Ambassador Sansa who said that they did notice it was brighter.

After all the festivals David told Kit well it has been a long time lets go to Tistana.

Chapter 36

The Counsel Decision

David and Kitaracta were back in Tistana facing the council, Mr. Nulls re energize a sun that was quite a feat, I do not believe anyone would have thought of that, let a lone want to try it. Can we talk to you in privet?

Yes certainly.

Come with us as all of the council members stood up and went through the door behind them.

David not knowing what to do for sure so he followed. Once in the small room the council took off their robs and hung them on the wall that had no hooks but look like there was a space made for them.

Mr. Nulls you have notices that there is a space for one more robe and there was an empty chair at the counsel table. That is because Councilmen Astinkcana has passed away.

I'm sorry to hear that, David said.

Oh do not feel sorry for Astinkcana he had a good life all 426 years his species usually only live around 300 years, he knew it would soon be his time to go. Are problem now is to find his replacement, and you are the most qualify to take his place.

I'm honored that you thinking that way of me, but I'm just not the kind to set on a counsel all day, I'm more the adventure type. Being the Kula Ambassador would be a better way I could serve the Kula.

This set the entire councilman mind talking. This had never happen before; that someone would turn down an appointment to the counsel was unthinkable. And David had seen the counsel room, where only the council members were allowed to see.

Finely one of the councilmen said STOP and got the other counsel man attrition. I have an ideal that might work. How about we eliminate the position of Ambassador and appoint Mr. Nulls to the counsel and have him do the duties of the Ambassador and when in Tistanna he sits on the counsel. He has shown in his own special ways that that he can handle any situation. He would have more authority as a counsel man especially when he is in other Galaxy's.

I think that would be a great ideal. It will show that we, the counsel want to do more than sit here and enforce the rules. It will give us an inside ideal of what is going on out there in the Federation, it was the Counselman Snoipmahc the one who had mentioned not to change history when David had left on his first assignment.

Mr. Null what do you think of this ideal, asked Counsel man Elttae.

Well I could live with that, David answered.

WHAT, came the question in unison from the Councilmen?

Sorry I meant that I would accept the position on the counsel under those conditions, David corrected.

Good we will announce it tomorrow at the opening. As for now thank you Ambassador Nulls if you will leave us now and return tomorrow. We have many things to do before your annunciation.

David turned and walked through the door back to the main council chambers where Kit was waiting.

Well are you the new counsel man and I'll be a counsel man wife, kit asked?

I think half of that will all happen.

You mean they don't want you for the counsel.

Oh that part might happen, David answered.

I see I'm not good enough to be a counsel man wife and live in an apartment on the top floor of the highest building in Tania.

Ha you are too good to settle down and live in the city. You would go crazy in a week. And run off with some shuttle jockey.

You are right but I sure would like to try it for that week.

Well I'll see what I can do, about get it for you to hang around with me for a week or two.

Ooh you are a real, what you call a jerk sometimes.

Hay now remembered you try to kill me one time.

That was a long time ago back on your planet. I have saved your butt many times since then.

Yes you have and I appreciate that. It just this wife thing, you may get tired of me and kill me in my sleep.

OK I'll just be your lover on the side and we will sneak around meeting, till your new wife founds out and she kills you.

And just what makes you think I'm going to get a wife.

All the Counsel man have wives, they throw big parties for the upper class people.

You told me that all citizens were equal here on Tistanna.

They are, you know what I mean, and the rich they get to do things other don't get to do.

Well for now I'm just the Kula Ambassador, with a very special space Jockey as a real good friend. What do you say friend we go out and celebrate an assignment completed, and maybe later we can go up to my apartment, for a little frolicking around.

Kit smiled, that sound like a lot of fun. Come on I'll show you what Space jockeys do when they hit a port.

The next morning David woke up with Kit in his arms. With Knight at the door telling him the counsel wanted to see him. David jumped up and went to the water less shower and was met by Kit coming in to join him. He kissed her saying good morning are you going with me?

You're kidding I would not miss this for rippin.

A what David asked?

A Rippin, when two stars collide only happen once in six trillion of you years.

In that case I'll wait for you.

A few minutes later David and Kitaracta transported to just outside the counsel doors, and were imminently ushered in as they walked in David looked around the small council chambers were turned into an gymnasium there were hundreds of aliens there. The word had got out a new counsel man was to be appointed. Kitaracta was stopped half way and David was escorted ahead up front as he approached all the Counsel man stood up.

Ambassador Nulls they announced in English it sounded like. The office of Kula Ambassador has been desolated and you have been asked to join the counsel of the Kula Federation, to be and not only be a council member but to also do the duties of the Kula Ambassador. To up hold the laws, and to serve the citizen of the Federation, putting them before your own personal wants and believes.

I do David thought.

You must say it out loud, came a message in his head.

I do David said again.

Then two aliens came up to him and took off the uniform of the ambassador and replace it with another. Only it was not like the other council members. As Snoipmahc announce, this is the new uniform of the new counsel man to show all galaxy's that where counsel man Nulls goes it will be known that he is a full Member of the Kula Federation counsel with all the power of the counsel. Come counsel man Nulls and take the seat at this counsel.

David walked up and stood at the table. In his head he heard sit down and with that, all the counsel sat down. And then the whole gymnasium came alive with cheers and yells and applause.

After all the cheers and applauds quieted down. The escorts who had escorted David up to the front escorted Kit up to the front. Captain Kitaracta your space shuttle will be refitted to make it presentable for Counsel Man Nulls to use at his digression you are here by promoted to Admiral and you will be given the best crew we can put together.

As he turned David could almost swear Snoipmahc winked at him.

Kit step forward I would be honored to shuttle around Counsel Man Nulls but, I have the best crew now and if it means giving them up I will have to refuse your offer.

David had to put his hands in front of his face as if thinking. But in reality it was to cover up a smile, that if he didn't get control he would break out laughing. He took a deep breath. I have seen this crew and they are very efficient and if Admiral Kitaracta is that loyal to this crew and believes they can do the job. I see no reason why they should be replace with a crew she does not know.

You are right Counsel Man Nulls Admiral Kitaracta should be able to pick her own crew.

David could hear the other counsel men discussing this few were a little skeptic but they all agreed

Counsel man Snoipmahc lean forward Admiral Kitaracta take your XZZ5 to bay 1 and have it outfitted to accommodate counsel man Nulls and you can pick your own crew.

A cheer went up in the back of the room, David was sure it was Kits crew.

Now Snoipmahc continued there will be no more business today. Today is to celebrate our new Counsel Man Nulls appointment.

For several weeks David sat at the counsel table and help solve problems from different Galaxies He was moved up to an apartment like Kit had said he would and she would come visit at night when she could get away from supervising the work on her space ship. David would go to the ship when he was done with the counsel duties.

When one day Admiral Kitaracta was called in the council chambers is your ship ready to transport Counsel Man Null to the Alosue Galaxy his presents is need there.

Yes the Tame is ready any time that Counsel man Nulls is.

Very well, Counsel man Nulls you know the problem whenever you want to go it is up to you.

We will leave tomorrow morning then David said.

9 781955 459112